Trailing Darkness

SAVIOR OF THE LIGHT BOOK ONE

A. L. GORDON

Copyright © 2024 by A. L. Gordon

All rights reserved.

No part of this publication may be reproduced, distributed, or transmitted in any form or by any means, including photocopying, recording, or other electronic or mechanical methods, without the prior written permission of the publisher, except as permitted by U.S. copyright law.

This is a work of fiction. The story, character names and descriptions, and incidents portrayed in this publication are the product of the author's imagination. Any resemblance to actual persons, living or dead, or events, past or present, is entirely coincidental. No identification with actual persons or events is intended or should be inferred.

Ebook ISBN: 979-8-9908192-0-7

Paperback ISBN: 979-8-9908192-2-1

Hardcover ISBN: 979-8-9908192-1-4

Cover by Getcovers

Edited by Dr. Michael with FirstEditing

Published by Lilabean Lit

Dedication

For my dad in heaven, who let me share a bit of this book with him during his last day on this Earthly plane. And to my mom, who read every chapter as it was written and supported me in pursuing my passions.

Content Warning

This book contains references to car accidents, brain injuries, chronic pain, depression, PTSD, murder, sacrificial rituals, and violence. Some of the scenes may also be considered graphic. If you find any of these topics triggering, please be advised.

Playlists

Listen to Brie's playlist on Spotify

Listen to Michael's playlist on Spotify

And check out the mood boards for both Brie and Michael on Instagram: @algordon.author

Prologue

BRIE

I adore the feeling of the sun's warmth as it washes over my skin and the feathers of my wings. I pause just outside the amphitheater entrance to soak it in. With my eyes closed and my head tilted up toward the sky, I can't imagine a more beautiful day than this. I breathe deeply, inhaling the scents of daffodil and honeysuckle carried on the breeze.

"Sabriel, my love, we should go inside."

I turn my head to the right without opening my eyes. A strong hand cups the back of my neck as warm lips descend on mine in a gentle kiss. He pulls away slowly, and I open my eyes to gaze into Michael's deep blue ones. His eyes are radiant and electric, a clear sapphire blue that you can fall into and get lost in, but which you could never forget. His hair is a rich brown. It's soft enough for me to love running my fingers through, without being long enough to tangle. At 6'3", he's solidly built and muscular in an athletic way, similar to a quarterback in the human sport called American football. Like all the archangels, Michael's wings are massive and match the innate strength of his body well. They are primarily a rich sapphire blue, matching his eyes perfectly, with waves of gold and yellow feathers throughout. I smile up at him as he gazes down on me with equal affection. Even after eons together, our love is still as potent as the day we married. Michael takes my hand, and we both turn toward the amphitheater entrance to walk inside.

The "Angelic Amphitheater", as it's formally called, is a massive semicircular tiered seating gallery that puts those of the Greeks and Romans to shame. The structure is made of solid White Thassos marble with gold and emerald adornments interspersed throughout. Each seat is a plush velvet recliner with massive arm rests. The seats are assigned based on rank. Due to Michael's high rank within the angelic community, our seats are front and center. My rank on its own is just below that of the archangels. I'm one of the most powerful in our community and a warrior in my own right. I imagine the power that Michael and I give off when we're together packs quite a punch. The other angels bow their heads to us in deference as we make our way through the crowd, automatically parting to give us a path as a show of respect.

The other archangels are already standing near their seats as we approach. I let go of Michael's hand and skip over to Raphael before wrapping my arms around his neck in a hug and beaming at him. Michael walks up beside me and places his hand firmly on Raphael's shoulder.

"Raf, we've missed you," Michael says, smiling. "How were things in the human realm?"

Raphael's forehead creases with tension as the smile he just showed us transforms into a frown.

"That's actually what this meeting is about. Things are worse than they've been in a very long time, brother. My healers are completely overrun. I fear drastic measures have become a necessity."

I stare at Raphael with dread pooling in my chest, siphoning the air from my lungs. If Raphael thinks we need to take drastic measures, then the human realm must be poisoned with more darkness than I can even imagine. How could things have gotten this bad? I glance over at Michael who shares a look with me right back. I can see his unease through the tightening of his jaw as he reaches out an arm and pulls me closer to him.

"Well, we're glad to have you back, brother," is all Michael allows himself to say in response, but I know we'll be having a much longer conversation with Raphael in private.

A booming voice echoes throughout the amphitheater, "Angels, please take your seats." I sit in my assigned seat to the left of Michael. Raphael is on his right and Uriel sits to my left. I look over at Uriel and give him a small smile. I think of Uriel as an uncle of sorts. Though we're not actually related, Uriel has acted as an advisor and teacher for me for as long as I can remember. He's known throughout the angelic realm for his wisdom, so I'm incredibly lucky to have been blessed with his guidance, especially during my formative years as an angel. I'm not sure why he took me under his wing—figuratively speaking, of course—but I am infinitely grateful that he did. Gabriel, the last member of the powerful foursome surrounding me, leaves us and walks onto the podium in the center of the amphitheater.

Like the amphitheater itself, the stage is solid marble with gold and emerald adornments. It also has angelic runes etched into the front of the platform and four Corinthian style pillars lining the back, each one encircled by twining vines filled with gladioli and snapdragon flowers. These pillars are meant to represent wisdom, courage, mercy, and faith. They are considered the ideal attributes of an angel, although some surmise the pillars are actually meant to represent the four archangels, as wisdom, courage, mercy, and faith are the main characteristics of Uriel, Michael, Raphael, and Gabriel respectively. I once asked Michael if there were any truth to those rumors. He just laughed and said vanity didn't exactly fit into that list.

"Angels," Gabriel begins, "welcome, and thank you all for taking the time to be here. I have received an important message from the divine spirit which I will now relay to all of you. Following Raphael's most recent trip to the Earthly plane, it has become apparent that the human realm is in danger of falling to the darkness completely. Demons have secured a much stronger foothold in the human realm than our lightbringers can successfully counter. As such, the divine spirit is asking for volunteers among our angelic community to live on Earth as humans in an effort to restore the balance. Should you volunteer, it is important to note that during your time as a human, you will retain no memories of your angelic past nor of your full powers. While you may innately retain some of your power, you will not know how to use it or why you have it. That being said, those who are willing to make such a sacrifice, please approach the stage so we may compile a list of candidates."

I'm shocked into silence by Gabriel's announcement—as, it seems, is the rest of the amphitheater, given the absence of sound throughout the large venue. You could literally hear a cricket right now—if we had crickets on this plane. This is insane. I mean, yes, most of us have spent time in the human realm before, but we've always gone as angels. Even when our wings were retracted or we used a glamour on them to appear human, we still knew who we were and why we were there. We still knew who our loved ones were.

My heart stutters and I look over at Michael. He's staring at me with pain in his eyes and I know he's thinking the same thing. Michael takes a deep breath and cups the side of my face with a tenderness that makes my eyes burn with unwanted tears. I know what he's going to say, but it doesn't make sense. As the leader of the angels and a warrior through and through, Michael feels that it's his obligation to fulfil the request Gabriel has laid before us.

"No," I say before he can even open his mouth. "It doesn't make sense for you to go. For any of you to go."

I look past Michael to Raphael, and then meet Uriel's eyes as well so they both know they're included in what I'm saying. "The archangels are too important to our society for us to risk you not having your memories. Should the angels who go to the Earthly plane fail in their endeavor, the four of you will need to be ready to protect our realm when the darkness seeks to penetrate it. All of you need to stay here, knowing who you are, to keep our realm safe."

Uriel sighs as he transfers his gaze from me to Michael.

"She's right Michael. You cannot go, nor can Raphael."

Gabriel leaves the stage and strides over to us. The reason is obvious to me, and I resign myself to whatever the fates may have in store for me as I wait for him to tell his fellow archangels what I've already determined.

Gabriel looks at Michael and says, "No one is going to volunteer without a leader to set the example. They need to follow someone else's bravery into battle." Then, he looks directly at me. "Sabriel, it has to be you."

Chapter 1

BRIE

Coffee. I need coffee. It's the only coherent thought that my foggy, sleep-addled brain can put together as I stumble toward the kitchen with one eye still fully closed and the other opened to just enough of a sliver that I don't end up walking into a wall or tripping over furniture. I pull open one of the kitchen cabinets, and look over my selection of mugs. I have my favorites of course, but usually I pick whichever mug stands out to me on each particular day. I've learned over the years that it's best to always follow my intuition, even for something as trivial as choosing a coffee mug. Today I end up grabbing one that's bright pink and has "Heyyy Hot Stuff" printed on the side. I grab some almond milk from the fridge and pour a little into the bottom of my mug before pumping in some hazelnut flavored sweetener and pushing the start button on the coffee machine. I loaded the actual coffee grinds into the machine last night, because I tend to be fairly impatient about waiting for my coffee to brew in the mornings. Actually, let's be honest: I tend to be impatient about most things.

As I stand in front of the coffee machine watching the dark deliciousness stream down into my mug and breathing in the rich, smoky dark roast scent, I feel a warm, comforting pressure wrap around my body. The energy is all too familiar and yet consistently fleeting. A smile automatically curves my lips as I take a few seconds to appreciate the sensation before leaning back into a phantom embrace.

"Michael."

His name slips past my lips on a breath, unbidden, and I feel a caress of air down my arm in response. My coffee is ready, but I don't want to move quite yet. I don't want to break this moment. I fear that even breathing too heavily could break the tenuous hold of his energy on this plane. It's a good thing I live alone, because if anyone saw me like this, they would undoubtably question my sanity. I used to question it myself to be honest. I tilt my head back slightly and whisper, "I've missed you." An answering brush of air touches my lips and slides down the side of my cheek. And then, all too soon, the pressure in the room dissipates and I know he's left me. I sigh in disappointment, grab my enticingly full coffee mug, and amble over to the chocolate brown colored sofa that sits just past the threshold to the kitchen.

I've never seen Michael in the physical sense, I just know who the energy belongs to, as weird as that sounds. If I had turned around in the moment, there would have been nothing but air in front of me, hence the looking crazy part. It's possible that I've just contrived all of this in my head, but I'd prefer to think there's some greater cosmic explanation in play. I first registered Michael's presence in my life about five years ago, around the time

I started hearing voices. And yes, that development was exactly as disturbing as it sounds. Thankfully, I wasn't plagued with hearing voices *all* the time, because that definitely would have landed me in a mental institution. Instead, I only hear the voices after sunset and until dawn.

When they first started it was just a conglomeration of murmurs, like white noise, that would start every time I laid in my bed at night readying myself to sleep. After a few weeks of this, I would randomly hear a voice amidst the noise. Initially, I thought it was someone talking outside my apartment. It kept me awake for nights: I was constantly getting out of bed to peer through the windows looking for possible burglars. After several weeks of seeing nothing outside the windows that could be causing the voices I was hearing, I realized it was all in my head. That was a pretty nerve-wrenching realization. I wondered about my sanity and if I would ever be able to easily fall asleep again. I thought about checking myself into a psych ward or asking my doctor if there was some sort of medication I could take, but neither option was ideal. Then, one night, Michael visited me. I didn't know what the energy was at the time, but I felt him simply laying in the bed beside me. His energy curved around the back of my body as I lie there facing the blank white wall, wishing I could just peacefully fall into a slumber. I'm not sure if I absorbed some of his energy or if I was finally calmed enough to fully process what the noise was, but in that moment the murmurs finally became distinguishable and I realized with a shock that I was hearing people's prayers.

So, yeah, since then I've felt that comforting energy around me fairly regularly, and at some point along the way I started calling that energy by the name "Michael". I'm not sure why. It just felt right. I often wish Michael were an actual physical presence. It would make my love life (or lack thereof) so much easier.

Speaking of, I open my day planner to today's page and look at the 6pm entry: "Date with Chad". I barely hold in a groan and idly wonder how terrible of a person I would be if I cancelled.

When I was younger, I thought I would end up married at a young age and live happily ever after with my white picket fence, 2.5 kids, and a dog. Turns out life had a different plan for me and now, here I am closing in on thirty, painfully single, and working a retail job that just barely covers my rent. It's not that I don't want to go on this date with Chad specifically, it's more that I don't want to deal with dating at all. I moved to Los Angeles when I was twenty-two and I've had a lot of really disappointing dates since then. Most people call L.A. "The City of Angels" but in my mind it's "The City of Zeros". A bunch of beta males trying to come across as alphas. Sorry betas, you don't fool me. So, sadly, I'm still single, and wishing I hadn't scheduled myself a date for tonight. Oh well.

I check myself in the mirror one last time before leaving for this dreaded date that my sense of justice prevented me from canceling at the last minute. I think I look pretty decent. I always try to find the balance between looking too sexy and looking like I don't care at all. Tonight I'm wearing dark wash skinny jeans with heeled gray ankle boots. My top is a pomp and power shade of purple with an asymmetrical neckline, so it only covers one shoulder. My golden blonde hair falls to just below my shoulder blades in soft curls and I have the tiniest bit of purple eyeshadow on my eyelids, making the green and gold flecks in my hazel eyes pop. My skin is naturally tan from all of the hiking I do in my spare time, complementing the color of my top well. Not too shabby, if I may say so myself. Also, not overtly provocative, which is arguably more important.

After I use my phone to book a ride to the restaurant, I pull up my text chains. Facing the camera towards myself, I make an exaggerated expression of terror and take a quick selfie to send to my best friend Callie, along with the details of tonight's date just to be on the safe side. I found Chad on a dating app that Callie made me download a few months ago, and this is my first time meeting him so I have no idea what his creep factor will be. You can never really tell from message interactions.

My driver pulls up, and is thankfully more interested in listening to his music than in talking to me. It's not that I dislike people per se, it's more than I don't really see the world the way other people do, which makes it hard for me to relate to others. I can empathize with them, sympathize with them, and make conversation, but in the end, I usually feel like most people talk only to hear themselves speak. They don't actually care about making a genuine connection or learning about the person they are conversing with, so I'm always left wondering why I even bother participating in the conversation in the first place.

We arrive at the little family-owned Italian restaurant Chad picked out for our date and I thank the driver. As I get out of the car, I pull up Chad's picture on my phone, hoping I'll recognize him. Doubtful. None of these apps or dating sites have a great track record of people looking like their pictures. I once had a guy who kept texting me pictures of himself. He was super into how he looked, and he didn't even look that attractive in the photos. His vanity was pretty off-putting, but I figured I would give him the benefit of the doubt and met up with him anyway. When I finally met him in person, I realized all the pictures he sent were close to ten years old and he probably thought they were amazing pictures because they were taken during his glory days. I try not to judge people too much based on looks, but his personality was even worse than his appearance, which had obviously deteriorated in the previous decade. I was genuinely unable to identify any redeeming qualities. Needless to say, that date wasn't a very enjoyable one.

I'm pulled out of my thoughts when I see a guy who looks like he might be Chad sauntering up to me. He has dirty blonde hair several shades darker than my own golden locks, looks to be around 5'7" with a wiry build, and is trying to pull off a high-schoolish skater vibe, which doesn't really work for someone who is clearly in their mid-thirties. As I watch him walking towards me, I also notice that his eyes are focused too low on my body to be looking at my face. Great, that would be strike one.

"Bri—ennnnna" he says in what I'm assuming is supposed to be an alluring purr. Sadly, the way he said it just sounds smarmy and vulturine.

"Hi, you must be Chad. Yes, I'm Brienna," I respond, forcing a smile. Chad doesn't respond to my statement verbally. Instead, he takes a step back and very obviously lets his eyes rove over my body before licking his lips and smirking. Now I'm wondering if I should just dip out before we even get a table. This guy is definitely not winning me over and I feel like I've wasted my time already.

We did have some decent conversations through the app, though, so maybe I should give him more of a chance.

"Let's get a table," Chad finally says, apparently sufficiently satiated in his perusal of my very clothed body. He walks next to me as we approach the door and I wait for him to pull it open. I always like seeing if my date will walk through the door first himself or if he will hold it open for me. Chad holds the door open for me, which I find somewhat surprising—until I turn around to thank him and I see that he's looking at my ass.

Chad swaggers past me and leans lightly on the hostess stand. "Hey sweetheart, how about a table for two?"

Ok, seriously? Sweetheart? Now he's calling random girls pet names and thinking that's acceptable. So not ok. At least he's looking at her face, though, and not staring at her chest. I wonder if it's because she's small busted so there's not too much to stare at. As the hostess leads us to a table, I pull out my phone and sneak a text to Callie.

I chuckle at her response. Callie has a very different approach to dating then I do. While I date in an effort to find a quality connection, Callie dates as a way of socializing. I always feel bad about my dates spending their hard-earned money on some girl they've never met before and might not end up interested in, but Callie revels in the free meals she gets. She sees it as a fair tradeoff for her time and attention. Part of me would love to be more like Callie, but my moral compass consistently gets in the way.

"Soooo..." Chad says once we're seated. "What's wrong with you?"

I'm pretty sure my eyes just bulged out of their sockets. That question was almost as bad as the one time a guy told me I was "basically a dude with boobs" because I said that I liked watching football.

"Excuse me?" I manage to choke out despite how dumbstruck I am right now.

"Well, you're obviously an attractive girl, from our messaging I know you can string together sentences, and yet you're still single. So why are you single? What's wrong with you?"

I feel like my jaw has hit the floor. Did he really just say that? Yes, yes he did. I don't care how good the food here is, no meal is worth putting up with this nonsense. Gathering my wits, I stand up and step away from the table.

"I'm still single because I haven't met the right person yet, and given the brief time we've spent together tonight, I can already tell that you're not going to end up being that person either. Enjoy the rest of your night Chad." Proud of myself for taking the high road despite my incredulousness, I turn on my heel and walk swiftly back out the door we entered through not ten minutes prior.

Chapter 2

BRIE

"Noooo!" Callie says in a low exaggerated whisper. "Did he really say that?! Like for real?"

My best friend has short, light brown hair that's cut into a bob, streaked with pink on one side and shaved close on the other. I like to think of it as an edgy, punk rock kind of look that I could never in a million years pull off. Callie, though, she makes it iconic. Her chocolate brown eyes are almost always lined in a cat eye style with heavy layers of mascara, and today she also has on bright red lipstick, making her porcelain skin look even paler than usual. Callie is around 5'5" with a slim build, and the look on her face right now is priceless.

"No joke, that is what he actually said to me verbatim," I reply.

I've just finished telling Callie about my 10ish minutes in Chad's underwhelming presence last night. Her expression conveys a mixture of horror and hilarity, like she's not sure whether to hate him on my behalf or laugh at how absurd the whole thing was. That pretty much sums up how I feel about the matter too.

Honestly though, I'm more upset about the money I spent getting to and from that epic failure of a date than I am about the date itself.

"At least you put yourself out there and gave it a shot," Callie says cheerily once she's recovered. "You don't know if you don't try—isn't that what they say? Nothing ventured, nothing gained. No pain, no—"

I cut her off before she can recite every phrase or idiom she's ever heard that could be even distantly relevant. "I'm not sure those sayings were meant to be applied to dating, but sure. Let's go with that." I let my amusement soak into my tone and place another flower-shaped piece of decorative soap on the shelf to my right.

Callie and I work at a cute little boutique called "Suds & Stuff" on Abbot Kinney Boulevard near Venice Beach. The shop specializes in decorative personal care items such as bath bombs, bath salts, bubble bars, and the aforementioned soaps. Most of the products are infused with essential oils or flower petals, which makes the interior of the boutique smell divine and helps to calm me. There's just something about being around those types of natural elements that I find comforting. Callie, on the other hand, is perpetually energetic despite her angsty appearance and isn't affected by the ambience of the boutique in the slightest. She's also the store manager and the reason I started working at Suds & Stuff two years ago.

Prior to that, I was waiting tables at one of the few remaining diners in West Hollywood. I didn't mind the work and made a decent amount from tips, but I started getting these sharp cutting pains between my shoulder blades about three years back, which made it hard to carry the heavy trays of food and drinks. That's when I figured it would be better for me to switch to retail so I wouldn't need to strain my back so much.

The pain has gotten progressively worse regardless, and now there is a constant ache between my shoulder blades with intermittent bouts of the sharp, cutting sensation. I've noticed over the years that the sharp pains tend to manifest more frequently when my emotions are high or when I'm helping people. I guess it lends weight to the saying "No good deed goes unpunished." Apparently, feeling like I'm repeatedly being stabbed between my shoulder blades is the punishment I get for being a good person. I've seen a few doctors about it, but none of them have been able to find what's causing the pain, and each one has mentioned that it might be psychosomatic. In their minds, since they can't find a source for my pain, it must be imagined.

I open another one of the boxes that arrived this morning in our latest stock shipment and find that it contains a silver pedestal bowl. I assume it's not real silver—the owner of the store would never approve an expensive purchase like that—but the silver plating is gleaming as if there are rays of sun shining on it, even while it's still inside this dark cardboard box. The bowl is probably meant to hold some of the bath bombs so their display will seem more decorative.

I take the pedestal bowl out of the box and examine it, slightly awed. It's absolutely gorgeous. The base of the pedestal is designed to look like three Florida horse conch shells propped up in a triangle, to connect to the center of the bowl's bottom. The bowl itself has wave-like shapes comprising its bottom half before transitioning to a web of fan coral. Atop the fan coral at the lip of the bowl is a row of beads painted in a way that makes them look exactly like real pearls spanning the circumference.

The pedestal bowl is so beautiful that part of me feels like it could be an artifact from the lost city of Atlantis. I peer into the well of the bowl wanting to examine the detail more thoroughly and then, I'm falling.

I'm not falling to the floor of the boutique though. Nope, that would be too normal, of course. Somehow, I'm falling from a sky filled with dark gray storm clouds periodically flashing with lightning within and booming with thunder. Below me lies a barren wasteland where high rises that once gleamed in the midday sun now lie blackened and destroyed. I'm still able to recognize the skyline despite its current state. What was once the busy cab-filled streets of New York City is now a desolate wasteland. There's not a soul to be seen. An inky blackness curves around entrances of buildings and alleyways, soaking up any light that may have penetrated the dark clouds above. The air is heavy with an acrid stench of rot, and has an arid feel—because despite the storm brewing, no rain will come. No rain has come in a long while and the city is now uninhabitable. But it's not just the city, is it? Somehow, I know that it is the whole of the Earth that has fallen into this state of chaos. All life that was once joyously thriving has ceased to exist.

Lightning crackles from the sky, bursting from the cloud in which it was contained and striking the broken ground, leaving scorch marks in its wake. I'm still falling as I take all this in. My body is just about to hit the dust-covered shards of pavement twenty feet below me when wings suddenly burst from my back, right where my pain is usually centered.

Instead of ending up splattered across the ground, my body is now hovering in place a few feet above it. Oh sweet baby angels, that was close. My heart pounds in my chest and my breaths come in quick gasps as I send a quick thank you to the powers that be. I look back at the literal wings that somehow just sprouted from my back with a mixture of disbelief and incredulity. They look sturdy and strong, and the feathers look soft. It's an odd juxtaposition. Each feather is pure white swirled with maya blue and has a thin gold strip down the center, as well as two thin silver strips that line the edge. As awe-inspiring as they are, I'm pretty sure I'm hallucinating right now, so I can't fully appreciate their beauty. I take a few deep breaths to calm myself so I can think more clearly. I was at work and we had just gotten a new shipment in...Callie and I were stocking the shelves with the new arrivals...The bowl. It had to be the bowl. Maybe there was some sort of toxic dust on it that I inhaled?

Now if only I could figure out how to stop floating. I pull my shoulder blades together and unceremoniously land face first on the disgusting portion of broken asphalt I'd been hovering above. As I push myself to my feet, I examine my body for injuries. Without the earlier momentum that I had while falling, the impact wasn't too bad. I've got a few scrapes, but nothing seems broken and I'm not gushing blood, so all in all it seems like a win.

I'm not entirely sure what to do now though. Most likely, I'll just need to wait out whatever drug ended up in my system. This place isn't exactly hospitable, so I don't want to sit anywhere or risk going into any of the decrepit buildings that surround me.

I slowly make my way through the rubble that was once a road. As I look at various buildings along the way, I'm suddenly struck by visions related to the demise of each one: the high-rise next to me is suddenly aflame before reverting to the burnt-out shell it started as, the building just beyond it has people running out of the main entrance in terror, their faces void of all color, as the sound of gun shots pierce the air. Then, as abruptly as it started, the street is suddenly empty again, with only the thunder from above to be heard. On and on it goes. Everywhere I look is another horrible scene filled with death and destruction.

I feel like I've been stuck in this torment for hours now. I stopped walking a while ago, hoping that if I didn't see anything new in my environment, the visions would exhaust themselves. They haven't. I see death and pain on a reel. Even when I close my eyes, the visions plague me through the darkness behind my eyelids. Tears pour down my cheeks as I fall to my knees and beg for the visions to stop, but no one is here to hear my pleas.

"Sabriel" I hear from a soft voice. A hand rests gently on my shoulder as the voice continues, "Brie, honey, please look at me."

I open my eyes and raise my head from where it was resting on my knees while I sat balled up in the middle of what was once a vibrant intersection but has become my own personal torture chamber. The first thing I see when I look up is a pair of soft baby blue eyes. They're looking down on me with sympathy, concern, and sincerity, although they are also somewhat distant, as if the mind behind them is only partially focused on what's going on around it. It almost seems like he's listening to something in the background despite the current silence of our environment. The man to whom the eyes belong is kneeling in front of me with his hand still resting gently on my shoulder. He has dark honey blonde hair and a strong jaw, and there's an air of command about him that makes you want to listen to whatever he has to say. It's as if anything that could possibly come out of his mouth would be of the utmost importance. He also has huge wings similar in structure to the ones protruding from my own back, though larger, and his are a checkerboard of silver and sapphire feathers. He smiles gently at me as I just sit here staring at him.

"How did you know to call me Brie?" I finally ask the man. "You said another name first though, I think. I'm not sure, but maybe you have me confused with someone else. I usually go by Brie, but my name is Brienna, not that first name you said."

"My apologies, it's hard to break some habits. Please allow me to introduce myself. My name is Gabriel. I know you don't remember me, but please trust that I'm a friend."

"A friend?" I question. His answer didn't make a whole lot of sense to me and I'm pretty sure I would remember this guy if we'd ever met before, considering the huge wings coupled with his good looks, but I have to admit there is something about him that feels familiar.

"Listen, Brie, we don't have long. It took me awhile to penetrate this prophetic vision you're having and I fear you will be pulled out of it soon. It's important that you hear what I need to tell you. What you see around you, the way this city looks right now, this is what the future holds for Earth if we can't purge enough of the darkness that has already infiltrated the Earthly plane. The measures we've taken thus far haven't been as effective as we'd hoped, and the darkness continues to grow despite our countermeasures. It's not enough anymore to spread hope and goodwill amongst the humans, we need to actively fight the sources of darkness and eradicate it completely. If we don't, this is what will happen." Gabriel spreads his arms, gesturing to our surroundings. "There are nine Hell Gates located throughout the human realm. As a safeguard to prevent war between Heaven and Hell, the Hell Gates can only be sealed by a mortal being. You, my dear, are an angelic soul of the highest order in the body of a mortal being, which means you have both the power and the capability to seal these Gates."

Gabriel's eyes start to glow bright silver as his voice falls into a deeper baritone. "Sabriel of the light, major angel on high, oracle, empath, warrior, sworn defender of all realms of light, you have been chosen. The divine spirit calls on you to close all Earthly Gates of Hell and purge the Earth of all darkness that seeks to decimate the material plane. Will you heed this call and accept this duty on your honor as an angel of the highest order?"

Gabriel's eyes are still glowing silver and it's kind of freaking me out. I also don't fully understand half of what he's said, but it's clear he's waiting for an answer and I get the feeling I can't say no. So, I do something that I'll no doubt regret in the future and give him the answer he's waiting for.

"Yes."

Chapter 3

BRIE

"Brie, did you hear me?" Callie's voice penetrates my consciousness as if from a distance. "Hello, Earth to Brienna. Are you with me here?"

Callie's voice seems closer now as Gabriel fades before my eyes. I'm suddenly back in Suds & Stuff, looking down toward that cursed silver pedestal bowl that somehow drugged me. A slender hand waves back and forth in front of my face. I raise my gaze from the bowl, looking around the shop surprised that I'm still standing and not sprawled out on the floor. I wonder how long that hallucination lasted. It felt like I was in that wasteland for hours, but if that were the case, I doubt I'd still be standing here in the same exact position as I was in when the hallucination started. Surely Callie would have become concerned enough to get medical help if I was unresponsive for hours on end?

"Sorry, what?" I say distractedly, remembering that Callie had been trying to gain my attention.

"I said I didn't order that bowl you're holding. Was there a packing slip in the box?" Callie responds with a bit of exasperation. I wonder how many times she tried to get my attention before I came to.

"Oh, um, let me check." I kneel down to rummage through the box at my feet. Instead of finding a packing slip, at the very bottom of the box I find a small white envelope with my name written on the front in gold ink. I flip the envelope over to find it has a gold wax seal embossed with an emblem of angel wings. The wings in the emblem look broad and full. They somewhat remind me of Gabriel's wings. Wait a second, I forgot about the wings. How could I forget about the wings? I jerk my head toward my shoulder so quickly that my body starts to spin around with the momentum and I nearly lose my balance. Re-centering myself, I peer over my shoulder more cautiously, exhaling with relief when I see that my back is once again free of the wings that manifested during my hallucination. The relief of this discovery is short-lived, however, quickly turning into a longing that makes my chest ache and an emptiness grow in the pit of my stomach. I know it's silly, but those wings felt like they belonged with me, and now that I've experienced that feeling, I can't forget the rightness of it, even if it was only in my imagination.

I return my attention to the envelope with a bit of melancholy, sliding my finger under the flap as I attempt to lift the wax seal in one piece, successfully avoiding ruining its beauty. Inside the envelope is a thick white notecard. The weight of the notecard reminds me of the expensive type of cardstock that people use for wedding invitations. As I pull the notecard out, I see that the message it holds is written in a neat, calligraphic style, with the same gold ink as was on the envelope. The lines of the text are thick and smooth in a way that only a practiced hand could manage, and there are little pools of dried ink at the beginning and end of each letter, signifying when the penman lifted their hand to move onto the next letter and giving me the impression that this note was written with a feather quill and an ink pot rather than a pen.

My darling Brie,

The time has come for you to reclaim the gifts that your soul has forgotten. The enclosed pedestal bowl was created for you long ago and blessed by the power of the sea to infuse your visions with the clarity of still waters and the fierceness of raging rapids. I hope you come to cherish it in this lifetime as you have so many times in the past. Let it inspire you to see the truth of what lies ahead so we can live in the light together for eternity.

I miss you more than one could ever imagine and will be seeing you soon.

With all my love,

Michael

I read the card three times, but I still can't process it. Michael? My Michael? My Michael who visits me energetically and has never manifested physically—that Michael? I run through everyone I know in my brain, checking to see if there are any other Michaels I've known over the years that this might be from, but no one else comes to mind. If I had told anyone about Michael, I'd take this as a practical joke, but I never have. Not even Callie knows about my visits from Michael. This is surreal.

I feel Callie's bright energy behind me and turn my head to see her peering over my shoulder to read the note. "Ooh, who's Michael? Brienna Celio, do you have a secret lover that you've never told me about?! Confess right this instant." She giggles as she then moves around me and bends down to get a better look at the bowl. Picking it up, she sucks in a breath then blows out a low whistle. "Wow, Brie. You do realize this is actual silver, right? And I'm almost certain these pearls at the top are real too. Your secret lover knows quality."

I gape at her, dumbfounded. "It's real? How can you tell?"

"There's a difference in weight between the fake stuff and the real stuff," she says looking at me intently. "And this right here, this is definitely real."

‹‹‹ ❦ ›››

I'm sitting on my comfy chocolate brown sofa in the center of my small studio apartment staring at the black screen of a turned-off television. It's been three days since I received the pedestal bowl and the note from Michael. He hasn't visited me despite the "be seeing you soon" message in his note. I didn't want to keep the bowl after what happened at the boutique, but there was no return address on the shipping label, so Callie made me bring it home. It currently sits on top of my bookcase with a large maroon bath towel draped over it because I'm afraid to look at it again.

Since that day, every time I close my eyes, my brain replays all the awful images I was forced to witness during my so-called vision. As much as I wanted to believe it was a chemical-induced hallucination, I can't deny the fact that both Michael and Gabriel referred to it as a vision. The uncertainty of what I actually experienced has been clawing at me. Thick strands of doubt have infiltrated my being and the anxiety of it feels like claws tearing through the inside of my sternum, raking against the fatty tissue of my flesh in an attempt to escape my body. Dread of the possibility that what I saw could transpire fills my stomach with a hollow emptiness no food can cure. The desire to prevent that actuality suffuses my limbs with uncomfortable tingles that attempt to spur me into physical action. It feels as though my muscles are attempting to hoard as much adrenaline as they can muster, leaving me shaky and twitchy. This is despite the concurrent exhaustion, because, on the rare occasions I can actually doze off in spite of my ruminations, I haven't been able to remain asleep for more than ten minutes at a time due to the nightmares I now suffer from. Fun stuff.

I've been here before. About a year before I packed up my belongings, loaded them into my little Kia and left my hometown without a single glance back through my rearview, I had been in a pretty bad car accident. Well, "pretty bad" might be an understatement. According to the doctors, I may have died for a few seconds. But they were able to revive me, so all good. Ok, maybe not *all* good. I broke some bones, tore some ligaments and tendons, but the worst was the brain injury. The trauma of the accident combined with my recovery really screwed me up. It was almost as if I came out of it as a different person. My personality completely changed, and I lost a good portion of my childhood memories, though I could still remember factual information. Turns out there are two different types of memory systems in our brains—episodic and semantic. Semantic memory is factual knowledge, whereas episodic memory is comprised of experiential memories. The doctors said that my episodic memory was likely damaged during the impact to my head and those memories may never return. Not being able to remember your own life coupled with the pain and grueling recovery of my physical injuries sent me into a downward spiral of depression. I was diagnosed with PTSD—post traumatic stress disorder—not long after. Because of this, I understand what I'm experiencing right now—the flashbacks and nightmares, the emptiness and fear, the twitchiness and inability to sleep. They're all symptoms of PTSD. But understanding why I feel this way doesn't make what I'm experiencing any less potent.

I continue to sit on my couch unmoving, in front of the blank television, and attempt to process at least some of what Gabriel said to me during my vision. I was so distressed at the time, and he was rushing through his words with such urgency, that I'm not sure how much of it I took in. I remember he said that what I saw could actually happen, and then he mentioned something about darkness. That we needed to get rid of the darkness. And then...oh, yeah, something about Hell Gates. He asked me to close the Hell Gates and purge the darkness from the Earth.

"Well, that shouldn't be too hard," I mutter sarcastically.

"What shouldn't be too hard?"

"Holy Heaven on Earth!" I scream, jumping away from the unexpected deep voice that I definitely should *not* be hearing, given that I've been sitting in here alone with the door and windows locked. My hand presses into the skin over my heart as adrenaline surges through my body. I try to spin around to find out who the voice belongs to, but give the spin a little too much power, and end up toppling to the floor, landing hard on my ass.

My heart is pounding wildly in my chest as I take in a pair of stunning sapphire blue eyes, a chiseled face with strong features, and rich brown hair that I suddenly want to run my hands through. He looks just as I had always imagined he would. My breath catches as my eyes hungrily devour every detail of his perfect features. I feel a deep yearning in the center of my chest, an urgency and warmth that breaks through the emptiness that was previously consuming me. I don't know how he's here, but he's here. Michael. *My* Michael.

And of course, he's laughing at me. "That was quite a tumble, love. I don't think I've ever seen you quite so floored before," he says with a wink, walking toward me smoothly and holding out one of his large hands to help me up. "Pun intended."

Logically, I realize that when a strange man magically appears in your apartment, the wise thing to do would be to call the police. Yet as I stare at the man in front of me, seeing the playful sparkle in his eyes and the easy smile on his face, I feel comforted by his presence. I feel like I know him, like I've always known him. Somehow, he brings me solace. Just by being near, he's pulled me from the deep dark waters I was drowning beneath and led me to a lush field full of calla lilies, daisies, and warm spring air. It's almost as if he brought the sun into my apartment with him, giving me hope and bringing me back to life. So as foolish as it may be, I don't reach for my phone to call the police or demand that he stay away while brandishing the nearest sharp object.

"Michael?" I ask, skeptically, staring at his outstretched hand without making any move to take hold of it.

"Yes Brie," he says softly. A flicker of sadness passes through his eyes and I feel a lancing pain across my heart in response. I never want to see him sad. The thought is so potent, the strength of it startles me. Collecting myself, I finally reach out and place my hand in his so he can pull me up off the floor. My delicate hand feels so small in his. When he closes his fingers around it, pulling me up as easily as though I'm a feather, I feel something I'm not sure I've ever felt before—I feel safe. Protected. As I continue to stare at him, trying to process this newest revelation, he leads me back to the couch and sits, turning his body at an angle so he's somewhat facing me while also sitting next to me. I get the sense that he's deferring to me in regard to starting a conversation so as not to rush me given the shock of his appearance. He must think I'm a complete nutjob by now with how much I've just been silently staring at him since he showed up. I should probably say something rather than continuing to stare at him in silence. That could get awkward fairly quickly.

"You're real? How are you here?" I blurt out. Smooth, real smooth Brie. Not what I meant to start with. It's a good thing he can't see my internal cringe.

"Here in your apartment or here in a physical sense?"

"Um, both?" I meant it as a statement, but it came out sounding like a question since my self-confidence has apparently retreated along with my ability to form intelligent thoughts.

Michael sighs and places a hand atop both of mine, clearly having noticed that I was wringing them together. He places his other hand on my knee, which was apparently bobbing up and down of its own volition.

"I think this is going to be a long conversation," he says. "How about I make you some coffee and then I'll explain everything?"

I nod. Mmmm, coffee. Smiling to myself, I wonder how this man knows me so well already.

Chapter 4

MICHAEL

Since the day Sabriel's immortal soul was placed in Brienna's mortal body roughly eight years ago, I've tried to prepare myself for the impending conversation. But how could one adequately prepare to tell the love of one's existence that she isn't who she thinks she is?

Even though I've only seen her apartment through my energetic form, I've been here enough times to know where everything is. I open the cabinet to the right of the one above the sink, where I know Sabriel keeps her coffee mugs. No, I remind myself, not Sabriel. It's Brienna now. I shake my head slightly. She may think of herself as Brienna right now, but she'll always be my Sabriel. Even when she doesn't realize she is. I've made a concerted effort to only call her by her nickname since I arrived, so as not to confuse or upset her by accidentally calling her Sabriel. I know Gabriel was required to use her angelic name when he penetrated her prophetic vision to complete her call to arms. He said she didn't respond too badly to being called Sabriel, but this conversation is going to be difficult enough without her thinking I don't know what her name is.

My gaze flits over the selection of coffee mugs and settles on a bright red one that reads "STRONG AND BOLD" in thick black lettering. I know Sabriel always chooses her mug based on her mood. Hopefully the message on this mug can help empower her through the bomb I'm about to drop on her life. I prepare her coffee just the way she likes it. As I stand in front of the coffee machine watching the dark liquid flow down into the mug, my mind takes me back to the last time I held Brie in my arms. We were standing in this exact spot just four days ago, her back pressed against my chest and her head tilted back to rest on my shoulder. I wasn't allowed to visit her in physical form until today, but even in my energetic form, I relished the feeling of being close to the woman I love. The coffee drips its last few drops into the mug and I steel myself for what's to come. Knowing I can't put this off any longer, I walk back over to the couch.

I hand Brie her coffee mug and sit next to her on the couch. I watch as she inhales the steam rising from it, relishing the scent before examining the mug. She gives me a smile of approval, and I give myself a mental pat on the back for choosing well.

Alright, time to man up. Taking a breath, I begin. "I think the easiest place to start would be to tell you who I am. I'm not sure how much you've figured out, so I'll just go ahead and explain as much as possible. Does that work?"

Brie nods but stays silent.

"As you know, my name is Michael. What you may not know is that I am an archangel. I've been keeping an eye on you for years, but was not able to show you my physical form until after the call to arms you received from Gabriel the other day."

In all honesty, I've been watching her since the night she arrived here in the human realm, but she doesn't need to know that. I came as often as I could to make sure she was safe and to be near her, while still taking care of my duties in the angelic realm. It broke my heart to see the state of the mortal body she was transferred into that night, but I know how strong my Sabriel is and knew she would survive the pain and come out the other side stronger for it. I tried to keep my distance as well as possible so as not to interfere with her journey, but when I saw how desperate she was to find peace that one night five years ago, I couldn't not go to her and provide what little comfort I was able to. Of course, she picked up on my energy immediately when I was in such close proximity to her, so it was pointless trying to keep any type of distance after that. She already knew I was here. I still couldn't interfere though, which is why I wasn't allowed to appear to her in physical form. The call to arms changed that. Now I will have an active role in my beloved's journey, guiding her and fighting by her side. As it always should have been.

Brie clears her throat. "I'm sorry, did you say *archangel*? As in from Heaven? As in *the* Archangel Michael who is known throughout history as the leader of the angels? The right-hand man of the guy upstairs? Top dog in the angel world? *That* archangel?"

Brie's eyes are wide and her face has gone a bit pale. Heaven, how I've missed this woman and her nervous rambling. I smile at her, hoping she'll see my amusement with her response through that small action.

"Some might argue that Gabriel is the right-hand man of the guy upstairs, since he is the messenger of the divine spirit," I say with a smirk, "but otherwise yes, I am considered the leader of the angels and oversee the angelic community."

Brie takes in my statement and then tilts her head slightly, intelligence radiating from her eyes as she narrows them. She places her coffee on the side table, rises from the couch and walks around behind it. I turn my head as she walks, tracking her movement and wondering what that brilliant mind of hers is puzzling out. Once she's standing directly behind me, I feel her hand reach toward me and my body hums with the anticipation of her touch. She pauses just before her fingertips make contact, whispering "May I touch you?"

I nod, and her fingertips close the final inches, stroking down the wings she can't see. It feels incredible. Touching an angels' wings in this way is considered an intimate gesture in our society. It's comparable to a kiss, although Brie doesn't realize that at the moment. Because it's such an intimate gesture, my wings have not felt touch like this since she came to this realm. I can feel the heat of her fingertips soaking into me as she explores the feel of my feathers ever so hesitantly. I allow my head to fall slightly toward my chest and close my eyes, relaxing into the softness of her touch.

"You have them hidden," Brie says, now letting her palms trace the tops of my wings, giving her a sense of their shape. "I can feel the energy of them when I'm close, but I can't actually see them."

"They're glamoured," I tell her. "Our wings are made of energy. Most angels are able to pull the energy that makes up their wings into their bodies. As the denseness of the energy in their wings is pulled back, the wings lose solid form and then disappear completely as the remaining energy is pulled internally. We call this retracting their wings. For all but the most powerful of angels, maintaining the solid form of their wings is extremely taxing, taking more energy than they can sustain, so they usually have their wings retracted. For the archangels, however, the energy of our wings is too potent and too powerful for our physical bodies to contain, considering the amount of energy our bodies already hold naturally, so we are unable to retract our wings. We can't pull enough energy out of them to transform them out of their solid state. So instead, we do the opposite. We push some of the energy normally kept within our bodies out to surround our wings and camouflage them. This is called glamouring our wings. In general, whenever an angel is in the human realm, we must keep our wings retracted or glamoured. There have been a select few exceptions where the divine spirit asked us to appear with our wings visible, but those exceptions had a meaningful purpose behind the display."

"Interesting," Brie responds as she withdraws her hand and comes back around the couch to sit next to me again. Picking up her coffee from the side table, she takes a long sip. I let her sit with her thoughts for a moment, allowing her time to process the new information before throwing more logs on the fire, so to speak.

"You sent me that pedestal bowl?" Brie finally asks, pointing to a lump of bath towel atop her bookcase, frowning at it with distaste. I can only assume the bath towel is covering the bowl in question, and I try my blessedest not to let the silent laughter that's now vibrating within my body burst out. Only Brie would cover an ancient, water-blessed, one-of-a-kind artifact with a bath towel.

"Yes," I say, keeping my expression blank and trying to hide the laughter that filters through in my voice with a cough. Probably not the best idea to be audibly laughing at her right now.

Brie looks directly into my eyes with the piercing stare she's always been so good at. The gaze is unnerving, penetrating the deepest depths of one's soul. It's one of her angelic gifts, reading the truth of a being's soul through their eyes.

"I had a vision after I opened it. Did you know?" she continues nonchalantly, revealing no emotion in her voice and continuing to stare intently into my eyes so she can read my reaction to her question.

"Yes, Gabriel told me about your vision. I'm sorry it was a difficult one." My chest fills with a fierce ache. It kills me to know the amount of distress Brie's vision caused her, and even worse is that I'm partially responsible. If I hadn't sent her scrying bowl to her at the boutique, she never would have had the vision. Although I know it was a necessary turn of events, I also lament the pain it has caused her.

I know Brie has read the truth of my words when her gaze changes from the preternatural soul-penetrating stare to a much softer regard, but she doesn't acknowledge my apology as she continues.

"In my vision, I had wings. And Gabriel, he said something about an angelic soul and honor as an angel. Am I...?" Her brow furrows as her question drifts off. It's clear to me she's debating between asking if she's human or asking if she's an angel. The prospect of the latter, although more direct, makes her balk, so she can't quite get the words out.

I spare her the discomfort by answering her unfinished question. "Yes, you're an angel, sweetheart."

An expression that I know well comes over her face at this revelation. It's a look of fervid concentration that tells me her brain is working a million miles a minute trying to process all of the ramifications of knowing her true nature and musing over past events to reinterpret their details within this new mental framework that has been thrust upon her. Brie looks down at her hands, which are now shaking in her lap. The expression of concentration evaporates from her face, and now she just looks so lost, it causes my heart to shatter into pieces. All I want to do is hold her in my arms and comfort her, but I'm not sure how she would react. She knows me as an energetic presence that visited her intermittently over the past five years, not as her husband of millennia. Not as her soulmate. I can't be certain she would welcome such a familiar gesture from my physical form, and I certainly don't want to make her feel uncomfortable. I need to regain her trust, not scare her away. I settle for covering her shaking hands with one of my own, trying to lend her at least a small bit of my strength.

"So, I'm one of those angels whose natural state is to have their wings retracted, and they came out in my vision as some sort of survival mechanism I guess," Brie says quietly to herself, still trying to process that she's not the human she thought she was.

"Actually no," I say, breaking her away from whatever new thoughts that conclusion would have triggered. "You are correct that your wings burst free of their bodily confinement as a survival mechanism, but your natural state is not one in which your wings are retracted. Your natural state is to have your wings out. You're not an archangel, so you are able to retract your wings when necessary, but you are also extremely powerful. Keeping so much power in your body is hard for you, so you prefer to leave your wings visible when given the choice." I know she's about to point to her back and make some tongue-in-cheek comment about not having wings for the past twenty-nine years of her life, so I continue before she gets the chance. "The reason why your wings have remained retracted since your soul entered this human body is simply that you didn't realize you had them, so you never consciously extended them. They won't pop out on their own unless you are in a life-threatening situation. Even so, their confinement has been hard on you. The buildup of excess energy has wanted release. It's why your back has caused you such pain over the past few years."

"My back has felt better these past few days than it has since the pain started. I thought it was just from the adrenaline boost," she says as she mulls over the information. "But if what you say is true, shouldn't my wings have come out when I had my car accident? That certainly qualified as a life-threatening situation."

My stomach plunges as apprehension fills my entire being. This is the moment I've been dreading since I arrived in her apartment today. It's why I delayed showing her my physical self after Gabriel told me of her vision. She may hate me after hearing what I'm about to say. Her whole perception of who she is will soon go up in flames, and I'm the one tasked with lighting the match. Even after she regains her angelic memories, she will retain the memories she has formed while living as Brienna. What if the sense of betrayal she feels toward me in this lifetime is so deep that it overrides our soul bond? What if her loss of trust is too deep to overcome and colors her impression of me even after her angelic memories return? I couldn't bear to exist without her by my side, but will she still want me by her side? When she was Sabriel, our love was all encompassing. It was intoxicating and unconditional and infinite. I can't lose that. I won't lose that. No matter how she reacts, we will come back from this. We have to.

Steeling my resolve and gathering all the courage I can muster, I look into Brie's depthless hazel eyes. "Your wings would have appeared during the car accident had the soul in this body when the accident occurred been yours."

Brie gives me a look of clear confusion. "Are you saying my soul wasn't in my body during the crash? That doesn't make any sense."

"The soul that was born into your body and named Brienna Celio by her parents died on impact the night of the accident. *Her* soul left the material plane for the astral plane, and *your* soul, the soul of the angel Sabriel of the light, major angel on high, was transferred into Brienna's body shortly thereafter. Your angelic memories were locked before your soul was transferred into Brienna's body, which is why you don't remember who you truly are. And since memories are tied to the soul who experiences them, Brienna's soul took her memories with her when she ascended to the astral plane. This is why you seem to have 'lost' the memories of Brienna's childhood. Certain memories, ones that are especially traumatic or create extremely strong emotional reactions in the host, make an impression on the physical body as well as the soul, which is why you are able to remember the accident itself even though you weren't the soul to experience it. Your memory of the accident is only an echo of the true memory, imprinted within Brienna's physical body."

Chapter 5

BRIE

I'm silent for a long time, trying to process the bomb that's just been dropped on my sense of self. Michael stays silent too, kindly allowing me the time I need to organize my thoughts. His large hand solidly encompasses the both of mine where they rest on my lap, a visible display of his care and support that I'm utterly appreciative of. There are so many emotions roiling inside me right now that half of me wants to laugh, while the other half wants to cry. I feel relief at finally understanding all the broken parts inside myself, but I mourn the fact that I was ever broken to begin with. I feel an empty well of nothingness in the hollow of my chest where my identity used to live, before it was ripped away from me and torn to pieces. Who am I if everything I thought I knew about myself was a lie? I'm not this Sabriel that Michael thinks I am, but I'm apparently not Brienna either, so who exactly am I? Maybe I'm just no one—a void of a soul lost right alongside the memories I no longer possess.

Michael seems to understand where my thoughts have led me, and he breaks the silence that bound the two of us. "You're still you, Brie. The core of who you are, that hasn't changed. The most important parts of us are soul-deep, and those parts exist regardless of whether you have your memories or not, regardless of your name or your age or your appearance. You're still the kind, compassionate, intelligent woman you've always been. Those parts of you haven't gone anywhere."

Michael's words wash over me and blanket my fears with comfort. I can feel the truth of his words despite my inner turmoil. It's hard having to redefine yourself, but he's right. I'm still the same Brienna I was yesterday. I may think about certain parts of myself differently than I did before, but *I* haven't changed, only my breadth of knowledge and understanding have changed. I need to reframe the situation in my mind. I haven't lost myself. Rather, I've gained a greater understanding of myself, and they do say knowledge is power. I need to grab onto this knowledge, harness its power, and mold myself into a stronger, more assiduous version of who I was before. As Michael said, who I am at my core hasn't changed, so why not "take those lemons and make some sugary-sweet lemonade," as Callie would say? Or more accurately for my tastes, turn the bitterness of black coffee into a delicious caramel latte. Yum.

"Ok," I say to Michael. "Where do we go from here?"

A brilliant smile spreads across Michael's face as he says, "Now, we train."

Michael's idea of training isn't fun. Much of it is actually quite painful, to be honest. We start out by letting the energy of my wings unfurl from my body and then pulling the energy back in. This part isn't too bad. Letting my wings out feels like getting a massage, which is a huge relief for my previously painful back, but pulling my wings back in feels like that overly full feeling I get when I eat too much. I feel heavy, bloated, and a little bit disgusting every time I pull them back in. The only difference is that the sensation is centered between my shoulder blades rather than filling my stomach. I definitely understand why Michael said I prefer to keep my wings extended.

I must have practiced extending and retracting my wings a few hundred times when Michael finally says we can move on. The next step, he declares, is learning to use my wings productively. Michael tells me that I need to be able to use my wings not only to fly, but also as weapons in battle. I'm secretly hoping he's joking about turning me into a living weapon, but he seems completely serious about it. I grumble a little bit about potentially being forced into battle against my will, and he narrows his gleaming sapphire eyes at me. I just huff and wave my hand in a "go on" gesture. The corner of his mouth quirks up slightly in amusement in response to the gesture as he tells me the best way to learn to fly is to put yourself into a situation where you need to fly and let instinct take over.

We drive to a trailhead in the Santa Monica mountains, arriving just past 11pm. Technically the trails are closed at night, but Michael says doing this during the day would present too much risk of exposure, so the archangel is breaking the rules. Apparently being an angel doesn't make you a rule follower. Good to know.

Michael and I hike through the mountains for an hour or so with only the light from the stars and a faint glow emanating from Michael's wings to guide our footsteps. We round a curve and end up alongside a deep ravine. Michael instructs me to let my wings out and places a steady hand on the center of my back, guiding me to the very edge of the ravine. I'm expecting him to give me instructions on how to use my wings to lift myself off the ground when, without the slightest hint of warning or hesitation, the hand on my back gives a solid push.

I'm falling. *Again.* Twice in one week. This had better not be my new normal. My mouth opens in a soundless scream as my breath catches while I plummet through the open air toward the imperceptible bottom of a deep ravine. All that lies before me is darkness while I remain in freefall. Part of me is wondering when I'm going to jerk awake, because I'm semi-convinced everything that has transpired over the past several days has been nothing more than a convoluted dream. The feeling of Michael's energy beside me pulls me from my panic-driven thoughts and I turn my head to see him lazily gliding beside me, seemingly without a care in the world. Are you freaking kidding me right now? If I don't die in the next five minutes, I am going to...well, I don't know what I'm going to do but whatever it is, I'm going to do it so hard! I'm seriously contemplating the potential repercussions of punching an angel in his smug smiling face when Michael starts laughing at me. No joke, he's actually laughing at me as I plummet to my death. Rage overtakes my fear and my entire body fills with hot white energy itching to burst out and attack him.

The wind is loud in my ears, but Michael's voice penetrates it nonetheless. "You always were one for righteous vengeance."

"What?" I call back to him, now faltering in my anger due to confusion.

"You got so angry with my nonchalance when I flew up next to you that your body went into battle mode, and you still haven't even realized it. You've been flying for the past minute at least," he replies.

I look down toward the bottom of the ravine, then to my left at the cliff which, sure enough, I'm gliding next to, then peer back over my shoulder to see that my wings are indeed extended. Well, at least I'm not going to die just yet. That's a win. I'm still angry at Michael, but I'm also a little giddy now too because I'm flying. I'm legitimately flying. This is amazing! I allow the tension to leave my body as I take in the feel of the air sliding along the feathers of my wings. Michael reaches out for my hand. I grudgingly allow him to take it because, although I'm still mad at him for literally pushing me off the side of a mountain, I also kind of want to be touching him in some way at all times.

Michael shows me how angling my body right or left will alter the trajectory of my flight, and then angles his body upward and gives me some pointers on how to flap my wings in a way that will allow me to fly upward without getting tired. By the time we arrive back at the trail, I'm having the time of my life. I feel like I'm releasing tension in muscles that were never allowed to slacken before and it's glorious, like an internal breath of fresh air. Michael gives me a few pointers on how to land and we settle back down on the trail still holding hands. Michael probably still deserves a good telling off, but in all honesty I'm too content right now to really care anymore. Between getting to fly and having my hand in his, this moment is pretty much perfect and I'm just trying to relish every second of it.

"You did well," Michael tells me as we begin the hour-long trek back to my trusty little Kia. Can I just say, by the way, how hilarious it was earlier watching Michael trying to squeeze into my compact sedan? I snicker at the memory. His discomfort during both legs of the drive somewhat makes up for him pushing me off a mountain, I rationalize.

"You always did like flying," Michael murmurs almost to himself with a small, sad smile. He looks so haunted in this moment and my instincts are screaming at me to comfort him. I push back the desire to wrap my arms around his neck and burrow my face into him while cupping the back of his head, letting my fingers tangle in that delightfully soft brown hair, an oddly specific urge that leaves me wondering where such a strong impulse came from. He may have been a presence in my life for the past five years, but we really only just met yesterday, and I know barely anything about him. Comforting him in that manner, in any type of manner, could scare him away. If it were unwelcomed on his end, it could strain our budding relationship. As it seems like we'll be working together for quite a while, that would be a foolish risk for me to take. The way he acted in his energetic form suggests he wouldn't take it as an affront, but maybe things are different now that he's in a physical form. I don't want to make things awkward, so I can't cross that line—at least not yet. Not until I know more.

"Did we know each other well?" I ask. "When I was an angel, I mean."

"You're still an angel. You're just temporarily in a human vessel," he says with a hint of frustration. "But yes, we knew each other very well. We were...important to each other."

He says the last part with a bit of hesitation, as though he's choosing his words carefully. I can't help but wonder about the subtext of those words. I want to ask how we were important to each other, what we were to each other, but his energy is telling me that he's completely shut down right now. It seems those few sentences were all he could bare to divulge on the topic. Not wanting to push the matter, I switch gears. "How did I end up being sent to Earth to take the real Brienna's place?"

"You volunteered," Michael says with a pained sigh, his sapphire eyes shining with regret. "The darkness on Earth had reached epic proportions. An imbalance of the darkness on Earth wasn't exactly a new development—it's happened several times throughout history—but in the past, there has generally been a fairly equal balance between leaders of light and leaders of dark. The leaders of light were able to rein in the leaders of dark. Right now, the majority of the world's leaders are slaves to the darkness, which *is* a new development. They are spreading their dark influence faster, farther, and more extensively than we've ever seen in the past. Without enough of our lightworkers in similar positions of power, our efforts to counteract the spread of darkness simply weren't effective. We asked for angels to volunteer to sacrifice their memories and live as humans, hoping that the greater strength of light in angels compared to lightworkers could tip the scales in our favor and rebalance the Earth. Unfortunately, it was too little too late, which is why Gabriel met you on the astral plane to deliver your call to arms."

"If you all were trying to balance out the world's leadership, why give me this body? Why not put me into the body of someone influential, rather than that of a twenty-one-year-old waitress?" I ask.

"Unfortunately, there were certain criteria that had to be met when choosing hosts for our volunteers. The outgoing soul had to be destined to leave their body within a certain time frame, due to the urgency of the situation, and couldn't be befouled by any darkness. Darkness can taint both the soul and the physical body. We couldn't risk putting an angelic soul into a physical body already corrupted by darkness. It takes the soul several weeks to adjust to being in another's physical body, and the darkness could have latched onto the angelic soul during that time, while it was in a weakened state, and corrupted it. If that were to happen, our selfless volunteers would become fallen. We protect our own even more fiercely than we protect the humans, so that just wasn't an option. Every individual with political or social influence who passed away during the time frame we were using was already infected by darkness, so none of our angels could be placed in a position of power. Had we taken this step sooner, we would have had more opportunity to find uncorrupted, influential humans for our angels' souls to inhabit. Waiting too long to initiate this measure was a failing on our part, and goes a long way toward explaining why our actions have not righted the balance."

"I guess that makes sense," I say, thinking of my many hours of volunteer work, all of which can easily be undone with one flippant change in a law or one haphazard comment from a celebrity.

Michael and I finish our hike back to the car in companionable silence, both lost in our own thoughts. It's nearing dawn by the time we arrive, but with this new information I've gained, the soft luster of the sunrise seems to have lost its glow.

Chapter 6

BRIE

I startle awake, gasping for air and darting my eyes around like scared prey looking for an escape route. Once I realize the adrenaline flooding my system is from nothing more dangerous than yet another nightmare, I groan and work to steady my breathing. Looking at the clock on the nightstand, I blow out a breath of frustration, seeing that I only slept for two hours. Given the adrenaline still coursing through my body and causing my muscles to tremble, I know I won't be able to fall back asleep anytime soon, so I get out of bed and stumble toward the coffee maker.

"Everything alright?"

I nearly jump out of my skin—I'd forgotten Michael had asked to crash on the couch for a few hours after we got back from our flying lesson. Placing a hand over my heart, I feel it pounding hard in my chest. Well, that's one way to drive away my fatigue, albeit temporarily.

"Yeah, I'm fine." I reply, turning toward the couch to find Michael's blazing sapphire eyes locked on me. He looks too heavenly for only having had two hours rest. I'm fairly certain I look like a cross between a chia pet and a drowned rat, considering I woke in a cold sweat, but Michael looks every bit the warrior angel. His hair is perfectly tousled from the pillow and his eyes are clear and alert despite the lack of sleep. He's still wearing the same clothes he was yesterday, but they don't look the least bit rumpled, and his shirt has ridden up just slightly to reveal a teasing inch of his deliciously toned ab muscles. He's like a living Adonis.

I belatedly realize I've been staring at him in silence again and hurriedly turn toward the kitchen to start on my coffee. Opening the cabinet that holds my coffee mugs, I pick one that's sky blue and says "To drink, or not to drink, there is no question" in white, cursive script. I prep my coffee mug with almond milk and sweetener and get the coffee machine running, then ask Michael if he would like something to eat. I'm not at all a breakfast person, so I have no idea what I can give him if he says yes, but I'm trying to be a good hostess at least. Since I'm hoping he'll decline, he of course accepts, and I rummage through my fridge and then the rest of the kitchen looking for something that could pass for breakfast food.

"Do you like blueberry muffins?" I ask. "I pretty much only have that or cereal."

"A blueberry muffin is perfect. Thank you," Michael replies.

I give him the muffin, hoping it will tide him over until he can get something more substantial elsewhere. Then I go to my normal morning spot, standing in front of the coffee machine and watching the dark liquid flow into my mug.

"So, um, last night was fun and all but—"

Michael chokes on his blueberry muffin and coughs hoarsely several times to clear his airway.

"You sound like you're breaking up with me, love."

"What? No! What? I...We're not..." I can feel the heat of a blush on my cheeks as I realize what I just said. "No, I meant the flying. Obviously, I meant the flying. There was nothing else that..." I trail off before I can dig myself in any deeper, mortified by how the start of this conversation has turned out.

"Given men that line a time or two, have you? It sounded very practiced," Michael teases—or at least, I hope he's teasing. There's a glint of amusement in his eyes, but his mouth has a hard line to it, so I'm not completely sure if the comment is as lighthearted as he wants it to seem.

"Look, I'm trying to say that I need to go back to work tomorrow. Today is the last of my sick leave, and I can't afford to take off any time unpaid. So as productive as the flying lesson was, the rest of our training is going to need to be planned around my work schedule. Staying out until dawn isn't really going to be an option anymore."

The part of me that always tells myself I'm not good enough, not where I should be in life at age twenty-nine, twinges with embarrassment at having to admit I can't afford to take more time off work, and I find myself looking vaguely into my coffee so I don't have to meet Michael's eyes. I know that I should consider my ability to admit the truth of my financial situation as a strength, but all I feel in this moment is shame. Shame at not becoming the successful adult everyone seemed to expect me to be. Shame at not achieving the life I strove for.

I'm buried so deeply in my spiraling thoughts of past failures that I don't hear Michael move, but suddenly he's standing directly in front of me with one finger under my chin, gently coaxing my head up so he can look me in the eyes.

"Honesty about one's capabilities is admirable," he tells me softly. "Don't ever think otherwise."

I peer deeply into his eyes, almost feeling as though I can see the purity of his soul, grateful for his words. He's so close right now that I can't help but think if I was to lift my heels off the ground and lean forward just slightly, I could close the gap between us and press my lips to his. I wonder if I could taste the remnants of that blueberry muffin on his lips. His breath feathers softly over my face and I'm just about to throw all caution to the wind when he suddenly takes a step back, increasing the distance between us and clearing his throat. I can almost see the wall we both keep between us being rebuilt brick by brick. I feel like the string tethering me to my fantasies of the man in front of me is forcefully cut, snapping back to hit me in the face with a sting of pain that is all-too-real.

"And no, you're not going back to work," he says—a bit too harshly and far too dismissively.

I flinch at the steel in his tone before metaphorical steam starts pouring out of my ears. "Excuse me? Don't tell me what I can and cannot do. I wasn't asking for permission. I was giving you the courtesy of telling you what was happening, which I didn't have to do, so maybe try again with a thank you. You don't control my life—it's *my* life, not yours. I'm the one living it, so I will be the one making the decisions about it and I don't fancy becoming homeless. How am I supposed to pay my rent if I don't go back to work? Where am I supposed to live if my landlord kicks me out?

I get that what you and Gabriel are asking me to do is important, but I can't just drop everything on a dime and forget about the real world. I need an income, so I have things like food that my very human body needs to survive."

Ok, I'll be honest: I was getting more defensive and upset than the situation really called for, but who does this guy think he is, coming into my life and telling me I can't go back to work? It pisses me off that he'd be so presumptuous and controlling, and I feel completely blindsided. That part of his personality came out of nowhere.

Michael holds his hands up in a placating gesture, looking taken aback by my outburst. "I'm sorry," Michael says, and now I'm the one with a taken aback expression. That he would apologize so easily shocks me more than his previous statement, and I concede that I may have misread his intentions. Maybe I've gotten too used to dealing with the off-putting excuses for men I usually encounter. "I didn't mean to tell you what you can or cannot do or try to control you. I should have phrased that better, so I apologize. What I meant to convey is that you've essentially been tasked with saving the world, and that is a full-time job in and of itself. We need you to eat, sleep, and breathe this mission, or the mortal realm may not survive. I understand you want a home to come back to after it's all over and that you don't want to disregard your own wellbeing in the meantime."

Well color me impressed. Also, I feel like a terrible person now. When he phrases it that way, my concerns seem pretty selfish. Yes, it's important to me to not be homeless, but what kind of a brat would I be to put my own needs above saving the whole freaking world? Ugh. I'm totally caught between a rock and a hard place here.

"What I should have explained before voicing my hesitance regarding your job," Michael continues, "is that as an angel, you have come to the human realm many times before. Although this is the first time you've lived here in a mortal body, we've both spent extended lengths of time here in the past for various missions, blending in with the humans. We have several bank accounts and properties throughout the world that were set up long ago, so you don't need to worry about going back to work. We have more than enough resources to get you through your training and this mission without you returning to the boutique. Now that you have this information, will you agree to focus on your training full-time without the added distraction of a human job?"

Once again, I'm flabbergasted. "Oh. Um, ok, I'm sorry I lashed out at you. Callie is not going to be happy if I leave the boutique, but if I do, will we be able to access these accounts? I'm guessing I don't look like I did as Sabriel. I certainly won't match fingerprints or something like that, and my ID wouldn't be the same. I guess if they're in your name, it wouldn't be a problem, but I don't want to freeload off of you."

I trail off. It also occurs to me that Michael must know the information of these supposed accounts if we are going to access them somehow, and I wonder, if any of the accounts are mine, how he has this information. Was it part of the intake process when I volunteered, or did he get the information from someone I was close to? *Or* was I close enough to him to give him the information directly? And when he says "we", does he mean we as in all the angels, or we as in him and I? I know asking these questions could send us into a much more tumultuous topic of conversation that I'm not quite ready for, so I keep them to myself.

"We have passwords and pin numbers set up on all of our accounts, allowing us to surmount the numerous hurdles that come with being an angel among humans."

Yeah, I can definitely think of more than a few issues being an angel in the midst of humans could present. Like not visibly aging at the rate humans do and being alive for generations upon generations. That could raise some suspicion.

"Accessing the accounts won't be a problem," Michael continues. "And you don't need to worry about taking things you didn't earn. You've contributed to these accounts just as much as I have. Though even if you hadn't, you should think of your mission and the training for it as a job, and every job deserves compensation, does it not?"

Well, he has me there.

"Also," Michael says hesitantly, "I'd like you to move into one of our properties. It would be convenient for us to be living in the same place, so we can train early in the mornings or late at night, without me having to travel to get to you and vice versa."

His reasoning makes sense and I'm sure he's simply suggesting we live together for practical purposes, but my breath hitches nonetheless. *Should* I be moving in with a man I barely know? Certainly not. But am I going to turn down the offer he's presented? No. No, I am not, because for some unknown reason, I implicitly trust the man standing before me with the entirety of my so-called angelic soul.

"Yes, I see how that would be productive for our training." I reply. "When?"

"Today would be best," Michael answers.

"Ok," I respond hesitantly. "I'll pack a bag once I finish my coffee."

Chapter 7

BRIE

"So how long should I be packing for?" I call out to Michael as I start pulling various items of clothing out of my dresser.

"Well, it will probably take us at least a few months of training before you're battle ready, so to speak, but the house already has most of what you'd need, so only the essentials, I'd say—and your scrying bowl of course. The clothes there may be a little out of date, but your angelic physical form was similar in stature to Brienna's, so they should fit for the most part. We can always purchase new items as well, and the property closest to here is the one we'll be staying at. It's not so far that you couldn't come back here to grab something every now and then. I'm assuming you don't want to give up your apartment quite yet?"

A few months?! Did he just say a few months?! No, I'm not giving up my apartment. This is my home. Panic floods me as the reality of my situation hits me like a Mack truck. It didn't seem real to me before. The flying was fun, and although the vision was disturbing, the concept of closing a bunch of Hell Gates was so abstract, I guess I didn't fully process what all of this would mean for my life. In this moment, I'm finally realizing that my life is drastically changing before my eyes, and I'm caught up in a whirlwind I can't push a pause button on. Everything suddenly feels like it's spiraling out of control as I reach for something to ground me only to find empty air. I'm in the center of a tornado and I can't get out.

"Brie!" The alarm in Michael's voice pulls me from the wreckage of my panic-driven thoughts. His left hand is firmly holding my right shoulder and his right hand gently cups my left cheek as his eyes look directly into my own. I realize I'm shaking and gasping for air. It seems I had forgotten to breathe while consumed by my panic attack.

"Are you with me?" Michael asks, his tone gentler now but still saturated with concern.

I can only nod as my heart continues to pound in my chest with so much force it's a miracle it hasn't cracked my ribcage. I take a few deep breaths, willing myself to calm down.

"Did you say months?" I finally whisper to Michael, my voice thick with emotion.

His eyes soften with understanding. "Yes, sweetheart. I know it seems like a lot right now, but it might help to think of your training like going to a fitness retreat. Then, once you finish the fitness retreat, you'll be like one of those travel bloggers, visiting different parts of the world. Does that help at all?"

It doesn't, but it's sweet that he's trying, so I just nod. "Thank you. I think... I need... Can I tell Callie what's going on? I feel like I need her support right now, and she's going to ask why I'm not coming back to work anyway. I don't want to lie to her, and

I don't want to lose her as a friend by dipping out on her with no explanation."

Michael grimaces and his lips purse. It's obvious he doesn't like the idea, but he also doesn't want to deny me if it would help me come to terms with everything that's expected of me. I can see his eyes mapping my face, searching for hints of my thoughts in my expression.

"You trust her?" he asks, his weighted gaze still focused on every miniscule change in my expression.

"Completely," I answer, staring directly into his eyes as I say it, because I do. I trust Callie with the entirety of my being. And right now, I need her support to be able to move forward in the way Michael wants me to.

"She will need to take an oath that she won't spread any of the information you give her. If she is willing to do that, then yes. It will be healthy for you to have someone to talk to about this other than myself. I can see that."

"What do you mean you're not coming back to work?!" Callie squeals as she bursts into my apartment two hours later. I always unlock the door for her when I know she's on her way over so she never bothers knocking. I had messaged her that some things had happened and I wanted to talk to her about all of it in person, but that I wouldn't be able to work at Suds & Stuff for a while so she should take me off the schedule. I knew she was at the boutique at the time and would come over as soon as her shift ended, but

I wanted to give her a head's up on the work thing, since she is the manager and it's not like I'm giving the standard two weeks' notice.

In the aftermath of the vision I had when I received the pedestal bowl from Michael, I had told Callie that I wasn't feeling well and needed a few days off. Thankfully, I was able to use my sick leave. She's been checking in on me every day to ask how I was feeling and if I needed anything. I hadn't told her about the vision or my resultant depression, just that I had gotten really dizzy and felt like I was about to pass out and wanted a few days to recover. I reasoned that it was probably low blood sugar or something of the sort, and she accepted that explanation.

"Hey Cals," I say, my tone somber. "We have a lot to talk about."

"Yeah, we do! What's going on?" Then she gasps as Michael walks out of the kitchen, where he was boxing up my coffee mugs. He explained that there were plenty of mugs at the house we're going to, but I insisted I didn't care how many mugs there were, I wanted to bring my own. As silly as it is, those cheap little mugs are special to me. He just chuckled and went out to get bubble wrap and boxes so the mugs wouldn't chip during transport. It was ridiculously thoughtful, and my stomach still has some butterfly flutters when I think that he cared enough to do that. He's been in the kitchen since he returned, wrapping each mug with a diligent level of care before tenderly placing it in the box.

Michael smiles charmingly at Callie and holds out his hand.

"Hello Callie, my name is Michael. It's a pleasure to finally meet you."

Callie looks from Michael's face to his hand, then to me. She ignores his hand and her expression transforms into a moue of pain and betrayal. "Michael?" she asks. "As in the Michael who sent you that silver bowl? Brienna, he's sending you gifts, and now he's in your apartment seeming as comfortable here as if it were his own home. You've clearly known each other a long time, how could you not tell me?"

Her voice breaks on that last question and I understand the implied question she doesn't ask. She had joked about Michael being my secret lover when she read his note. Now she thinks that he is and I didn't trust her enough to tell her. I can't blame her for feeling betrayed when she thought that we were the type of best friends who told each other everything. The truth is that her feelings of betrayal are legitimate. Michael may have only shown up in the flesh yesterday, but he's been a big part of my life for the past five years and I purposefully never told her. I thought she would laugh at me or think I was crazy if I admitted I had some sort of soul-deep relationship with an energetic presence that just happened to be invisible. I mean, that doesn't exactly sound like something a sane person would say. In keeping that from her and in not telling her I hear prayers whenever I lay down at night or that I had a vision of the world completely destroyed, I really haven't trusted her the way I should have. I told Michael that I trusted her completely, but my actions tell a different story. My eyes fill up with unshed tears, blurring my view of the room and Callie's pain-filled rageful face. I never meant to hurt her by not telling her the truth of my abnormality. I only meant to protect myself, but I've hurt her in the process and that in turn hurts me, because I care about her so much. My throat constricts with guilt and a single tear trails down my cheek. I quickly brush it away, embarrassed to display such emotion in front of Michael.

Before I can answer the accusation in Callie's question, Michael says, "My history with Brie is extremely complicated and there is much she would like to tell you, but it puts both of us in danger. She will explain everything to you, but first I need you to swear on your soul that you will not repeat any of what she tells you. The promise you will be making is not to be taken lightly. If you break this vow, if you don't uphold this promise, your soul will never be able to ascend to Heaven. That is the cost."

Callie looks at me with utter confusion. She seems to be torn between laughing, thinking this is all one big joke, and shuddering in fear of the thought that her soul could being kept from ascending. Callie's never been religious at all, so she may not even believe that there is a Heaven, but she wouldn't want to risk it just in case there is.

"Is he being serious?" she asks me.

I nod.

"Um, ok. I wouldn't tell anyone Brie's secrets anyway," she says pointedly—a bit of a slap on the wrist for me.

"Good," Michael responds. "We'll need to do this officially though."

Michael's eyes start glowing, and their purity transforms into iridescence. Unlike Gabriel's eyes, Michael's eyes retain the electric blue color as he delivers the oath, but they look as though they are backlit and his voice contains a power that sizzles against my skin, electrifying every cell in my body.

"Callista Corwin, do you swear on the purity of your soul that you will protect the secrets shared with you today—with your life, for all eternity, sharing them with no other?"

"That's so creepy," Callie mutters. Then, more loudly, she says, "Yes, I swear it."

Michael's eyes return to normal and he nods at me. "I'll give you ladies some space," he says, before walking out and leaving Callie and me alone to talk.

We sit down on the couch and I tell her everything. Absolutely all of it, from the car accident to the voices to the vision and the flying. I even show her my wings. When I finally finish, Callie simply stares at me. I've never seen her speechless before. Callie's the type of person who always has something to say and I expected for her to bombard me with questions once I had told her everything I knew, but it seems the knowledge that I'm actually an angel who has taken over the real Brienna's body has rendered her utterly speechless. She didn't know the real Brienna, since the car accident was before I came to Los Angeles, so at least she's not mourning on top of all the other revelations I just threw at her.

After a few beats of both of us sitting on the couch in silence, Callie jumps off the couch like she was electrified and starts jumping up and down in front of me, full of energy.

"Holy shit, Brie!" she squeals. "You're an angel! That's incredible. So cool. I always knew you were special. Wait, did I just get a ding or something for swearing in front of you? That's bad right?"

I can't help but laugh and just like that, my heart feels lighter. This is exactly why I needed to tell Callie all that's happened, because I knew she would support me no matter what and help me see the good in it. She's always super enthusiastic, and I need that excitement to help me tame my natural response, which is panic.

"Honestly, I don't really know how it works. We can ask Michael about the swearing when he gets back. Do you forgive me for not telling you everything sooner?"

"Of course! I probably would have been hesitant to tell anyone else if I were in your shoes, and I'm grateful that you decided to tell me now. Thank you for sharing this with me. I can't imagine how scary all of this must be for you. You know you have to do it though, right? I mean, the entire world is at stake here—no pressure of course." Callie winks at me.

"Yeah, no pressure," I say, rolling my eyes.

"You'll be great," Callie reassures me. "Plus, you get to spend lots of time with Hottie McHotson." She waggles her eyebrows at me.

"Yeah, that's definitely a perk," I say lightly and bite my bottom lip as I suddenly envision what Michael would look like, sword in hand, going into battle. Callie laughs at me, clearly aware of where my mind fluttered off to, and I feel my cheeks heat as I blush, giving her a look of abashment.

"Let's finish getting you packed," Callie says. "You have a world to save."

Chapter 8

BRIE

It's a three-hour drive to the vast estate which will become our training grounds for the next few months. The property is hidden to the outside world, completely fenced off by a fifteen-foot gray stone wall that surrounds the whole of the property. There are boxwood hedges lining the wall, softening the harshness of the stone. I can barely fathom the amount of work it must take to keep the hedges so neatly trimmed. We pull up to an intricately designed iron gate. It's a smooth, broadly arched blue-tinged sheet overlaid with a red-tinged, highly detailed motif of angel wings, but instead of feathers forming the interior of the wings, there are leaves, hearts, musical notes, and symbols of the natural elements woven into an exquisitely interconnected design. Several feet in front of the gate is a keypad with what looks like a small peephole camera built in. I punch in the numbers Michael tells me and the glass of what I thought was a peephole camera rotates down into the body of the keypad. I feel a pull of air coming from the open hole in the keypad, before the glass rotates back into place and the gate opens, each side parting inward to allow us passage. As I drive through the gate, my eyes also find a multitude of security cameras placed intermittently atop the wall. They blend in well with the wall from a distance due to their coloring, so I didn't notice them before.

"Why is there so much security?" I ask Michael. "And what was the deal with that hole in the keypad? I've never seen anything like that before."

"The hole in the keypad was an energy sensor. All beings emit a portion of their energy. It's not just contained within the body; a small bit is constantly flowing out of you into your environment. The energy sensor in the keypad sucks in air and scans that air for any traces of darkness. Dark energy leaches out into the environment more extensively than light energy. It permeates the air in a large radius around its source and impacts that environment without the source even trying to spread it, so if anyone of dark influence were nearby during the scan, the sensor would detect their darkness and the gate would not open," Michael explains.

"As for why there is so much security," he continues, "I am the general of the Angelic Army and leader of our society. You are one of the most influential members in our society and a high-ranking officer of our army, not to mention my most trusted advisor. Dark entities are constantly seeking to destroy those of us who are notable members of the angelic realm in an effort to gain more power and prestige among their kind. They only have access to us when we are on this plane, so we must be extremely diligent in our security protocols here. We have a team in place that maintains the grounds of properties owned by high-ranking angels. They update our security and keep all of our properties in pristine condition."

I'm an officer in an army of angels *and* Michael's most trusted advisor?! Holy mother of all that is good and pure, this must be a dream. I mean, I accepted the whole angel thing because of the wings, but this whole situation is really getting harder and harder to believe. It's very possible I've lost my mind and everything I've experienced is just an elaborate machination within my mind. If it is real... I don't even know how to react. This is so much to process and the surprises just keep piling up. My questions also keep piling up, because I'm not ready to deal with them, and this revelation adds a mountain of additional unknowns for me.

Assuming this is really happening and everything Michael tells me is indeed true, I should at least try to process the knowledge that I'm an officer of the Angelic Army. Or was, I guess. It's not really a tidbit of information that I can just gloss over and put a pin in to process later. I wonder what an army of angels would look like. I also silently applaud myself because apparently my angel self was a little bit of a badass. I gloat internally for my forgotten badassery. Then I feel a pit open up in my gut as I continue to explore this new knowledge. If Michael's the commander of the Angelic Army and I'm an officer and advisor, that means we had a close *working* relationship. I think back to our flying lesson and how carefully he chose his words when I asked if we were close. He said we were important to each other. Did I completely misconstrue the intimacy of our connection? When he was nothing more than an energetic presence in my life, were the hugs he gave meant as gestures of support and comfort rather than romantic endearments? He calls me love and sweetheart sometimes, but maybe those are just pet names that he uses with lots of women, or maybe he sees me like a younger sister rather than... I've never liked it when men use pet names for women who aren't actually special to them, and I didn't think Michael was the type, but what if I was wrong? In truth, I don't really know who he is. My heart plummets as I realize that I may not be important to him in the way I wanted to be. Our ties might have been strictly professional. My lungs constrict and every cell in my body turns frigid. How could I have been so stupid to think this powerful, respectable man could reciprocate my feelings? A weight forms in the center of my sternum as I'm infused with a sense of despair so intense that I can barely keep my bearing.

I don't want Michael to see my inner turmoil, so I try to keep my voice and expression neutral as I turn my focus to what *should* be my priority, and that is the task at hand, not my relationship with him.

"If these dark entities are constantly after us, why haven't I been attacked since coming here? You'd think I'd be an easy target given that I didn't even know I *was* an angel."

"Your lack of memories coupled with your human body actually protected you. Your human body acts somewhat like a buffer. It's meant to keep your energy contained within, and most of your angelic powers were dormant since you weren't aware of them, so the light energy you put out, even when helping others, was just slightly stronger than that of our human lightworkers. Nowhere near strong enough to raise suspicions. Any dark entity you may have encountered would have thought you were the lowest tier of angel at most. Your light would have made you too hard to infect with darkness, so trying wouldn't be worth the energy it would cost them, and they wouldn't have considered you important enough to be worth killing."

Not important enough to be worth killing. I guess I should view that as a good thing in this case. It's not like I've ever felt important anyway. As we get out of the car, I try to stabilize myself by examining the grounds in front of the house. Like the exterior, boxwood hedges also line the interior of the stone wall. The driveway is circular with two entrances, and I see the second gate is a duplicate of the one we entered through. Lush green grass surrounds the driveway and in the center is a grove of netleaf hackberry trees, with several stone bird bath fountains scattered among them. Each fountain is unique, yet they all seem to complement each other. I walk around the front of the car toward the house. Smooth cream-colored limestone covers the exterior of the house, accented by white casing trim surrounding the many large windows and massive front double door. Michael unlocks the front door and motions me inside.

As I cross the threshold, I'm struck by how light and airy the house feels. The walls are a soft white with minimal décor and the floor is white birch hardwood, making the space seem large and open. The entry area holds no furniture other than a single marble table set directly in the center of the circular space, beneath a spiraling helix-patterned chandelier with dangling strands of brilliantly clear crystals. It is clearly meant to be the focal point of the room. Atop the table sits a shallow circular silver tray covered with large white granules of sea salt surrounding three standing crystal towers. I remember reading once that these crystal towers are called wands. They don't look like the wands you think of when you think of witches though. They're more like the Empire State Building in design.

My fingers twitch and my feet carry me towards the table before I even realize I've moved. My hand reaches out to touch the point of the middle crystal, the largest of the three. *Black tourmaline*, my mind whispers, and as a single finger connects with the tip of the crystal, my body is engulfed by a feeling of safety and security. Warmth flows through me as the protective crystal shares its cleansing energy with me. I don't know how my subconscious knows what type of crystal it is, but the whisper was definitive, so I won't question it, and to be honest, it just feels right.

I lift my finger from the black tourmaline wand and move it to the crystal standing to its right. This one is turbid white. My finger touches the point and I'm nearly overwhelmed by the calm that rushes over me. *Selenite*, my mind tells me, as I revel in a level of calm I can't remember ever feeling before. I don't want to let go of the crystal's calming energy, but the last of the three calls to me, begging for the same acceptance I gave the other two.

I languidly pull my finger away from the selenite wand and move it toward the third crystal. This one is a warm yellow hue, clear enough that it looks like tinted glass. I touch my finger to the tip and a bright, giddy sensation filled with vitality dances through my body. *Citrine*, my mind whispers happily. Feeling more energized and clear-headed than just a moment ago, I remove my finger from the revitalizing citrine and take a moment to appreciate the beauty of the setup before moving my gaze away from the table and glancing back towards Michael. I probably should have asked before just touching his stuff.

I walk farther into the house, noticing a closed door to my left and a staircase on my right that begins near the door and curves upward along the wall, creating a mezzanine balcony that circles the remainder of the foyer. I continue forward in my exploration, not wanting to intrude on personal spaces by opening doors without an invitation to do so. Clearing the foyer, I find the living room, dining room, and kitchen are all connected in an open concept. Like the entry area, these rooms feel light and airy. The dining area, which lies directly in front of me, is relatively small and sparsely furnished, with only a round white table and five white chairs, but my eyes pass over these to gaze upon the back wall with awe. The back wall of the dining room and the living room is pure glass. One giant wall of glass, broken up only by the sliding glass doors in the middle of the dining area that open to the breathtakingly beautiful grounds of the property. I swallow a gasp at how impressive the grounds are, and my body itches to go out and explore those instead of the house. I've always been drawn to nature and the lush greenery of the vast grounds call to me.

I start walking toward the sliding glass doors, but Michael places a hand on my shoulder, stopping me. I turn and look up into his brilliant blue eyes with an unspoken question in my own.

"There will be plenty of time for you to explore the grounds," Michael says. "Right now, it would be better for you to get comfortable in the house so we can get the items you brought put away and resume your training first thing tomorrow morning."

Right. My training. With the beauty of this house, I completely forgot that was why I was here. This house makes it feel much more like a vacation than a boot camp. I nod to Michael, acknowledging his statement, and transfer my focus back to the rooms in front of me.

The white birch hardwood flooring of the foyer also encompasses the dining area and continues through the kitchen. Beneath a rectangular geometric chandelier with dangling strings of crystals, a white breakfast bar with two beau blue upholstered bar stools separates the dining area from the kitchen. The kitchen itself is quaint, with white cabinets and white marble countertops. One accent wall is painted beau blue, though the others remain the soft white that fills the rest of the house.

The white theme continues with the living room, which is filled by a cushy-looking white L-shaped sectional with beau blue accent pillows. It looks so comfortable and inviting, it's just begging to be curled up on. Filling the space in front of the sofa is a square, white coffee table. On it there's a white serving tray holding three white candles of varying heights, and on one end of the couch is a white end table topped with a blue lamp and a glass bowl filled with small blue stones. Literally everything is white with hints of blue. I feel like it would be easy to get dirty, but it's currently pristine. Maybe there's some angel mojo I don't know about that keeps everything so impeccably spotless. Before I can register what's happening, my feet are carrying me over to the bowl with the blue stones like it's magnetized. I automatically reach out and pick up one of the stones. I'm not sure why I keep getting pulled toward these things, but it doesn't feel like something I can control. The urge to absorb the energy of the crystals is overwhelming and my body just acts on autopilot.

The stone I'm now holding is smooth and has banded layers of varying shades of light blue. I close my fingers around it and close my eyes, automatically tapping into its energy like I was made to do just that. Immediately, I feel grounded, rooted to the solidity of the hard ground beneath the soft cream-colored carpet I'm currently standing on. My throat feels more open and my spirit feels more free as the stone's energy seeps into my being. *Blue lace agate*, my mind whispers to me and I smile. I may not know *how* I know what all these crystals and stones are, but I appreciate that I do. I open my eyes and place the stone back into the glass bowl with its companions, retaining that feeling of freedom the stone imbued into my soul.

Resuming my exploration of the room, I admire the white marble fireplace and the sleekness of the built-in television above it. The third wall in this room has a set of elaborately designed white double doors, but like the door in the foyer, they're closed, so I turn back towards Michael. "This is a beautiful home," I tell him.

Amusement floods his eyes as his lips turn up into a broad, waggish smirk and he teeters on the edge of laughter. "Of course it is," he says. "You designed it."

"What do you mean I designed it? Is this... Exactly whose house is this?" I stammer.

"Ours," Michael states unhelpfully as he motions for me to walk up the stairs to the second level of the house.

"Ours as in...?" I trail off, trying to get clarification without outright asking the question that's been burning in the back of my mind since we passed through the gates of this property less than an hour ago. *What are we to each other?* I want to shout. I'm starting to get frustrated with all of the vagueness in Michael's replies to questions that could clarify what our relationship was. It feels like he doesn't want to share the truth with me, and I don't know why, but I do know it makes me feel like there's a boulder beneath my sternum.

"Could you provide names please?" I snap after a beat goes by and Michael hasn't answered my previous question. I'm finally allowing my frustration to boil over into the tone of my voice and his expression blanks at my outburst. It's like he's suddenly erected a wall between his emotions and his facial expressions so I can't get any read on what he's thinking or feeling. It's a bit disconcerting.

"This will be your bedroom," Michael says flatly, ignoring my question. He's stopped at the end of the hall in front of a set of ornately carved cherrywood doors and is very pointedly refusing to make eye contact with me. I walk into what appears to be the master bedroom and my eyes immediately find a long cherrywood dresser, but it's not the dresser that has captivated my gaze and captured my intrigue. It's the framed photograph sitting atop the dresser. This is the first personal object I've seen in the house, and to say I'm curious about it is an understatement. I gently pick the photograph up from the dresser and hear Michael inhale a shaky breath. I want to turn and look at him, ask if he's ok, but instead, my eyes lock on the photo.

I can feel the solidity of the thin copper frame in my hand as my eyes greedily take in every detail of the photo. It pictures a couple embracing amidst a field of daisies. An awe-inspiring sunset saturated with blues, pinks, and just the slightest bit of yellow fills the background, but the couple is seemingly unaware of the beauty that surrounds them as they stare into each other's eyes like nothing exists beyond one another. The flaming passion of their undying love is so intense, it has been clearly captured through the camera's lens as the woman leans into the man, the fingers of her left hand curling into his hair as her right hand cradles his neck. His right hand peeks out as it presses on her lower back, bringing her as close to him as possible, and his left hand rests gently on her right hip. Their foreheads and noses touch in intimate devotion, yet their lips remain a hair's breadth apart. The woman's dark brown hair blows softly behind her with the wind, and the skirt of her white sheath wedding gown lies daintily amongst the flowers, billowing out around her. The man's light gray suit is a perfect complement to the woman's white gown. This is without question the most stunning photo I have ever seen, clearly depicting a bride and a groom in the kind of love that most of us can only dream of. But that is not what has my hands trembling and the pain of pent-up tears prickling the backs of my eyes. No, the influx of emotions I'm feeling is because the groom in the photo is undeniably Michael.

Chapter 9

BRIE

The bedroom is filled with thick tension. I swallow and it sounds like a bass drum against the blanket of silence permeating the air. I'm trying to temper my emotions and process this new information rationally. Michael still won't look at me when I glance up at him. It seems as though he's bracing himself for rejection. I'm once again staring at the photo, stuck on their devotion to each other, when Michael finally answers the question I had asked earlier.

"Ours as in you and me. We built this home for the two of us."

Home. The two of us. So that means...

"Is this me?" The words come out as a whisper, cutting through the silence harshly despite their softness.

"Yes." Michael replies, finally tilting his head up from the floor and meeting my eyes. I can see his uncertainty through them. He's scared of how I'll react to this information—scared that he'll lose me if it's not something I'm ready to hear. His eyes glisten, but no tears fall as he skirts the edge of pain.

"That is your soul's true form," Michael explains. "We were married—*are* married. We've been partners for eons. Every century we renew our vows." Michael looks down at the photo still in my hands. "This picture is from our most recent vow renewal ceremony a few years ago." He then looks at me tentatively. "You and I are soulmates. Mortals don't truly understand what that word means. Our souls are literally bound together and intertwined. It allows us to always find each other. It's how I was able to visit you in my energetic form. What we have, Brie, it's special. I know you don't remember, but I hope that in time you will love me again as you did before, even without the memories of our past."

Michael looks up toward the ceiling and I can tell he's trying to keep the tears that have been pooling in his eyes at bay. The depth of his pain takes my breath away as I realize he's been tortured by my ignorance. He's had to watch his wife of millennia go on dates with other men and look at him with no recognition of who he is. I can't even fathom how painful this must have been for him.

A single tear slides down my cheek as I share in his pain and take on the burden of knowing that I'm the cause of it. I want to apologize to him, but the words stick in my throat. It's clogged by sorrow and grief. I traverse the chasm between us and place the palm of my left hand on Michael's right cheek with a surety that surprises even myself. He tilts his head down to look at me, and I close my eyes and press my forehead to his own. The gesture is less intimate than in the photo, but provides a closeness and acceptance that we both need in this moment.

Michael wraps his arms around my waist and pulls me into a hug. His body feels strong and sturdy against my own, and I'm filled with a penetrating sense of peace and security as I relax into his hold. Neither of us speak. We just stand there clinging to each other as though we've been waiting for this moment for years, and we have been. The embrace says what words never could. For the first time in my life, I feel like I've found my home. Michael is my home. My heart beats strongly in my chest and stutters as he gently pulls away.

"It's getting late and you've had a long day. I'll let you get some sleep," Michael says to me, before placing a gentle kiss on my forehead.

I give him a small smile and watch him softly close the door behind him. My mind is still reeling. I can't quite wrap my head around the concept that my old self was married, but I also can't help the grin spreading wide across my face as I explore the rest of the bedroom, change into sleep shorts and a tank top, and curl up beneath the fluffy down comforter on the bed.

I gasp awake with a silent scream. Despite the goofy grin I fell asleep with, my dreams were still filled with nightmarish terrors. Picking up my phone, I see that the time is 5:45am. Michael had told me to set my alarm for 6am, so I may as well just get up and start the day. No point in trying to go back to sleep right now anyway with the amount of adrenaline currently pumping through my body.

As I trudge down the stairs with the sole purpose of consuming some delicious coffee, I'm equal parts excited and terrified to see Michael after the information bomb he dropped on me last night.

I'm still reeling from the news and have a lot to sort through in my head regarding everything I've learned over the past several days, but I also feel like a giddy teenager with a crush right now. It's a feeling I haven't experienced since moving to Los Angeles. And considering that the experiences before that weren't really mine, I guess the last time I truly experienced these types of feeling were with Michael during a time I can't even remember.

I stumble towards the kitchen as the butterflies filling my stomach increase their little flutters and my heart pitter-patters in my chest, but I quickly realize the common areas that I explored yesterday are empty. Michael's not down here as I expected he would be, and an aching disappointment replaces the butterflies. Maybe it's for the best, I tell myself. I don't know what I'd say to him right now anyway.

The box with all the mugs I brought from my apartment is sitting on the kitchen counter. We didn't have time to unpack it last night. I unwrap a few until I find the one I'm looking for. It's a rich teal color and reads "Keep Calm and Coffee On". Yeah, I definitely need to channel some calm right now. My emotions are up and down like a rollercoaster.

Just as my coffee finishes brewing, I hear Michael coming down the stairs. I turn around as he clears the bottom of the staircase and give an awkward wave. Ugh. I just waved at him. Really, how dorky can I be? Good job Brie. Way to play it cool. I internally roll my eyes at myself while Michael just chuckles.

"Good, you're up," he says, apparently reverting to business mode. Alright then, guess we're going to ignore the elephant in the room. And I don't mean my awkward wave.

"Yep."

Why is it that I seemingly lose my ability to say anything intelligent in his presence? I wonder if I was this pathetic when I was Sabriel. Probably not, considering I was some sort of Angelic Army badass. I doubt I'll ever compare to my old self. Will Michael still want to be with me when he finds out that I don't measure up?

"Finish your coffee quickly. I'm giving you fifteen minutes and then we're doing a conditioning run," Michael says after he downs a glass of water. He's already wearing workout clothes. I...am not. I'm still in my sleep attire. Oops, forgot about that.

I rush through my coffee, not happy about that at all, and change into some yoga pants and a sports bra. I quickly pull my hair up into a messy ponytail and dart down the stairs just as Michael calls out, "Thirty seconds!"

Michael means business right now. He leads me out the sliding glass doors of the dining area onto the area of the property behind the house. We walk for a bit to warm up our muscles and then he starts jogging along a path that weaves throughout the grounds. I've never been great at running and I'm already huffing and puffing two minutes in. Michael gives me an incredulous look as I start to wheeze before we've even hit the mile mark.

"You've got to be kidding me," he says with blatant disbelief. "How are you this out of shape?!"

I would love to give him some sort of snarky reply, but I'm too busy trying to breathe right now. Talking is just beyond me in this moment. I develop a stitch in my side, the muscles of my diaphragm cramping fiercely and stabbing me with pain. I slow to a walk and Michael looks at me with wide eyes, like he just can't fathom how anyone could be so unfit.

"Why are you stopping?" he asks me with sheer confusion.

"Cramp," I pant out, not even trying to attempt full sentences. I drink some of my water and then stop walking altogether, bending over and digging my hand into the area that's cramping, in an attempt to release the muscles. Michael grumbles something under his breath, but otherwise just stands next to me patiently while I try to work the cramp out.

Eventually, I start walking again and what was supposed to be our first conditioning run turns into a breathless stroll on my part. Michael keeps glancing over at me with looks of dismay but doesn't say anything else until we get to a big building at the very back of the property.

"This is our training complex," Michael tells me, gesturing to the large building. He unlocks the door using a keypad and gestures me inside.

The training complex is mostly just a massive open space. Half the space is covered in matted flooring while the other half is sprung wood flooring. One wall is covered in mirrors and there are a few machines in the corner of the matted part. Michael walks over to the far wall and presses a button on a panel near the end. A door slides open, revealing a large weapons room.

"We won't be using weapons today, but you should know this is here," he tells me.

I nod, feeling a little gobsmacked. And also greatly alarmed that old me felt the need to install a weapons room in the first place.

"Alright, so every day we'll start out with a conditioning run—notice I said run, not walk," Michael says, eyeing me like I'm purposely slacking. "Then you'll be doing an hour of yoga."

Yoga goes slightly better than the run went. I'm pretty flexible, but it's also intensive so my muscles are shaking and I'm dripping sweat by the time the hour is over. Who knew yoga could be so hard? At least I got through it. Michael and I walk back to the house for breakfast, and since the walk is meant to be a leisurely cool down from the yoga, we're finally able to talk.

"So, um, I guess that lore about you having a human wife wasn't true?" I really should learn to keep my mouth shut. Of all the things I could have used to breach the topic of our relationship, I start with that. Hopefully, he doesn't see my cringe.

"I think it's more accurate to say my wife occasionally pretends to be human," Michael tells me with a smile. He looks like he's remembering those times with fondness and a pang of jealousy hits me. I think I'm actually jealous of myself right now, which is admittedly a little pathetic.

"Did we come to the earthly plane often?" I ask.

"Yes, our time has been relatively evenly split between the heavenly plane and the earthly plane. Sometimes, we would come down for missions, but we also vacation here quite a bit. You always enjoyed experiencing the cultures here."

"How exactly do we get here? You never really explained that part. Like, you pretty much just appeared in my apartment. I know you didn't come in through the door, so how does that work?"

"Our energy can travel through the different planes," Michael explains. "Just as you can manipulate the density of your wings, we can manipulate the density of our bodies. When we travel between planes, we spread out our energy and become incorporeal. When we want to retain a physical form, we just pull our energy in closer, and our physical body reassembles."

I contemplate this for a moment before asking my next question. "Why can't humans do that?"

"Our physical bodies are made from the energy of our souls. They are an extension of our essence. Some humans can disengage their soul from their physical body and travel to the astral plane in that way, but their physical body is not part of their soul, so the energy composition is different. That is why they cannot manipulate their physical body as we can. Also, our souls have a higher vibration than those of humans due to the intensity of our light. The higher a soul's light, the higher it's vibration, the more easily it can manipulate its own energy."

I guess that makes sense. It's actually pretty cool when you think about it, and it almost sounds like an extension of the glamouring Michael uses on his wings. Speaking of which, "Angel's wings are usually depicted as white, or black in the case of fallen angels, but our wings have color. Is that normal?" I ask.

Michael laughs. "Yes. Think of light shining through a prism and how it can create a rainbow effect. Since our wings are made of light energy, they reflect the colors of our souls. Fallen angels do have black wings, and that is because their energy is filled with darkness. Color doesn't permeate darkness as it does with light."

"On the topic of prisms, when I touched the crystals and the stones in the house, each one gave me a different feeling. How is that possible?"

"Everything with energy is alive. Just because something doesn't breathe or eat, doesn't mean it doesn't contain energy. Rocks and crystals come from the Earth, one of the most potent sources of energy on this plane. They retain a portion of that energy. When you feel certain sensations from the crystals, you're tapping into their energy."

Interesting. But if I can tap into that energy, could something tap into my energy? Maybe that's how darkness infects people. It connects to their energy and corrupts it.

Chapter 10

BRIE

Descending the stairs after rushing through a quick shower, I hear an engine cut off in front of the house, followed by muffled voices approaching the front door. I stand indecisively at the base of the staircase, unsure if I should make my way to the front door to greet our visitors, or call Michael into the room and let him take care of it. He's more likely than I am to know whoever our guests are. My conundrum disappears when I hear a key disengaging the locks on the front door before it is suddenly flung open and a deep masculine voice booms, "Honey, I'm home!" followed by, "Never fear, the cavalry is here," in a singsong tone.

A large man strides into the foyer as if he owns the place. He stands around 6'5" with a rich chocolate skin tone, penetrating brown eyes, and hair so dark it is nearly black. He has the build of a basketball player—ripped and muscular, but lithe rather than bulky. His movements are confident and graceful as he walks to meet Michael, who has just emerged from the opposite end of the foyer. The two embrace in a synchronized bro hug, that type of hug where men maintain their masculinity by pounding each other on the back while hugging. Yeah, that kind of hug.

A few steps behind the unfamiliar man, Gabriel also enters the foyer, chuckling at his companion's antics. As Michael and the new man separate from their bro hug, Gabriel gives Michael a sheepish, puppy-eyed grin.

"Hey, big bro," Gabriel says, looking at Michael.

"Come here, runt," Michael responds as he holds his arms open, inviting Gabriel in for a real hug.

Michael and Gabriel embrace and I hear Michael whisper, "Thanks for coming" before he turns his body slightly, moving one arm around Gabriel's neck to hold him in a headlock before rubbing the top of Gabriel's head with his other fist. My jaw drops as I realize my stoic warrior is giving the archangel a noogie. What is happening right now? Have I entered a different dimension where Michael is suddenly playful?

"Yield, I yield!" Gabriel hollers and Michael laughs as he releases the poor man, slinging an arm over his shoulder and turning to face me as I try to clear what must surely be a dopey look of confusion from my face. Though I met Gabriel in my apocalyptic vision, I certainly didn't realize that he and Michael were brothers. Seeing the two men standing next to each other, though, I can now see the similarities in their features.

"Brie, you remember Gabriel, I'm sure," Michael says warmly. "And this dufus," he continues, gesturing toward the large man who entered the house first, "is Raphael. He used to be my best friend until you stole him from me."

Raphael booms with laughter while Michael winks at me.

"Don't be sour, brother," Raphael responds. "You're still my third favorite."

"Wait, does that make me or Brie your second favorite?" Gabriel asks, looking genuinely concerned.

"You two are tied for first place." Raphael states, walking over to me and wrapping me up in a comfortable hug.

"Um, hi," I say awkwardly.

Raphael laughs softly in response and releases me.

"I wish we could give you your memories back," Michael says. I can tell that he's frustrated, though he's trying not to show it. "It would make all of this so much easier."

"When she transcends, everything will be as it once was," Raphael reassures Michael in a comforting tone.

Michael nods silently.

"Are you saying that when I die, I'll get all of the memories from my time as Sabriel back?" I ask Raphael in confusion.

It's Michael who answers, though. "Yes, your memories were locked into your energy, but they will automatically unlock when you ascend once again and reassume your true form. Unfortunately, we cannot unlock them while you are in a human body, as it would overload the human brain, causing the brain matter to liquify." He then sighs heavily.

"Got it," I respond, once again dumbfounded and possibly also slightly terrified at the thought of my brain turning to mush.

"Soooo..." I say as I shuffle my feet nervously, "you two are brothers?" I move my finger so that it points at Michael, then swing it to point at Gabriel, before pointing at Michael again.

Raphael, who appears to be the most jovial of the bunch, chuckles again. "Let's move this into the dining room," he says. "I'm starving. It was a long drive."

"It was an hour," Gabriel says dryly, rolling his eyes.

"Exactly!" Raphael exclaims as though Gabriel just validated his previous statement. "I still don't understand why we had to drive at all, when we could have just manifested inside the house. Such a waste of time."

That's a really good point actually. If they can just disperse their energy to travel between planes and then compact it to reappear at their destination, why bother driving?

"Why *did* you drive?" I echo curiously.

"Because it's bad manners to simply materialize inside someone's house," Gabriel states, giving Michael a stern look. "Also, because we didn't want to startle you with our arrival," he continues, this time giving Raphael a stern look. "Plus, acting as humans does give us a better understanding of them. We strive to act as human as possible when on Earth, so we can better aid new angels in their adjustment and integration into our society when they ascend."

I nod in response, visibly accepting his explanation as we all make our way into the dining room. Gabriel, Raphael, and I sit around the table as Michael starts grabbing containers out of the refrigerator and arranges plates for each of us.

"So, about that brother thing," I state, returning to my original question. "Are all the archangels considered siblings, or is it just you two?"

"Michael and Gabriel were made of the same energy, so they are true brothers," Raphael states simply. "Angels do not have blood as humans do. We are solely made up of energy, just as souls are. The difference in density and our ability to manipulate energetic density is what gives us our forms, but we are not of physical matter as humans are. Their blood contains the energy of their souls, which is why it is considered their lifeforce, but it is the energy within that blood that causes true familial connection, not the blood itself. Angels can maintain familial connections through energy as well. Most angels ascend, so their familial connections are established long before they become angels, but the seven of us who are called archangels were made. Of the seven, Michael and Gabriel are the only ones who were made of the same energy, so they are the only true siblings among us."

Wow, that's super interesting. I briefly wonder if I have siblings or parents in the angel world, but decide I should finish processing the whole husband thing before learning about any other potential family members. I'm not sure how many more identity-altering facts my poor human brain can handle.

Michael sets a plate in front of me that's filled with delicious looking berries, yogurt with granola, cheeses, baguette slices, and various spreads. It's a gigantic step up from my usual breakfast of a 99-cent muffin or whichever cereal is on sale when I make it to the grocery store, and my mouth is watering just looking at it.

My attention is now solidly on my food, though I try not to inhale everything too quickly so I at least look like I have some manners.

Michael sits next to me and turns his piercing blue eyes on me. "Brie," he starts. "Raf and Gabriel are here to help with your training. While I will be in charge of your physical conditioning and weapons training, Raphael is going to help you reconnect with your healing and energy transference abilities and Gabriel is going to work with you on your visionary abilities."

I nod my head silently, wondering what the heck energy transference is but not questioning it aloud. I'll find out soon enough. My nod seems to be enough for Michael, since he then gives me a blinding smile before turning back to Raphael and

Gabriel, barraging them with questions about how things are going in the angelic realm.

An hour later, I find myself sitting amidst a thriving garden, Raphael by my side. The garden is quite vast, comprised of vegetable plants, berry bushes, fruiting vines, and an abundance of colorful flowers. It's a dream garden, the type of garden I thought I'd see only in my imagination. And yet, here I am, sitting right in the middle of it.

"Brie, did you hear what I just said, or were you too distracted by all of the plants?" Raphael asks, breaking into my thoughts.

Admittedly, I did not hear what he said, too immersed in all of the beautiful plants surrounding me.

"Well, the flowers are quite colorful," I respond, with a good amount of sass added into the inflection of my words.

Raphael chuckles, repeating his words for me since I clearly wasn't paying attention the first time. "I said that you have the ability to heal both yourself and others. Basically, you can heal anything with energy," Raphael explains.

"I thought healing was your gift?" I ask, confused.

"It is, but the ability to heal is not exclusively mine among the angels. Just as the sureness of sword and high aptitude for battle strategy are not exclusive to Michael. If they were, the Angelic Army would not exist. We would only have Michael as a lone warrior amongst all angels. That being said, no two archangels share the same gift, and we are masters of the gift we have. The archangels are unique in that we each have only a single gift, but that gift is extremely powerful. Conversely, all other angels have several gifts, but they are weaker in strength. Your gifts are among the strongest in our society, but even so, the gifts of the archangels are at least a hundred times stronger than yours. Still, you have several gifts whereas we only have one," Raphael explains.

"So, it's like the saying 'Jack of all trades, master of none.' You and the other archangels are the masters and all the rest of the angels are the Jacks," I affirm.

"That's correct. Now, there are some abilities that all angels possess. These abilities are considered basic abilities. They are not considered gifts."

"So, the archangels have these abilities too, in addition to their gift?" I clarify.

"Yes," Raphael says. "These abilities are things like flying, glamour, and energy transference. Now there are different levels for each of these abilities. For example, weaker angels may only be able to partially glamour one hand, whereas the archangels can glamour our entire beings, but still, all angels have the ability to some degree."

"Ok," I say, understanding the concept if not really the scope. "Where do I fall on that spectrum?" I ask.

"Normally, you would be able to glamour your whole being like myself and the other archangels can, but while you're in a human body, you won't be able to manipulate your own energy as well as you could in your angelic form, so you'll only be able to glamour your wings or maybe a few small things," Raphael tells me.

"Well, that's disappointing," I sigh, before letting Raphael continue with his lesson.

"Anyway, we are going to work on both your healing gift and your energy transference ability for the next few hours. I think it will help you to picture energy as a physical entity. Look at this flower in front of you and picture a green light flowing through it. This is its lifeforce. Healing energy is always green, so you can picture the plant's lifeforce as green as well. Can you envision the path by which the flower's lifeforce flows?" Raphael asks.

I nod as I picture a green light flowing from the roots, up through the stem of the flower, and then out into its petals and leaves in a loop.

"Good," Raphael continues. "Now I want you to place your hand at the base of the flower and picture that green light flowing out of the flower and into your hand."

I concentrate as hard as I can, picturing the green light being sucked out of the flower through its roots and traveling through the soil into the palm of my hand.

"Good, that's enough," Raphael instructs, and I let my concentration break, seeing the world around me again rather than focusing on the image I was imagining. And when I look at the small flower in front of me, I gasp, seeing that it is now wilted and I immediately feel guilty for harming it.

"Now," Raphael says, oblivious to my inner guilt trip, "that was energy transference. In this case, you transferred the energy from the plant to yourself. As a light entity, if you are transferring energy to yourself, the being that is giving you the energy must be a willing participant in the transfer and you should *never*, under any circumstances, transfer energy to yourself from a being that has been corrupted by darkness. If you do, the darkness within their energy will infect your own and you will fall. Your soul will no longer be pure, and you will not be able to return to the angelic plane."

"I understand," I say solemnly. "I won't."

"Good. Now, this lovely flower gave you its energy willingly. To thank it, you are not only going to transfer its own energy back to it, but you are also going to give it a piece of your energy as well," Raphael instructs. "So, picture a ball of green healing energy forming in your chest. Then, let a dribble of that energy flow through your chest and into your arm, down your arm into your hand, and then through your palm into the ground where the flower's roots can soak the energy up."

I do as Raphael says, following his instructions with my full focus.

"Well done. Now shut off the flow of energy and let the energy remaining in your body disperse throughout your being and settle where it wants."

I once again do as I'm told, picturing the flow of green light ceasing before dispersing into speckles of green throughout my body. Once I feel comfortable with the visualization in my mind's eye, I come back to reality, looking at the flower in front of me in awe. The small flower, that was originally only about three inches high, has now doubled in both height and circumference and appears to be flourishing. It looks much healthier than it did when we started the exercise. I can't help but smile, happy to have helped it in its growth.

"You did well," Raphael says, as he sees the smile bloom on my face, but then he ruins it by saying, "Now, you just need to do that about a hundred times more, on progressively larger plants, and then for wounds on both yourself and others."

"Wounds? What wounds?" I gape at him.

Raphael shrugs, not looking at all concerned by the alarm I'm certain I'm projecting.

"I'm sure you'll end up with some during your weapons training. If not, we can always create some simply for the sake of your healing practice."

I can't tell if he's joking or not, but I really hope he is.

Chapter 11

BRIE

Raphael walks me back to the house for lunch. We were outside practicing for hours, and I'm exhausted from having to focus so intently for so long. I didn't realize how tiring something as simple as concentration can be.

After washing my hands thoroughly, I head toward the boisterous voices in the dining room, claiming a seat as Michael places a filled plate and a glass of water in front of me. The plate holds what appears to be a perfectly cooked and seasoned salmon fillet with a side salad. I eye the salad warily, glancing around at the others' plates, all holding the same combination of food but in different portion sizes.

"Um, do we have any ranch?" I ask, scooching my chair out and getting up to walk over to the refrigerator and check.

"Your salad has lemon juice on it already," Michael responds.

"Oh, um, ok but I'm looking for salad dressing. Do we have any ranch?" I repeat, confused, and continue my journey to the refrigerator, pulling the door open and searching for some ranch dressing.

"The lemon juice is your salad dressing," Michael says assertively.

"Lemon juice isn't salad dressing," I state, feeling the need to educate him on such matters since he obviously doesn't understand how salads work.

"I can get you the vinegar if you'd prefer it to the lemon juice," Michael replies, a bit of amusement slipping into his voice.

I look over at the table. Raphael and Gabriel are ping-ponging their gazes between Michael and myself as Michael watches me and I stare incredulously back at him.

"You really don't have ranch?" I ask desperately.

"No," Michael states plainly.

"Really?" I ask again.

"Really," he says, his lips twitching as I sullenly make my way back to the table and focus on my fish. It is delicious, but I'm not sure how I feel about eating the salad with only lemon juice as dressing. I guess this training is going to be full of new experiences, and not only where my angelic abilities and gifts are concerned.

We all eat fairly quickly, light conversation throughout the meal making the experience as enjoyable as it could be in the absence of my coveted ranch dressing. Once we've finished, Raphael grabs my empty plate from the table, bringing it to the sink, and Michael does the same with my glass. The only one remaining with me at the table is Gabriel, and he turns to me with a gentle smile.

"You'll be working with me for the next hour or so. It will give your food time to settle before you have to engage in any strenuous activity. Then, the drill sergeant will get you back," Gabriel says softly.

"I heard that!" Michael calls from the kitchen and Gabriel pulls an oops face, before rising from the table and letting me trail after him back out onto the grounds. There was a square by the entrance to the garden that I found interesting earlier, and it looks like that is where Gabriel is leading me now.

"We're going to work on your scrying," Gabriel tells me, gesturing for me to sit on one of the benches at the edge of the square.

The path to the garden cuts straight through the center of the square, and on each side of it lay two unique items, each faced by benches along the very edge of the square. To the left of the path, there is a large circle of solid black obsidian and a fire pit next to it. To the right of the path, there is a large pedestal holding a large ball of quartz crystal, and next to that is a small pond filled with shimmering, crystal clear water. It's really quite mesmerizing, seeing the juxtaposition between the black obsidian and the white quartz crystal, coupled with the juxtaposition between the fire pit and the pond.

"Each of these items before you can be used for scrying," Gabriel explains, gesturing to the four items within the square. "You won't need these items specifically to scry. Any reflective, glowing, or smoky medium can be used for scrying, but we will use these while we're here for convenience. If you can scry on one medium, you can scry on them all. Some will be easier for you than others, but any of them will work. You experienced a taste of scrying when I delivered your call to arms. Scrying itself will be easy for you, but you, specifically, are very sensitive to strong energy imprints, so anytime you touch something that contains a strong energy imprint during your journey, you're likely to fall into a natural, unprompted vision. So, we'll use the scrying as a tool to go over how to recognize when you've fallen into a vision, and how to distinguish if the vision you're experiencing is an event from the past or a possibility of the future."

"Ok," I say, rubbing my arms in comfort as I remember that vision of the future I had when I looked into the scrying bowl Michael sent to the shop. That was not an experience that I would like to repeat. I can already imagine that, although this practice may not require as much concentration as Raphael's lessons or the grueling physical conditioning of Michael's lessons, it will be just as difficult for me.

"Wait, if I'm likely to fall into visions naturally since I'm sensitive to energy or whatever, why hasn't it happened already? The only vision I've had was the one with that cursed bowl Michael sent me," I ask.

Gabriel looks thoughtful before answering, "There's a combination of factors that prevented you from experiencing spontaneous visions before now. First, just as your human body acted as a buffer in preventing dark entities from understanding the true strength of your light, it also has acted as a barrier from psychic energies. Second, since you were unaware of your ability to have visions, your energy was less reactive and therefore less likely to trigger a vision. The blue lace agate stones in the living room will have negated some of that by freeing your energy when you first held them. Another contributing factor is that you probably haven't been in a place with very strong energy imprints. The strongest energy imprints are in places with very dark histories, and you've had no reason to be in such a place before now. Plus, your light energy would have urged you to stay away from such places had you gone near any. You would have felt an unease about the place and automatically tried to avoid it."

"Gabriel!" Raphael shouts, running out of the house and waving both arms in the air to get Gabriel's attention. "Gabriel, wait!"

Gabriel's whole face lights up as he laughs at Raphael, who is still waving both arms as though we haven't already seen him.

"Gabriel, you forgot!" Raphael says, waving only one arm now that he's directly in front of us. Since he's now much closer, I can see that he's not just waving his arm, he's waving around a small black case. "She needs the rune first."

Gabriel slaps his palm to his forehead before smiling back up at Raphael. "You're right, I did forget. Thank you, Raf."

Raphael smiles back at Gabriel, before looking at me with a mischievous quirk to his lips and saying, "Tell me, Brie, darling. How do you feel about tattoos?"

"Tattoos?" I parrot, utterly confused. "I guess I like them if they mean something," I answer, shrugging.

"Lovely!" Raphael replies enthusiastically. "That's great, because we need to tattoo an angelic rune onto your body somewhere so that you can understand other languages without having to learn the language itself. Any language you hear will be automatically translated into English for you, and you can even reply in the original language if you need to. It will be important for interacting with people you meet during your travels, but also for your visions."

"That sounds pretty cool. I've always wanted to speak another language but, um, a tattoo? Really?" I ask. "Can I at least see what the rune looks like first? If it's ugly, I don't want it permanently tattooed on me."

"It's not ugly," Gabriel assures me. "And we can always position it somewhere inconspicuous. Let's go back inside. I honestly did forget we needed to do this since you now have a human body, and it'll take up the rest of our time today. We'll have to start on the actual scrying tomorrow."

"Oh, ok," I say, my disappointment evident in my tone, and follow Gabriel and Raphael back to the house.

Raphael leads me to the white sectional in the living room and gestures for me to sit. I hesitate, nervous that I'll end up dirtying the pristine white fabric. Don't get me wrong, the house looks great from a design perspective, but angel me really should have chosen a different color for the couch. White is just a no-go for me when it comes to furniture that will be sat on.

Gabriel joins us a few seconds later, holding the case that Raphael had brought him earlier and a small sketch pad with a pen clipped onto it. He examines me as he approaches, rubbing one hand along the back of his neck.

"Why are you standing in front of the couch and scowling at it?" Gabriel asks me as he sits on one end of it.

"It's white," I reply simply.

"And you have a vendetta against the color white?" Gabriel asks in confusion, Raphael barking out a laugh at the sheer sincerity of the question.

"I don't want to get it dirty," I explain, both men huffing out a small laugh in response to my words.

"Just sit down, Brie. You'll probably end up sitting or lying for the tattoo anyway," Raphael tells me.

"Wait, what? Aren't you taking me someplace to have it done?" I ask, slightly panicked.

"Of course not. I'll be doing it for you," Raphael replies.

"Are you even qualified for that? Do you even know how to tattoo? Does Heaven's big boss healer have a tattoo parlor on the side or something? Not enough healing work so you decided to branch out? Is tattooing your side hustle up in Heaven?" I ramble, my panic growing.

"As you said, Brie, I'm Heaven's big boss healer. Who better to serve as your tattoo artist than a healer?" Raphael asks me calmly.

"But you're qualified?" I ask again. His logic may have cut through my nerves to a degree, but there is no way I'm letting him put a permanent tattoo on my body if he doesn't know what he's doing.

"Yes, I'm qualified. We spend quite a bit of time on the Earthly plane, and we've all picked up hobbies along the way. Tattooing is one of mine. I actually worked in a tattoo parlor here on Earth for about a year."

"Oh, I didn't realize. That's pretty cool," I say, feeling much better about the situation now that I know he has experience and actually knows what he's doing.

Gabriel, who had been seemingly doodling during my exchange with Raphael, rips a piece of paper out of the sketchpad and hands it to me.

"This is the rune," Gabriel says, and I look down at the paper, examining the symbol that will be permanently adorning my body. "Let us know where you want to put it."

The symbol is small, less than the size of my thumbpad, and looks like a partial circle with a bunch of lines inside of it. It's not too bad, but it's not exactly what I would consider pretty, and definitely not a design that I would choose for myself if it didn't have the purpose that it does. Now knowing what the design will look like, I contemplate my options for where to place the tattoo. Since it's small, my immediate thought is to hide it behind my ear, where it won't be very visible, but the thought of having a tattoo needle that close to my brain kind of creeps me out. How do I know the ink won't seep into my brain matter and infect it somehow? No, better to keep it away from my brain. Just to be on the safe side.

My next thought is to put the tattoo on the inside of my wrist. That's pretty inconspicuous, but a nice area. But this is my first tattoo, so I'm worried about my body reacting to it somehow. It would be very problematic if it somehow affected the nerves that run down through my hand, and I lost my ability to write or type or hold stuff. No, that won't do either. Too risky.

Maybe my ankle then. Or my foot. Even if I lost some nerve control in my foot, I'd probably still be able to walk and it's pretty much the furthest location from my brain, so that'll be safe. Decided, I look down at my foot, planning the exact position on the inside of my foot, a spot equidistant between my heel, arch, and ankle. Be brave, Brie. It's just a tattoo. People get them all the time. I point to the spot on my foot and look up at Raphael, saying, "I want it here."

Raphael instructs me to lie down on my side on the couch. He removes the tattoo pen from its case, and I turn my head away since it's just making me more nervous to watch what's going on. The pen whirs to life, startling me, and I jump.

"Calm down, Brie. You're fine," Raphael soothes as he imbues the ink with his light energy. "I'm not going to use a stencil on you because I've drawn this rune hundreds of times. I could draw it in my sleep. Just try to stay as still as possible and we'll be done before you know it."

"I doubt that," I mumble.

"Plus, you won't even need to wait for it to heal on its own like the humans do," Raphael says cheerily, and I can't help but agree that is a bonus.

I feel something swipe against my skin in the area where the tattoo will be. Next, I feel something rubbed on my skin in the same area. I brace for the needle and at first, it's not so bad.

"Holy bunnies in Heaven!" I yell, as the pain increases after a few seconds.

"Raphael put some numbing cream on the area. It should kick in soon," Gabriel says in a poor attempt at comforting me.

"Why couldn't he wait until it had already kicked in before he started?" I whimper.

"I'm sorry, Brie, but Michael wants you to become more accustomed to pain. This is part of that. It will help you in the long run. When you are sealing the Gates, you'll need to still be able to function and fight, even if you're injured or in a vast amount of pain. We can't necessarily change the level at which you feel pain, but we can help you condition yourself to be able to work through it," Gabriel replies.

Obviously, I am none too thrilled with his answer, but the numbing cream does start working pretty quickly so I don't need to endure it for long. I think I need to have a discussion with Michael about these plans though.

Chapter 12

MICHAEL

"Michael!" Brie shouts from somewhere in the house, her melodic voice hardened by her you're-in-trouble tone. "Where is he?" I hear her ask in exasperation, though it's unclear to me whether she's asking herself or one of my brothers.

I rise from my desk, pushing in the desk chair before striding to the door and pushing it open to cross into the foyer. Brie strides into the foyer just as I'm re-closing the office door behind me. Her eyes focus on me intently and she stands right in front of me, looking up at me with what she thinks is her tough face. I try as hard as I can to keep my face impassive, because honestly, I have a strong urge to laugh at her expression and I know that would just make her mad. Or I guess, at this point, madder than she already is.

"You were looking for me?" I ask politely.

"Yes, I was looking for you," she says frankly. "We need to talk."

Those four blasted words. We need to talk—the kiss of death for men everywhere, humans and angels alike.

"Ok, love. What is it we need to talk about?" I respond calmly, quickly adding, "Oh, did Raphael finish your tattoo? May I see it?"

"Yes, he finished the tattoo and it's right there," she says, pointing down toward the inside of her right foot. "Now, stop trying to distract me."

She knows me so well. She may not have her memories or remember me on a conscious level, but the fact that she realized I was asking her about her tattoo to distract her and delay the conversation she has planned, demonstrates that she does still know me on a level that is soul-deep.

"I was told you have some insane agenda to make me more accustomed to pain. That's not happening. Nope, not happening at all. A big no," Brie rambles, and I hide my smile behind my hand as I pretend to cover my mouth in thought.

"It certainly will bring me no pleasure, Brie," I tell her honestly. "If I could prevent you from ever having to feel pain again, I would in a heartbeat. Unfortunately, we know that there will be obstacles near the Gates. We may not know what those obstacles will be, but we do know there will be some, and I won't always be able to protect you from the obstacles we encounter. We will need to fight them side by side. There's a chance that you may get hurt in the process, and you'll need to be able to fight through the pain until you are able to heal yourself. I'm sorry, but I'd rather you learn to endure pain here, in a controlled environment, than see you die because you falter from it in the middle of a battle."

Brie stares deeply into my eyes, reading the truth of my words in my soul before she breathes a heavy sigh and throws her head back, briefly looking up at the ceiling. "Ugh. Why do you always have to make things sound so logical and reasonable?" she groans.

Then, she turns on her heel, striding out of the foyer toward the sliding doors in the dining room.

"Well, aren't you coming?" she calls back to me. "We have training to do."

I huff a laugh under my breath and follow her out of the house. Brie may not like what I have planned, but she'll suffer through it nonetheless. Her soul has never shied away from hard work, no matter how monotonous or unappealing the task.

We walk down the path that leads to the training complex, my long strides quickly overtaking her and forcing her into a brisk walk to keep up. I notice that she'll fall behind every now and then, and then do some weird walk-hop-skipping thing to catch back up to me. I've never seen such an odd movement before but it does seem to be effective, though goodness knows how.

Brie is once again out of breath when we reach the training complex, but at least this time she didn't stop at all. It's a small bit of progress, I guess. Better than nothing. As we walk into the air-conditioned space, Brie beelines for the water cooler and gulps down water in between her panting. Finally, after she has drained the cup, Brie rejoins me in the center of the sparring area.

"We're going to start with a small strength workout and then we'll move into sparring technique," I tell her.

She just looks at me blankly.

"I'll teach you to throw a punch," I clarify.

Her whole face lights up as she bounces on her toes in excitement. "Oh, ok!" she says enthusiastically.

"We need to work on building up your strength first though," I remind her, and her face falls but she nods in understanding.

I take Brie through a short strength circuit comprised mostly of bodyweight exercises. Her level of strength is woefully low, and I can only hope that I can get her to where she needs to be physically before the darkness forces us to move on our plans. I'm not exactly sure how long we'll have, but at the infestation's current rate of growth, I estimate we'll only have three to six months before that happens. And once we do start, we'll need to seal each Gate as rapidly as possible. I hope I'll be able to prepare her in time. I can't even fathom what will happen if we fail on this mission.

I guide Brie into a fighting stance, explaining each part of the positioning in detail so that she understands and can recreate the position on her own. Despite her lack of conditioning, she's a surprisingly quick learner and as soon as I show her something once, she retains it and can recreate it fairly well. It gives me hope that she will be able to progress as rapidly as I need her to in these areas. Her punches lack power, but her form is nearly perfect as I guide her through a jab-cross combo and then let her shadowbox the combo to practice it. I only have to remind her to keep her guard up once and she doesn't let it fall again, which is pretty impressive for a beginner.

As I watch her shadowbox, I can't help but feel a sense of satisfaction at how much she's enjoying it. Brie has a huge smile on her face and as she starts to get more comfortable with the movements, she starts cheering herself on in her uniquely Brie way.

"Take that!" she yells as she throws a jab at thin air.

"Ha! Gotcha!" she cheers after another jab-cross.

Then, she decides to take a break from her shadowboxing to do a victory lap around the room, her hands in the air, vocally cheering herself on and giving herself words of encouragement. Unfortunately, her jogging is still as bad as it was this morning, so after just a few seconds of her victory lap, she starts breathing heavily, mutters to herself that the rest of the lap isn't worth the effort, and walks slowly back to her water bottle to take a few gulps. I only just manage to keep myself from laughing at her antics.

"Back to work!" I call out to her. "You're not done yet."

"Yeah, yeah," she grumbles, resuming her fighting stance and restarting the jab-cross combo. Given how good her form is still looking, even after abandoning her fighting stance and then resetting it, I think I'll bring out the pads tomorrow and focus most of her training on building the power of her punches.

I let Brie practice her punches for a little over an hour before directing her to stretch. I'm sure she will end up being quite sore in the morning. She's used a lot of muscles today that her body is unaccustomed to engaging. I wanted to give her a first run through our obstacle course today too, but after seeing her fitness level, it seems that's something I'll need to ease her into. Maybe I'll try it out with her tomorrow when we have more time.

"So, how are you feeling?" I ask her as we start walking back toward the house for dinner.

"I'm feeling ok. It was a lot of hard work, but I did enjoy most of what I learned today," she says honestly, then pauses and quickly adds, "Other than the running. I hated that."

I chuckle at her bluntness. "It will get easier."

"I seriously don't understand how people can run for fun. Like, seriously, what kind of a person likes running?"

"I like running," I tell her.

"I'm questioning your sanity right now," she teases, but the skeptical look she gives me betrays the grain of truth her declaration holds. I just smile back at her unconcerned.

We enter the house, and my olfactory nerves are immediately engulfed by the delicious scent of food. Gabriel is in the kitchen, stirring something on the stove, while Raphael hangs out at the breakfast bar, keeping him company.

"Food will be ready in a half-hour if you want to shower, Brie," Gabriel says, looking over at her.

"You're a godsend!" she says before running upstairs.

I make my way over to the breakfast bar, taking a seat on the open stool there.

"How did she do?" Raphael asks me.

I pause, thinking about my response before answering. "She's a fast learner and she really enjoyed the sparring introduction. I think she'll take to the fighting and weapons well, but she's alarmingly out of shape. It's like she hasn't worked out at all since she was dropped into Brienna's body. I don't know, guys, I'm a little worried to be honest. I don't know if we have enough time to prepare her. The conditioning she needs—it would take most people years, and we only have a few months."

"She'll be fine," Raphael assures me. "It's Brie. When has she ever come up against a challenge and not succeeded?"

"Raphael's right," Gabriel agrees. "When Brie sets her mind to something, she accomplishes it no matter how out of reach it seems. It's part of who she is. She hasn't lost that part of her simply because her soul is inhabiting a different form."

"Thanks guys," I say. "I needed to hear that. The stakes on this mission are so high. I guess I'm just worried. Failure is not an option, and she's our only chance of succeeding."

"You'll get it done. You and Brie have always been unstoppable together," Raphael says, squeezing my shoulder in reassurance.

"How did she do with your stuff?" I ask Raphael in return.

"She did well. I think her soul remembers her gifts, even if she doesn't. It was like working a muscle that you haven't used in a while. She didn't have as much stamina and control as she did before, but I think it will rebound rather quickly. We should only need to practice once a week after these first few sessions, so you and Gabriel will have more time for your lessons," Raphael asserts.

"That's a relief," I say, and Gabriel makes a vague sound of agreement from the kitchen as he cracks open the door to one of the ovens, peeking inside as more mouthwatering smells permeate the air.

"What are you making us tonight, Gabe?" I ask. He's always been a phenomenal cook and it's been too long since I've enjoyed his food.

"Crab cakes, broiled lobster tails, and seared scallops with a lemon beurre blanc sauce, cauliflower mash, roasted vegetables, and a strawberry kale salad," Gabriel answers nonchalantly.

I can't help but lick my lips in anticipation as Raphael groans "yum" from his seat next to me.

We hear Brie stomping down the stairs just a few minutes later. Her tread's not usually so heavy and I'm a bit confused as to why she's walking like this, but my confusion is immediately resolved when she stumbles into the room muttering to herself.

"Stupid exercise. Stupid sore muscles. How am I even supposed to sit in the stupid chair now? I seriously think my legs might give out when I try to bend them to get into the chair," she mutters lowly as she approaches one of the dining chairs with a look of pure loathing on her face.

Raphael bursts out laughing, and I realize I wasn't the only one entertained by her display. She looks up, noticing us staring at her, and a soft blush covers her cheeks before she turns back to the chair, pulling it out, and practically falling into it.

"Feeling a bit sore, sweetheart?" Raphael asks her jestingly with a grin.

"Ugh, you have no idea. I think my drill master over there overdid it a bit," she groans, pointing at me.

"Maybe this would be a good time for you to practice self-healing," Raphael responds patiently, his grin growing wider.

"Oh, right. That's something I can do now," she whispers to herself, looking abashed.

I watch as she closes her eyes and her brows scrunch together in concentration. She looks so adorable as she focuses internally. Finally, after only a few seconds, her body seems to relax, and she slumps further into the chair as she opens her eyes.

"That helped a lot. Thank you. I'm not sure why it didn't occur to me sooner," Brie says.

"You're just not used to it. It will become habit soon enough," Raphael comforts and Brie smiles back at him in response.

"Dinner's ready! Go set the table and sit," Gabriel instructs.

Raphael and I do as we're told, setting the table and getting everyone drinks before taking our seats. Gabriel brings over plates for Brie and Raf, setting the plates in front of them before going back for mine and his. The food is perfectly portioned for each of us and looks incredibly delicious.

"I've missed you, Gabey, but I've missed your food more," I joke with a completely straight face.

Gabriel looks at me and smiles, then pauses and furrows his brow. "Wait, you're joking right? That was a joke?" he asks, and Brie and Raf both burst out laughing.

"Yes, of course it was a joke," I reassure him. "I missed both you and your cooking equally," I continue, trying not to chuckle myself. I love messing with my brother. Almost as much as I love him.

Chapter 13

BRIE

I blearily descend the stairs, still half asleep, with only one eye partially open. I almost lose my footing twice, but thankfully my grip on the railing keeps me upright. Tottering into the kitchen, I head straight toward the cabinet filled with my coffee mugs and tiredly look them over. I finally grab a black one with yellow lettering that reads "NEED CAFFEINE ASAP" and begin preparing my much-needed coffee. Deciding I'm in a grumpy mood today and need a pick-me-up as well, I glance around the room. When I've confirmed that I am indeed alone, I creep over to the alcohol cabinet, pulling out a bottle of Irish Cream liqueur and adding a shot of it to my coffee. I'm almost in the clear when I hear a deep voice. Dang it, so close.

"What are you doing?" the deep voice asks suspiciously.

I whirl around, bottle still in hand, to see Raphael standing a hair's breadth away from me, looking over my shoulder.

"Um, nothing," I say, trying to act as innocently as possible. "Just making my morning coffee. Nothing to see here. Do you like my mug?" I ask, trying to distract him from the bottle in my hand.

Raphael pointedly looks down at the bottle of liquor I'm holding, quirks an eyebrow, and smirks at me.

"I hope you've made one for me too," he says, a mischievous glint in his eye.

I sag in relief and nod enthusiastically, then start preparing a spiked coffee for him as well.

He licks his lips as he takes it from me and whispers, "Let's not tell Michael about this."

"Let's not tell Michael about what?" Michael asks from the kitchen entrance.

Raphael and I both freeze.

I quickly turn around, holding the bottle behind my back and acting nonchalant. My luck is not so great today apparently. I mean, for Heaven's sake, I was caught red-handed not once, but twice, and I've only been awake for maybe twenty minutes max. That has to be a world record or something.

"So?" Michael prompts, since neither of us have answered his previous question and we're both just staring at him like deer caught in headlights. "What is it you aren't telling me?"

"Ummm..." I rack my brain for any response that won't get my coffee taken away from me. Considering how healthy my meals have been since we came here, Michael probably won't be so happy I'm drinking alcohol right before our morning run. "Ummm, I was just telling Raphael how much I'm looking forward to jogging today."

I internally facepalm as soon as the words leave my lips. If there was a list of least believable excuses, I'm pretty sure that one would have been at the top.

"Hmm, I'm sure," Michael hums. "Be ready in fifteen. Oh, and Brie?" he continues with a smirk turning up the corner of his mouth. "Next time you don't want me to know you've spiked your coffee, maybe close the cabinet door."

I burst out laughing as he turns away and confidently strides out of the room. I feel like every time I expect Michael to react to something in a negative light, he always surprises me in the best way possible. I down my coffee quickly, then run upstairs to change. Like yesterday, I throw on yoga pants and a sports bra, pulling my hair up into a ponytail as well, before rushing back downstairs to put on my shoes.

"We're going to do a walk-jog split today so your body can acclimate to the jogging. I don't want a repeat of yesterday," Michael tells me as I join him outside. "One minute of walking followed by one minute of jogging, repeating the whole way to the training complex."

"Got it! Let's do this!" I say enthusiastically, the spiked coffee running through my system having improved both my mood and my motivation. Also, survival. I kind of want to live through this whole closing all the Hell Gates thing, so I need to work hard and improve rapidly with everything the guys are trying to teach me.

Michael and I set off along the same path we took yesterday and today's jog goes much better. The minute-long walking breaks save me from getting any cramps, and although I'm dripping sweat and feeling the work by the time we reach the complex, my breathing is labored but not unhealthily difficult. I really feel like I worked. I grab some water from the cooler and then Michael guides me in the yoga routine. The yoga is much harder today since I did more jogging, but I manage to get through it. I *barely* manage it, but I do manage it. Michael encouraged me to practice my self-healing a few times during both the jog and the yoga, which also helped a lot. I'm sure Raphael will be happy to hear that I'm getting practice in that even outside of our lessons.

"How are you feeling about the tattoo?" Michael asks me as we walk back toward the house.

"I guess it's ok. It's not a design that I would have chosen for myself, but it's not terrible and I understand its purpose," I tell him.

"Did Raphael or Gabriel check to make sure it activated correctly?" he asks.

"No, I don't think so," I say.

"Well, let's do that. Can you understand me?" Michael asks.

"Yes, of course I can understand you," I answer, eyeing him like he might have lost a few marbles in the last few seconds.

"Good. Can you understand me now?"

"Yes, I can still understand you."

"And can you understand me now?"

"Why do you keep asking me if I can understand you?" I demand, wholly perplexed.

Michael chuckles at my exasperation and confusion. "Sweetheart, I asked you if you could understand me in three different languages—Russian, Spanish, and Mandarin."

"No, you asked me in English all three times," I correct.

"The rune translated the sound to English for you, but I didn't ask the questions in English. Your brain just processed it as English. You also answered me in the language that I had spoken in, though to you it seemed that you were answering in English."

"Oh," I say dumbfounded. "I didn't realize I wouldn't even hear the original words. I expected a delayed translation or something like that. So, the rune works then?"

"Yes, it's working perfectly," Michael assures me.

"Well, that's good. It would have been very unfortunate if it needed to be redone or something," I say with a shudder.

We walk in silence for a few moments, before I break it, asking, "Can I ask you about something Raphael mentioned in our lesson yesterday? It's been bugging me and I don't want to forget to ask."

"Yes, of course. You can ask me anything," Michael responds earnestly.

"Raphael said that I should never transfer energy to myself from a being that has darkness, but how can I know if someone has darkness or not?"

"As a being of pure light, when you encounter a being that has been corrupted by darkness, you will automatically feel a wariness about them. In all honesty, that's about ninety percent of the population on the Earthly plane at the moment. You won't feel completely comfortable around them no matter how charming they try to be. Think of how you feel around me, the guys, and your friend Callista. We are all uncorrupted beings of pure light. Even being unable to remember Raphael and Gabriel, you automatically knew that they were trustworthy. You won't feel that way around beings that have been infected by darkness," Michael explains.

His response leads me to think about when I first met Callie. We hit it off right away. I connected with her immediately, like I had never done with anyone before, and being friends with her just felt easy. I didn't have to worry about what she might say behind my back or any of the other catty games girls sometimes play. I knew from the get-go that I could trust her implicitly and she would always have my back. While I'd like to think that at least some of that is purely Callie, I guess part of it is because her soul doesn't carry any darkness.

"If nothing else," Michael says, breaking into my thoughts, "you'll know as soon as you look into their eyes. You, in particular, have a very unique angelic gift. We won't be training it because it's something that you do inherently, but you should know that it is a gift you possess. Your gift is the ability to read the truth of a soul through a being's eyes, so if you're not sure if a being is solely of the light, just look into their eyes, and you'll no longer have any doubt."

Reassured by that, I thank Michael for his explanation and his insight. I have always felt like I could judge someone more clearly by looking deeply into their eyes. It's good to know I was subconsciously using one of my angelic gifts and not just giving meaning to something that had none.

As soon as we re-enter the house, I pop upstairs for a quick shower. It only takes me around fifteen minutes before I'm back downstairs, especially since I leave my hair to airdry. My nose is assaulted by the delicious scents of breakfast as I sit in my seat at the dining table, curious to see what Michael and Gabriel are whipping up for all of us this morning. It's cute to watch them work side by side. Their intuitive understanding as they dance around each other in their preparations, without any need for speech, makes clear how close they are.

It's not long before Michael and Gabriel turn off all the appliances they were using and make their way over to the table, carrying two plates each. Michael places one of his plates in front of me as Gabriel does the same for Raphael, and my mouth waters when I see the spinach and mushroom eggs benedict they've prepared. I absolutely love eggs benedict. It's one of my favorite foods, and definitely my favorite breakfast. I wonder if they knew that when they decided to make it.

The first bite hits my tongue and I can't hold in my moan at the explosion of flavors. It's just so incredibly good. I hear a fork clang onto a plate as someone starts coughing and I look up at my tablemates in a panic, worried that one of them is choking, but pause when I observe Raphael and Gabriel looking highly entertained as they watch Michael. I then look over at Michael, who has now stopped coughing but is still red-faced and looking like he's trying to regain his composure as he stares back at me with hunger in his eyes.

Confused, I ask, "What happened?"

Raphael and Gabriel completely lose it, laughing their bums off. Michael gives me a sheepish smile and answers, "Nothing, love. You can go back to your breakfast."

For some reason, that just sets Raphael and Gabriel off even more, to the point where they can barely stay in their chairs and are both leaning heavily on the table for support as they laugh uncontrollably. I'm still confused as to what happened, but I just mutter "Ok" and dig back into my delicious breakfast. I finish eating far too quickly and frown down at my empty plate, wishing there was more food on it. I'm actually quite full, but it was just so good I wish it was unending.

Gabriel takes me out first today since we didn't get a chance to start on the scrying yesterday. I'm actually pretty nervous about this part, and I wouldn't mind if it was delayed even further, though I know I'll have to delve into it sooner or later, so I might as well just get it over with and jump in the deep end.

"We'll start with the black obsidian circle. Mirrors and bowls used to be your preferred scrying mediums," Gabriel tells me, directing me toward the bench next to it.

As I sit on the bench, Gabriel continues with his lesson. "All I want you to do now is look into the circle and let your eyes relax. We want a vision to come to you right now in the most natural way. I don't want you to mentally focus on anything specific, just let whichever vision wants to make itself known find its way to you."

Gabriel falls silent and I stare at the circle, letting my eyes relax as he instructed. Several minutes pass and I'm starting to get bored. I'm about to look at Gabriel to tell him it's not working when I notice shapes forming in the blackness of the stone. Is this the scrying, or is my mind playing tricks on me because I've been staring at the reflective surface for so long? Before my mind can run away on that train of thought, I feel a falling sensation and the world around me changes.

The bench beneath me has disappeared and I'm now sitting on the bare ground. As I look around, I spot the house and the training complex in the distance on each side of me, but the rest of the grounds are bare. The natural pool and jacuzzi that butt up against the back of the house aren't there, nor is the square with all the scrying mediums that I had just been staring at. There's no garden or greenhouse. The grounds around me are vast, but empty.

I hear humming in the distance, coming from my right, and I turn my head in time to see a beautiful brunette emerge from the house. Recognition strikes me: she's the woman I saw in the wedding picture upstairs. This is the angel version of my soul. Sabriel.

The melody she hums is full of joy, and it makes me think of the musical notes that adorn the front gate of the property. She carries a sketchpad and some pencils as she walks right up to me, plopping down on the ground to sit cross-legged next to where I'm sitting. She continues to hum as she draws in her sketchbook. I peek over to see that she is outlining the design of the grounds. She's drawing boxes with labels for the garden, the pool, and so on. After she's finished the main design, she flips to the next page and draws the design for the garden in more detail, specifying which plant she wants where. She's about halfway through when she pauses and smiles, then she looks right at me and says, "Hello Brienna," in the most melodic voice I've ever heard.

Shocked, I gape at her. Can she see me? Will the people in my visions be able to see me or interact with me?

"No, I can't see you," she answers my thoughts with a knowing lilt to her voice. "I had a vision of you telling Gabriel about seeing me in this moment. I'm glad we get to meet each other—even if it is in a roundabout way."

I don't try to respond, guessing that if she can't see me, she won't be able to hear me either. I just sit here, waiting with anticipation for whatever she'll say to me next.

"Do me a favor?" she asks lightly. "Give Michael some time. He'll love our soul no matter where we are or what form we take, and he's fiercely protective and infinitely loyal, but he's still a man, and not always the best at verbalizing his feelings or showing them in the ways that we might expect. I'm sure this whole situation must be very confusing for you, but know that even though we look different, and we don't share our memories, he still loves you and would go to the depths of Hell for you if he needed to. Never doubt that he has your best interests at heart, even on his grumpy days."

She lets out a tinkling laugh and I can't help but smile as well. I like her—me—angel me. She looks like she's about to say something else when Michael emerges from the house, calling her name.

"Sabriel, my love, we've been asked to return to the angelic plane. Gabriel has called an urgent meeting."

"Of course," she responds and gracefully stands, turning back to give me a wink before walking to the house with Michael, hand in hand.

Chapter 14

BRIE

I'm suddenly sitting on the bench again and it takes me a minute to acclimate. The scenery change is jarring and a bit disorienting. Hopefully that will get better with time. Once I've adjusted to being back in the present, excitement overtakes me.

"Gabriel!" I squeal. "You'll never guess what I just saw! I was here but not, and the grounds were totally bare and angel me came out and talked to me. At first, I thought she could see me because she plopped right down next to me being all graceful-like and started drawing the layout for the grounds and the garden. She turned and looked right at me and said, "Hello Brienna," and then said she couldn't actually see me and then I thought maybe she was a mind reader, but she explained she'd had her own vision of me telling you this. It was crazy!"

Gabriel smiles at me in amusement before answering, "I'm glad you received a pleasant vision. Now, what did you notice that will help you, in the future, to identify that you've just entered a vision?" he asks, getting right down to business even though I'm still bouncing in excitement.

"Well, the scenery changed," I answer, thinking back.

"Good. That's a pretty clear indicator, though not something that you can always count on. What else?"

"Um, I felt like I was falling and everything kind of blurred for a second," I say.

"That is a clear indicator that you will always be able to identify," he tells me.

"But how do I know it's a vision and I'm not just passing out or something?" I ask.

"Well, what other things can you think of that were different while you were in the vision?" Gabriel pushes.

"I guess it felt like everything that I wasn't specifically focused on was a little fuzzy around the edges," I answer.

"Good, that's another clear indicator. When you get the sensation of falling, there's a momentary blur of your surroundings, and the visual stimuli you aren't focused on seem fuzzy, you'll know you are in a vision. We'll practice so you get used to the change and become able to pick up on those three things without thought."

"Ok," I agree.

Three visions later, I ask, "Isn't it time for lunch yet? It feels like I've been doing this for hours!"

Gabriel smiles as his eyes light up in amusement. "Time works differently when you're in a vision. It's as though time is compressed in the real world and expanded within the vision, so for every minute that you experience within your vision, only a fraction of a second will pass outside of it. You may experience a vision that seemingly lasts for hours, and only minutes will have passed when you come back to yourself. That being said, you've been practicing for about an hour, and since it's new for you, I can imagine you're finding it to be quite taxing. We'll break for the day and pick back up tomorrow."

"Thank you, Gabriel," I say, feeling genuine gratitude.

It really was draining and I'm relieved for the break. Maybe I can grab a quick snack before I'm inevitably ushered off to my next practice session.

Just as that thought crosses my mind, I spot Raphael walking over to us.

Gabriel stands as he arrives, saying, "We just finished."

"Good," Raphael responds. "Michael sent me out. He was worried the visions could overtax her. We're supposed to work on flying until lunch. Would you like to join?"

"Sure, why not?" Gabriel answers with a shrug.

"Michael says he already gave you an introduction to flying?" Raphael says questioningly.

"Only if you consider pushing me off a cliff an introduction," I drawl sarcastically, punctuating my statement with an eyeroll. "Ok, I guess he did also teach me a bit after he pushed me off the cliff," I relent, and Raphael chuckles as Gabriel mutters, "Sounds like Michael."

Flying feels more like playing than working if I'm being honest. I really enjoy it, the feeling of freedom it gives me lightening my mood even further. They work with me on flying technique until it's time to go back to the house for lunch, and part of me wonders if Michael could somehow feel how much I needed that sense of freedom today.

We return to the house, ribbing each other along the way. Even though I don't remember these two, my friendship with them feels so easy and natural. It's easy to forget that we haven't been friends for as long as I can remember. I guess that makes sense, since we were friends for a much longer time that I can't remember.

I sit in my spot at the dining room table and Michael places a large bowl of chicken Caesar salad in front of me. I thank him and dig into it, extra hungry from both the visions and the flying.

"I believe I've identified the location of one of the Hell Gates," Michael announces to the table, and I nearly spit out the food I'd been chewing.

"You don't know where the Hell Gates are?" I ask incredulously.

"Not exactly. We know there are nine remaining in this realm, and I have made a list of possibilities that I'm currently narrowing down. I believe I've been able to identify one of them as unequivocally being one of the Gates. I still need to determine which of the locations on my list comprise the other eight," Michael answers.

"That's great, Michael. Good job. I know you've been putting a lot of time and effort into your research. It's good to see that's paying off," Gabriel says, giving me a warning look.

"No, yeah," I stutter, "I mean, I'm not discounting your effort or criticizing you. I appreciate that you're researching it and training me and everything, I just... Doesn't Heaven get a ping or something when a Hell Gate opens on Earth? Like, how can a Hell Gate be here and Heaven doesn't know about it?"

"No, we don't get some sort of text notification whenever a Hell Gate opens telling us the location," Michael answers me dryly, though clearly amused. "It would make my life a lot easier if we did. We know the number of open Gates because we can calculate that based on the maximum amount of darkness each Gate is able to emit, combined with the rate at which the darkness is spreading throughout the world. Beyond that, I have to use historical accounts and local lore to determine where each Gate is located."

"Wow, that sounds like a lot of work," I admit, impressed. "I've always enjoyed research, if you need any help."

"Thank you for the offer, but for now, I need you to focus on your training. Sealing the Gates is something only you can do, and I need you to be ready when the time comes," Michael says firmly.

"I understand," I acquiesce, and I really do understand. It won't matter if he knows where the Gates are if I'm not strong enough or capable enough to actually seal them.

The guys chat more about Michael's research and I leave them to it, merely listening in and absorbing the information they divulge. Apparently, Michael has narrowed down his list of probable Hell Gate locations from twenty-one to thirteen, and the one he's sure is a Hell Gate is located in Iceland. He makes some comments about adding rock climbing and mountaineering into my physical training regimen. After that, I tune out of the conversation so I don't become too overwhelmed by how daunting his plans for my training are.

I finish eating and bring my plate over to the kitchen sink to rinse before placing it in the dishwasher, then I follow Raphael out to the garden for more energy work and healing practice. Our hour seems to come and go in the blink of an eye, and before I know it, I find myself standing in front of a massive obstacle course that was hidden behind the training complex.

"What in Heaven's name is this nonsense?" I ask Michael in horror. "You can't possibly think I'm capable of completing an obstacle course like this. I'll probably die halfway through, and then who will close the Hell Gates for you?" I ask, gesticulating emphatically.

Michael, who is in an annoyingly upbeat mood this afternoon and is clearly taking joy in my misery, just chuckles in response before launching into his instructions.

"We'll start out jogging the path. You need to jog or run between the obstacles—no walking," he tells me firmly. "I'll come along with you, mostly to spot you. Today your only goal is to complete the course, no matter how long it takes you. It will give me a baseline so we can make sure your performance is constantly improving."

"So, back to my comment about dying halfway through—"

Michael cuts me off, "I'm timing you starting in three...two...one. Let's go."

With a groan, I start jogging next to him, since he hasn't given me much of a choice in the matter and being able to complete this obstacle course is somewhat important to my survival in the long run. The first obstacle is a ditch filled with water. I have to run down the slope into the ditch, wade through the water, and then pull myself up the opposite slope with a rope that hangs down into the watery ditch. The rope bites into my hands as I grip it tightly and try to balance the work for my ascent evenly between my arms and my legs. I don't have much arm strength though, so my arms are already tired and shaking after just the first few pulls. I honestly don't think I'll make it the whole way up, and this is only the first obstacle.

I hear Michael grumble "I'm going to help you, but I have to touch you to do so. Is it ok?"

I automatically answer, "Yeah, sure." A heartbeat later, a hand on my butt distracts me for a second, and with all logical thought fleeing my brain, I'm just about to turn back toward Michael to ask if turning me on is part of the challenge. Thankfully, my brain comes back online before I do so, and his words reverberate in my mind, helping me to realize that he's pushing me up, helping me climb up the slope so I don't fail before making it to the top of this first obstacle. Well darn, I was kind of hoping he just really liked how my bum was looking and couldn't help himself from copping a feel when the opportunity arose. I mean, usually I'm against that kind of thing, but Michael is my one exception. He can check out my bum anytime he wants.

Realizing that I'm getting far too distracted by my wanting thoughts, I refocus on the task at hand and make it up the slope solely due to Michael's help. I definitely would not have made it otherwise. He joins me at the top, seemingly without any real effort, and we take off jogging again, toward the next obstacle. I'm really hoping whatever is next doesn't require any arm strength.

Unfortunately, my hopes are soon dashed when I find that the second obstacle is climbing up a vertical wooden structure and then climbing back down it on its other side. I manage the climb up with great effort and then hang onto the top for a bit, gaining my strength back with a little break so I don't end up falling off on the way down.

"You know you can't just lay there forever, right?" Michael asks me as he chills next to me, looking far more poised than I do.

"I don't see why not," I answer primly, but quickly worry that talking could dislodge the tentative hold I have on my position, so I immediately cut off what I was planning on saying next.

Michael is sitting atop the wooden structure nonchalantly, as though it's something he does all the time, one leg on each side of the beam, his back perfectly straight, his arms hanging naturally by his sides. I, on the other hand, am clinging to the beam like my life depends on it. While I'm also straddling the beam, my entire chest is pressed against the top of it as I lay flush against it, my arms and legs both hugging it tightly. I'm pretty sure that even with my death grip on the beam, there's a good chance I may still fall off of it.

Eventually though, my thoughts of falling off the top of the structure terrify me enough that I decide it's safer to start climbing down, so I roll-climb onto the back side of the structure and wobbly start my descent. I'm shaking fiercely from both fear and adrenaline, which makes the climb down even harder, but I do end up making it and breathe a sigh of relief as soon as both feet touch the ground.

Michael is right next to me when I land, and although I'm tempted to kiss the ground in my appreciation of it, I start jogging again instead. On to the next obstacle I go. I totally got this. Ha! Who am I kidding, I don't have this at all. Nope, not even a little bit.

The next obstacle involves rolling and army crawling under a net stretched taut a foot above the ground. I wouldn't say it's easy or pleasant, but it's the most palatable of the obstacles that I've encountered thus far. I'm starting to feel a little better about the obstacle course, thinking maybe the obstacles will get easier and easier, when we jog up to a sparkling lake. I pause on the shoreline, wondering if that was the end, though even I can admit that having an obstacle course with only three obstacles doesn't seem very likely.

"You need to swim across," Michael tells me.

"What?" I ask, even though I heard him perfectly well. "Is there anything in there that can eat me?"

"Not the last time I checked, but you never know," Michael answers. He says it with a straight face, but the mischievous glint in his eye gives him away and I can tell he's mocking me a bit.

"Well, no time like the present," I say, and dive into the lake.

Chapter 15

BRIE

I climb out of the lake after swimming freestyle over to the other side. My clothes are heavy as they drip water, forming a puddle around my feet, and I realize that all of the obstacles to come will be that much harder due to the added weight. Michael resumes the jog toward the next obstacle and I grimace as I follow along behind him, my shoes making a slopping noise with every tread.

I nearly turn around when we reach the long line of monkey bars. As we've already established, arm strength is not my forte. Add in the extra weight from my wet clothes and how slick my grip will be from the moisture remaining on my palms, and I can already imagine the disaster this will become. Nevertheless, I know I can't quit before I even try, so I climb the ladder at the start of the line of monkey bars and reach for the first rung. As predicted, I only make it to the second bar in the line of twenty before my grip gives out and I crash onto the ground. Michael rushes over to make sure I'm ok, which thankfully I am, and encourages me to try again. I do, mostly just to placate him, but I fall again almost as soon as I begin so he relents, telling me that I can skip the rest of it and jog to the next obstacle.

Next, there are some hurdles that Michael bounds over easily, while I hop-rotate-fall over each one. The hurdles are followed by a sandbag carry, though I don't have the strength to even pick the sandbag up, so I end up alternating between pushing, rolling, and dragging the sandbag. Michael easily tosses his over his shoulder and strides on, pausing to wait for me every few seconds with the sandbag perched atop his shoulder the whole time as though it weighs nothing.

Suspiciously, I ask, "Are our sandbags the same weight? Because that wouldn't be so fair. I'm much smaller than you in size so, logically, mine should weigh less."

"Your sandbag does weigh less. It's also in the lighter range of what would be appropriate for your size," Michael answers humorlessly as he watches me try to kick the sandbag forward in an attempt to rest my arms.

Unfortunately, my kicking idea doesn't work, the sandbag not budging even a single millimeter, so with a huff, I go back to my pushing, rolling, dragging rotation. I finally reach the line marking the end of the obstacle, feeling like I'm about to keel over, but Michael doesn't give me time to recover, immediately taking off jogging as soon as I let go of the sandbag.

We arrive at a rope hanging about five feet in the air above a pool of water. Michael instructs that I'm supposed to scoot upside down along the length of the rope. Ironically, although it looks difficult and I had no idea how to get onto the rope to begin with, this is one of the least overwhelming obstacles for me. I simply cling to the rope like a monkey and use my shoulders and my legs to scoot myself along. It works pretty well, and although my arms are total mush, my shoulders haven't given out on me yet, so I'm feeling pretty confident about their durability right now. I have to say, though, my shoulders are burning hard when I reach the end. Of course, now I need to figure out how to get myself onto the ladder to climb down. That is arguably more difficult than the obstacle itself was.

The next obstacle is pretty easy compared to the others. I scoot along a balance beam slowly, teetering only slightly.

"You do realize that you're supposed to run across the beam, not crawl across it at a snail's pace, correct?" Michael calls up to me once I'm a few steps in.

"You said my only goal for this course today was finishing. That implies I can complete the obstacles at whatever pace I deem appropriate," I counter, pausing while I talk because multitasking is not my strong suit, and I really don't want to fall.

"Touché," he mutters quietly.

I finish with the beam and then climb through some gigantic tires. I guess you're supposed to hop through them, but I need my hands to help lift my legs high enough to simply climb over them, so the hopping is definitely not going to happen this round. It probably won't happen in the near future either, if I'm being completely honest with myself.

"The next obstacle is the last in this course," Michael tells me.

I almost cry with joy, but then the obstacle comes into view. It looks like one of those basketball machines that arcades have, where you earn tickets every time you make a basket. At first, I think that's not so bad. My arms are mush, but surely I can rally and make it happen. Once I'm standing in front of the machine and I pick up a ball, however, my delight quickly fizzles. The balls are weighted. I can barely lift my arms with just their own weight to account for, and yet I'm supposed to throw a weighted ball through the net? And now that I'm really looking at the setup, I'm pretty sure that the net is higher than it's supposed to be as well. I try to throw the ball—I really do—but I can't even lift it to chest height, let alone gather the necessary momentum to throw it. Frustrated, with both myself and the situation, I let my wings unfurl, cuddle the ball to my body, fly up so I'm hovering directly above the net, and drop the ball straight through it.

"Well, that's one way to do it," Michael laughs. "I'll give you points for ingenuity, but in the future, you'll actually need to throw the ball up there, not just drop it in."

"Yeah, yeah," I begrudgingly agree.

"Let's stretch a bit and then you can rest for the remainder of the day," Michael tells me and I am so grateful to hear the word "rest".

I mimic Michael's movements as he transitions from one stretch to the next. My body is so wiped from that obstacle course that even holding each stretch feels like it's taking more energy than I have.

We've been at it for a few minutes when I notice movement in the distance, coming from the direction of the house. "I think we might have company," I say to Michael, gesturing over his shoulder.

Michael turns to look as Gabriel jogs closer, and I'm able to make out Gabriel's expression for the first time. He looks almost panicked, which is completely out of character for him from what I know about him so far. Dread suffuses me and I wait with bated breath to hear what he needs to tell us. Michael stands up and walks toward Gabriel, reducing the distance between them. I struggle to my feet and follow behind him, even though every muscle in my body is trying to convince me to spread eagle on the grass and not move for the next decade.

"Michael, there's been a development," Gabriel calls when he's close enough to be heard. "You'll need to leave for the first Gate, sooner than you'd hoped, at the lowest end of your timeline, and you need to hasten Brie's preparation schedule. Three months at the very most. The lower plane somehow found out that we plan to seal the Gates and there are rumblings that defenses are being put in place to make the task harder to accomplish. The longer we take to prepare and to train Brie, the longer the lower plane has to prepare as well."

"No!" Michael gasps, his voice wavering in fury.

"I'm sorry to be the bearer of bad news. I just received the message from the divine spirit directly," Gabriel says solemnly.

"There's so much to prepare. I don't know if we can be ready in time," Michael worries.

"You'll have to be. There was one surety in the message that I received, and that surety was that if you wait any longer than three months, there will be irreversibly disastrous consequences. Far worse than any of the possible futures that could occur otherwise," Gabriel replies seriously.

Turning to me, Michael says, "Brie, heal yourself. I'm sorry, I know you're tired, but we'll need to start on your weapons training now and work more on your sparring later tonight as well. I know I said you could rest for the remainder of the day, but we no longer have that luxury. I'll give you fifteen minutes to rest and recover, but then we're jumping back in."

I nod, meandering my way toward the entrance to the training complex and leaving Gabriel and Michael to continue their conversation. I pause briefly to envision my healing energy dispersing throughout my body, but even after I do so, I feel bone weary. My limbs, though no longer sore, are still alarmingly shaky, and I feel like any strength I had at the beginning of the day—which, let's be honest, wasn't much—has seeped out of my body completely.

I enter the training complex, dragging my feet with the fatigue overwhelming me, walk a few paces to the side of the doorway and slide down to sit with my back against the wall. I pull my knees up in front of me, fold my arms on top of them, lean my head down atop my arms, and close my eyes. Within seconds, I feel sleep pulling me under.

"Brie, sweetheart, wake up," Michael's voice says.

"No, too tired. Sleeping," I slur.

"Brie, come on, love. I know you're tired, but we need to continue training. Don't you want to learn how to use some of the weapons?" Michael asks enticingly.

He knows me too well: I really do. Despite my alarm at the presence of the weapons room, I'm itching to play with whatever it contains.

Peeking one eye open, I gain awareness of my surroundings. I'm still propped up against the wall near the door of the training complex and Michael is kneeling in front of me, watching me fondly. He must have been in here for a few minutes before trying to wake me, because I can see that the door to the weapons room is already open. Slowly, I raise my head and start to get up, feeling slightly re-energized from my short nap and too curious about what the weapons room contains to try to go back to sleep.

Michael chuckles in amusement as I pad over to the weapons room and peek inside, gawking as soon as I get my first glance. Have you ever seen a super large, well-organized celebrity closet, like on television shows? That's what the weapons room reminds me of, except with all different kinds of weapons instead of clothes, shoes, and accessories.

The weapons room spans the length of the training center and appears to be organized by weapon type. Each section has glass cabinets lining the walls, along with at least one center armoire with a glass display top and drawers, each one filled with the weapon type of that section. The first section when you enter the weapons room seems to be dedicated to firearms, holding everything from pistols and revolvers to shotguns and even some machine guns. The next section appears to be the most expansive, holding different types of swords and knives, including katanas and glaives. Then there's a section with spears, followed by a section with axes. The section with bows and arrows appears a bit smaller, without as much variety as I observed in the previous sections. Then, at the very end, are a few flamethrowers and a small collection of explosives. Well, at least we're well equipped.

Walking back over to Michael, who has been watching me from the doorway, I grin and say, "So, what am I starting with?"

He throws back his head and laughs at my eagerness. "Well, you always had fun wielding a short sword and some daggers, so let's start there."

Chapter 16

BRIE

Three months later

My courage is a little wispy thing floating around inside my chest. It is seldomly present, frequently absent, and as I look out at the tarmac through the little window next to my seat as our jet's wheels find purchase on the runway of Massachusetts's New Bedford Regional Airport, I can't help but wonder if my coming here will lead to my death. I don't feel ready, despite the intensive training of the past three months. If one were to measure the amount of courage floating through my chest right now, it could possibly fill a teaspoon. Maybe. Probably not. And considering I'm about to venture into a place known as "The Cursed Forest of Massachusetts", a teaspoon of courage feels somewhat inadequate at the current moment. Regardless, we're here and Michael is ushering me off the plane. Too late to back out now.

The drive to our accommodations is short and pleasant, filled with greenery and silence. I'm far too nervous for conversation and Michael seems content to let me stew in my own thoughts. The hum of anxiety below my ribcage shallows my breath and I feel like there are ants crawling beneath the skin of my arms. It's a welcome relief when we arrive at the bed and breakfast we reserved.

The house itself is a cute little two-story colonial with white siding, black shutters, and a bright red door. It looks old, but well cared for. There are two wooden chairs by the front walkway and a sparse sprinkling of bushes lining the front of the house, but no other decorations beyond that. Michael and I grab the two bags that hold our clothes, leaving our weapons and travel supplies in the trunk of our rental car, and walk up to the bright red door. I reach out to ring the doorbell, but before my finger so much as brushes the little round button, the door flies open and we are greeted by a short pudgy woman with a heart-shaped face and white hair tied up in a bun. She is a bundle of energy as she bounces on her toes and smiles broadly at us.

"Oh, welcome, welcome! You must be the Angelus newlyweds! Congratulations. Such a lovely couple," the woman exclaims excitedly.

Michael had the idea of telling people on our journey that we were newlyweds in an effort to "ensure we receive maximum privacy and minimal interruptions while in our rooms so we can strategize in peace"—his words, not mine. I'm not sure he considered the additional ramifications of his lie, and I consciously hold myself back from laughing at the shocked expression currently painted across his face. It's like he can't possibly fathom how anyone could be as jovial as the woman in front of us. I can't help but smile at her though. Her mannerisms and energy remind me so much of Callie. I bet this is exactly what Callie will be like as an older woman. A pang of longing hits me at that thought. I really miss my best friend.

"Yes, that's us," I answer the woman with a bright smile.

It's actually not us, to be honest. Angels don't have last names, just titles. I suggested using my human last name, but Michael didn't want to give away any information that could be traced back to us, so we are using "Angelus" as a contrived last name. I thought it was an appropriate choice, as I love irony. I put on an air of extreme seriousness and made sure I maintained a straight face when I made the suggestion. Raphael was with us at the time and burst out laughing. I winked at him when Michael wasn't looking. Michael scowled, but his laughter shone through in his eyes as he grudgingly agreed, encouraged by Raphael's enthusiasm on the matter.

"Oh, lovely. My name is Cara. I'm so happy to have you both here. Come in, come in!" the woman responds, waving us through the doorway. I step through the threshold and before I know it, I'm being enveloped by the woman's plump frame as she gives me a tight, smothering hug. My arms are pinned to my sides and it's super awkward. Thankfully, it only lasts a few seconds before she moves onto Michael, hugging him with the same level of overt friendliness. He rigidly pats her back, refusing to embrace her in return, though his arms aren't pinned as mine were. His expression is that of an animal trapped in a cage as he stares imploringly at me, silently begging for escape. I just smile back at him, unbothered.

Michael manages to disentangle himself from Cara and gently guides her away from his body. It's sweet how careful he is not to hurt her with his powerful strength while still firmly putting space between them. He gives her a tight smile and moves partially behind me as though he's using my body to shield himself from the woman so she can't hug him again. It's kind of adorable and makes me love him that much more. Wait, love? Nope, didn't mean that. It's way too early for an emotion that strong. I totally meant to think "like".

Shaking my head at my own thoughts, I follow Cara as she shows us to the room we'll be staying in. When she opens the door, my eyes bug out of my head and I nearly choke on my own saliva. It's pink and floral *everywhere.* And I do mean *everywhere*: the draperies, the wallpaper, the bedding, the carpet—all insanely ugly pink floral patterns. Even the furniture is made of distressed wood that has been painted a French rose shade of pink. I cough a few times to clear my throat and Cara gives me a wide smile.

"I know, it's beautiful isn't it? This is my favorite room in the whole house. Only the best for my newlyweds!" she titters. "I'll leave you two to get settled. Just come downstairs if you need anything. I'll be in the kitchen."

"Thank you," I manage, walking into the nausea-inducing, disgustingly pink room.

Michael follows me into the room, closing the door behind him, and starts grumbling as he puts his bag on a floral armchair in the corner. I can barely make out what he's saying, but I do hear him mutter that he didn't reserve the Pepto Bismol room, followed by something about wanting to gouge his eyes out. The room really is terrible, but I'm entertained by the fact he seems to take this personally. Placing my bag on the awful pink dresser, I flop onto the bed only to find that the ceiling has been painted pink as well.

I laugh humorlessly at that and close my eyes for a brief respite from the styling of the room.

"When do we leave?" I ask Michael. After seeing this room, I already feel better about journeying into the forest. At least it won't have pink floral patterns.

"Two hours," Michael responds. "The forest will empty of visitors before nightfall, as even the most skeptical of visitors is wise enough to not risk wandering the forest after dark. We will enter after nightfall to avoid being seen. We should rest to conserve our energy until then."

Michael opens the window in our room and pops out the screen, propping it up against the wall just to the right of the where we will be exiting the room. I extend my wings and wrap a glamour around them, just as Michael taught me, and he does the same. We both slip silently through the open window into the dark night and set down by the trunk of our rental car. Michael opens the trunk and unzips one of our weapons bags, careful not to jostle the contents. We both start strapping on holsters and weapons atop our all-black attire. Knives, swords, sai, guns, and throwing stars each find their designated holding spots along our bodies until all three weapons bags are empty and we are both fully armed. Next, we both snap on belts filled with pouches containing other supplies that may be necessary for our survival tonight. Despite all of Michael's research, we don't fully know what we may or may not encounter on our journey to the Gate, though we do expect it to be protected somehow. Once we are fully loaded down, Michael and I start walking in the direction of the forest, having decided not to risk alerting Cara to our absence by starting the engine of the car. Walking will take longer, but will ensure that our absence at the bed and breakfast goes unnoticed.

We enter the woods among the massive trees, careful to stay off the paths that hikers and bikers use during the day, just in case some fool did decide to stay in the forest after dark. It's unlikely, but one can't be too careful. A light wind whispers through the leaves of the large, ancient trees, causing a faint rustling sound. The trees creak, seemingly at random, and as we continue deeper into the forest, those creaks transition to moans and wails. Eerie is an understatement. Between the dark of night and the canopy of leaves above us, the forest is pitch black save for the slight glow emanating from our wings.

Michael and I move through the forest silently, careful of where we place our footfalls. We soon come across an area with three uprooted trees, fallen atop one another like a row of dominoes. The trees are gargantuan, with the rooted portion towering above both Michael and myself by six feet or more. I briefly wonder what kind of storm could cause such an upheaval, when an intense urge shudders through my body, causing me to reach out a hand and touch one of the exposed roots before I even realize what I'm doing.

As soon as my hand connects with the ancient tree, I'm tumbling through a murky blackness into a vision of the past. The forest reforms around me in a previous reality where the three felled trees have not yet fallen. I hear a commotion to my right and hastily follow the noise. Not far from the trees lies a small brook, filled with blackened water. Hateful spirits emerge from below the water, moving with the tantalizing grace of a lethal serpent. I can feel their malevolence in my very being. They focus their gaze on a man who looks to be in his mid-forties. He has ruddy brown hair, an unkempt mustache and beard covering a round face, and dark, emotionless eyes. He is carrying a young girl, also with brown hair, though her features are soft and filled with kindness and innocence. She is unconscious and defenseless.

The spirits start to hiss, entrancing the man and encouraging his already evil soul to blacken further. A loud squawk pulls my gaze upwards, where a bird of great size streaks across the dark, starless sky toward the spirits. The bird opens its mouth and squawks again, eyes focused directly on one of the spirits, and a lightning bolt bursts from the sky. It crashes into the spirit the bird was staring at, singeing the spirit's energy from its core. The spirit wails in pain as the lightning streaks through its center and webs outward, eating up the spirit's energy. When the webs of electricity disappear, the spirit is no more. The bird focuses its attention on another of the spirits, readying for a second strike, and the man starts to run, carrying the girl over his shoulder. The spirits flee the bird, dipping under the water, and the bird turns, chasing the man. I run as well, trying to save the girl from this evil being masquerading as a human.

This is what demons look like on the Earthly plane, I realize. They are ordinary people filled with darkness and capable of terrible things. They don't have horns or tails. They look like anyone else one might encounter on a daily basis, and those that cannot see darkness or sense evil might never know that they are in the presence of a demon until it's too late.

I reach the man and jut out my leg, trying to trip him, but my leg sweeps right through his ankle, completely immaterial. Of course:

this is a memory of the past, so regardless of what I do, I won't be able to save this poor girl. I am forced to let this memory play out and watch what transpires with utter helplessness. Just like the man's unconscious victim.

The bird squawks again, closing in on the man, and he throws the girl in a show of desperation, trying to lighten his load so he can run faster. I hear a loud crack as her head hits a nearby tree and her body crumples lifelessly to the ground at its base. Blood pools quickly on the ground in a circle surrounding her head and traveling outward. She is unquestionably dead. A tear traces down my cheek as I stare at her broken, unmoving body in shock. I watch as her unblemished soul releases from her body and dissipates as it travels to the next plane of existence, to either continue its journey or find peace above.

My attention then returns to the man who is now huddled against a giant tree, cornered by the large bird. The bird hovers in the air in front of the man and beats its wings. Thunder explodes from where its wings beat the air and the powerful boom is focused right at the man. The man is crushed against the trunk of the tree before the tree itself topples back, roots tearing up from the ground in a deafening roar. The tree hits the one behind it, toppling two others before shuddering to a rest. The air fills with a heavy silence. Justice has been served, but not without great tragedy. The trees that have fallen whimper and I feel their pain as their lifeforce seeps out of them and flows into the forest floor on which they now lie. The bird lands next to the first tree that fell and nuzzles the rough bark with its head, in apology, before taking to the sky and letting out one last mournful squawk.

Michael has his hand on my shoulder when I come back to the present. I sink to my knees and bow my head, resting my forehead against the exposed roots of the fallen tree as tears flow freely from my eyes from the reverberations of their pain still plaguing me.

"I'm so sorry," I whisper. The forest floor shudders as it weeps with me and the trees surrounding us let out anguished moans. I know the tree I'm resting my head against is no longer alive as it once was, but the forest contains the energy that once filled the tree. That energy is still scarred by what happened, and it's all around us. I picture peaceful green energy filling the center of my chest. I infuse the energy with as much feeling of comfort and healing as I can, then picture the green energy expanding to encompass the entirety of my body, until I'm a silhouette of green glow. I place my left hand on the tree's roots and my right hand on the forest floor, trying not to think about spiders or snakes or any other creepy crawlies that I may unwittingly be touching, and push the green energy out through my hands until it has all been expelled. The forest seems to sigh with relief, and the dark eeriness that has engulfed us since we entered the forest lessens minutely. The forest requires much more healing than I can offer in this moment, but at least I gave it what I could. Finally, I turn my head toward Michael. He gazes back at me with concern etched across his features.

"Are demons real?" I whisper almost inaudibly.

"Yes," he whispers back, his eyes flooding with compassion. "You had a vision."

He says it as a statement rather than a question, already knowing the truth of his words.

"Yes," I murmur.

"Many supernatural creatures exist," Michael says. "We will likely meet some of them on this journey. Supernaturals are not as humans think. Humans interpret things too literally, when most attributes of supernaturals on the Earthly plane are essentially metaphorical. As it seems you've just realized, the demons that inhabit this plane are simply humans filled with the capacity for evil and hastened to action by the darkness that infects them. They are filled with darkness to the point their soul is completely black. Supernatural creatures have two forms. The darkness or light penetrates their soul during their time on the Earthly plane, but only influences aspects of the personality until the soul crosses over into a higher or lower plane of existence. Once the soul does cross over, that is when the being's visage will change. For most beings that humans think of as supernaturals, the way humans depict them tends to be more representative of the form the creature takes when their soul is not in the Earthly plane. It can get more complicated than that, as you can see by the fact that I didn't inhabit a human vessel to come down to this plane, but that's the basic explanation."

I nod.

"We should continue," Michael says softly.

I nod again. I knew coming into this that the forest has an extensive history of murder, satanic cult activity, sacrifices, and spirits—Michael briefed me on its history before we left California—but seeing the memory of one of those murders right before my very eyes has shaken me to the core. It didn't seem real before, but it's real now. I now understand the magnitude of responsibility resting on my shoulders and the necessity of completing this mission successfully.

"I think there's something we need to do before we venture further," I say to Michael.

I explain my vision to him, telling him all about the malevolent spirits that emerged from the water in the brook. While the focus of our journey is on closing the Gates of Hell, Gabriel also said that I needed to purge the darkness from this world, and I feel in my gut that this is where we need to start.

Chapter 17

BRIE

I open two of the little pouches on my belt, removing a bundle of white sage, a stick of palo santo wood, and a small lighter. With tools in hand, I close my eyes and picture a bright white energy in the center of my sternum. I think of protection and safety as I let the energy flow outward until it rests atop my skin like a bodysuit, then I nod my head to Michael, signaling that I am ready. Michael and I decided that one of us would need to perform the banishment while the other holds a dome of containment around the spirits to keep them from escaping. Since I will need my light energy to close the Gate to Hell, it made sense for Michael to hold the containment while I perform the banishment. Lucky me.

I make my way toward the brook from my vision, Michael following closely behind me. When we arrive at the edge of the small downhill slope that the brook borders, we stop walking and Michael lifts both hands in front of him. I can just barely see the stream of white energy flowing from his palms, encompassing the area of the brook in front of us in a dome of protection. Since the spirits are contaminated by darkness, they cannot pass through light energy and will be unable to flee the dome, locked inside until I finish banishing them from this plane. Since I'm a light entity, I'm able to pass through the barrier with nothing more than a warm tickle across my skin. I stride through, relishing the pleasant sensation.

I flick the lighter a few times before a tiny flame appears at the end of it, then place the flame at the end of the bundle of sage and palo santo, watching as they both start to smoke. I beat my wings a few times, fueling the smoke and lifting myself off the ground. As the smoke grows, the spirits start to rise from the depths of the water. They likely sense the danger of expulsion. I start to fly counterclockwise along the edge of the dome, while also circling the sticks clockwise in front of me as their smoky scent fills my lungs.

The spirits become more and more agitated as the ones closest to me begin to fade out of existence. As one, the spirits fling themselves toward me, trying to cease my efforts. I wish I could fly faster to escape them and finish this, but I can't risk extinguishing the embers fueling the smoke that will inevitably cause their banishment. The first spirit reaches me, and a jolt of pain sears my abdomen as it digs claw-like hands into my stomach. The hands pass through me without leaving a physical wound, but they do damage my energetic shield, and that hurts just as much as a physical wound would.

I keep moving counterclockwise while gritting my teeth through the pain of each attack. They are weakening, but there are so many. Occasionally, I'm able to throw some light energy at the ones closest to me with my free hand, but it's difficult to do while also flying and circling the sticks. Almost like patting your head while rubbing your stomach but much, much harder. Every time one spirit is pulled from this plane, another takes its place, digging claws into whatever area of my body they can reach. I desperately want to flee and avoid more pain, but if I leave the dome, the spirits would follow as soon as it fell, and Michael can't hold the dome indefinitely. We need to finish what we started. My shield is in tatters and their claws are starting to reach my innate energy. I cry out as the energy of my being is damaged for the first time. I'm only halfway around the dome and I don't think I'll be able to make it the full circumference, but my intuition is telling me that I must extinguish all of these spirits or we won't be able to close the Gate here.

With pleading eyes I look across the brook to Michael, who is still sending a constant stream of energy into the dome. We didn't expect the spirits to be this strong. We thought that they might be able to pierce my shield in one or two places, but we never considered they would be strong enough to shred it completely. They are absorbing energy from a Hell Gate though, so I guess it makes sense. Note to self: don't underestimate your opponent. Still, even with them damaging my energy, having me doing the banishing is still the better decision. Healing tears in my energy can be done fairly quickly, but filling a depleted energy store would take hours, if not days, and no one could help with that. Michael's face is filled with pain as he watches the spirits tear into me, but he knows just as I do that neither of us can deviate from our positions. He meets my eyes and determination crosses his features.

"Azrael!" Michael bellows into the blackness of the sky.

Not a second later, an angel with black and silver hair and piercing hazel eyes filled with flecks of orange and yellow is hurtling down through the sky. He flies straight through the top of the dome and heads for the spirits closest to me, thrusting his arm through their incorporeal chests and grabbing on to their essence before jerking his hand out harshly, causing the spirit's energy to dissipate. If I weren't still in agony from the claws raking through my being, I would be very impressed by the Angel of Death's raw power and ability. He is literally thrusting each spirit into the next plane for judgement. I wish I could do that, but we all have our gifts and, unfortunately, that is not one of mine.

With Azrael's help, the spirits clawing through me lessen and I'm just barely able to finish my circle before collapsing to the ground. With the circle finally complete, the remaining souls are sucked into the center of the dome and their energy explodes in unison. Trickles of dark energy rain down onto the surface of the brook before dissipating, leaving no remnants of the evil beings that once inhabited this brook. Michael releases the dome and rushes to me in panic. He places his warm palm atop my heart and pours his energy into me.

I gasp as his energy fills my body, dancing and weaving through the frayed pieces of my own energy. His energy covers the gaps and tears like a bandage, keeping the pieces of my energy from floating away from each other, but not healing them. He can give me his energy and it will mingle with my own because of our soulmate bond, but healing isn't one of Michael's powers, so his energy can only boost my own energy's natural healing ability. Michael closes his eyes and tilts his head down, quietly yet clearly saying, "Raphael, I need you."

Minutes pass. Michael is frozen in his position kneeling by my side. Even with Michael's energy holding my broken pieces together, I'm still too weak to move. Too weak to turn my head even. My energy is knitting itself back together ever so slowly. Too slowly. I hear footsteps approaching us and Michael finally opens his eyes, hope lighting up his face. Raphael kneels at my other side with a grave look on his face. I've never seen him so serious before. Michael looks up and stares into Raphael's eyes, silently begging the healer to help me. Raphael stares back at him for a moment before brushing a hand gently over my forehead and letting it come to rest near the top of my head. I feel the fingers of his other hand splay against my stomach. He closes his eyes and pours potent green healing energy into my body. I watch as the shreds of my energy knit themselves together as quickly as zipping a zipper, absorbing Raphael's green healing energy to use as thread. When all my energy is once again connected, Raphael's energy ripples in a wave from the top of my head to the tips of my toes and a sigh of relief escapes my lips. In mere minutes, my energy is whole again.

I slowly sit up and Michael wraps his arms around me, placing his head on my shoulder while one of his large hands cradles my head. I realize he is trembling as he holds onto me like his life depends on it. Guilt consumes my being. He's hurting right now because of me, because I made the decision that we needed to banish those spirits. Most men want to take over when a woman is in danger, but Michael offers support. He steps in when needed but lets me handle things on my own when I want to. It's one of his best qualities, but it also means he cedes control in those instances. He let me handle this, respected me enough to honor my choices, and had to watch me being torn to bits as a result.

The willpower it must have taken for him not to drop the dome and rush in to fight by my side is incredible, but having to stand back and watch made him feel helpless. That is the true cause of his pain. He thinks that by respecting my wishes, he is responsible for what happened.

With his head on my shoulder, I only have to tilt my own head down to whisper in his ear, "Thank you for respecting my wishes and keeping the dome up. You made the right decision calling for Azrael to help and I appreciate it. I appreciate *you*."

I feel the tips Michael's soft hair brush my temple as he raises his head to look into my eyes. His hand threads into my hair as his gaze penetrates the depths of my soul. Then his soft, full lips descend on mine as he kisses me with all the pent-up emotion from the past eight years and the passion of his unwavering love for the angel I used to be. I'm lost in sensation, loving the feel of his lips on mine when a throat clears loudly. Reluctantly, Michael and I break away from each other and Michael glares over my shoulder at Raphael.

"I just saved her life," Raphael says in a humor-filled voice. "That means you can't glare at me for at least an hour."

I chuckle softly as Michael narrows his eyes further and retorts, "I can glare at you whenever I want." Michael's tone then turns serious as he adds, "Thank you Raphael. I owe you a debt of gratitude."

Raphael's eyes twinkle. "No need to be so formal, brother. In all seriousness though, Brie, your energy was severely damaged. This could have ended very differently. I think from now on I should stay closer to you both so I can get to you much more quickly if you need me."

"Agreed," Michael states, and I nod my concurrence as well. Michael's mouth forms a sly smile as he says, "Let me give you the address of where we're staying. I'm sure you'll love the place."

Raphael flies off to the bed and breakfast shortly thereafter, fully glamoured so he won't be spotted flying by a human. I'm not sure when Azrael left, but he was nowhere to be seen once my energy had healed. I'll have to remember to thank him for his help the next time I see him. Michael and I resume our trek through the forest, no longer aiming for stealth considering the noise we've already made. As we slip through the trees, I notice ghosts of Native American tribesmen accompanying us. Their spirits are not malevolent. Rather, they ooze curiosity and a desire for peace and justice. I hope I can fulfill their wishes.

Every so often as we continue walking, I'm hit with a glimpse of the past. Nothing as extensive as the vision I had earlier, but the forest shows me its scars in brief flashes of past happenings. I'm shown cult rituals, animal sacrifices, and more death than one should ever have to see. I'm relieved when we finally come within view of our destination.

The rocky surface of the ledge we are approaching is covered with graffiti. Tingles of fear travel up my spine as we walk closer and closer to the edge. A ghost of a woman sits right on the edge, legs dangling over the side. She peers over her shoulder as Michael and I approach, eyes filled with sadness. Standing up from her spot on the rock, she takes a few steps toward us, staring at me unblinkingly.

"Is he your love?" she asks, thankfully not waiting for an answer before saying, "Hold him close my dear, lest he desert you. I used to meet my love here. Every night I would wait for him on this rock, cherishing the little time we had together. One night, he never came. I waited and waited, but he never came. It broke my heart. Hold him close dear."

Her words end in a whisper before she suddenly turns back to the awe-inspiring drop and launches herself over the rocky ledge.

"No!" I yell, lurching forward in an attempt to grab her incorporeal hand, not realizing in my panic that it would slip right through my own. I'm too late regardless, as her body is already in a freefall. Her form disappears before it reaches the water below.

I belatedly realize that Michael's arms are around my waist, making sure I don't tumble off the ledge as well. He starts gently pulling me backward, away from the edge. I squeeze his forearm gently, letting him know that my awareness has returned, and his arms unfurl from my waist. I turn to face him, an apology ready on my tongue. Before I get the chance to speak, though, I catch a glimpse of dark smoke emanating from the surface of the water below. Looks like I need to jump after all.

I silently point toward the black smoke, alerting Michael to its presence. He nods. Removing one of my daggers from its sheath, I cut the angelic rune for closure into my left palm. I place the dagger back in its sheath and look into Michael's mesmerizing eyes one more time before turning toward the cliff edge and taking a running leap off of it.

My wings slow my descent until I am just above the water and then I pull my wings in close to my body and tear through the surface of the water like a bullet. I dive rapidly toward the dark depths, where I can see the swirling black smoke, which is a physical manifestation of the evil seeping out of Hell, becoming thicker. The thicker the smoke is, the more evil is present. This smoke is what caused all those murders, suicides, and sacrifices in the surrounding forest. This smoke is what has caused the forest so much pain. The evil crept into the air, dispersing enough as to not be visible, while simultaneously infecting those who encountered it. Light can purge darkness in small amounts, but those whose souls were already tainted would become more and more dark just by breathing in the forest air.

My blood drips from the rune carved into my hand and is lapped up by the black smoke as though it's the finest wine on Earth. This is the key to closing each Gate. Each of the Gates of Hell have a sort of failsafe built into them, such that they can only be closed with a sacrifice of human blood. It doesn't need to be very much blood, thankfully, but because of this an angel couldn't just close the Gate on their own. To fully seal the Gates, angelic light energy must be infused with compatible human blood. Just like the human body can remember an echo of trauma experienced by a soul, human blood is tainted by any darkness that taints a soul. So for the blood to be compatible, it can't contain any darkness. Furthermore, since the blood must infuse the light energy, it needs to come from the same source. Both literally need to flow out of the same wound for any of this to work. Hence, the rune on my hand.

I fill my body with bright white energy and push it out through the rune in my hand. My energy and my blood meet the black smoke as one and the smoke laps up both, not recoiling from the pure energy as it would if my blood were not mixed in. Like acid, my light energy eats away the black smoke, consuming the evil it exemplifies and destroying it. Ever so slowly, the dark smoke recedes, consumed by my energy's light, which is good, because I've been holding my breath for a while now, and I'm going to need to resurface soon for some oxygen.

I grit my teeth and push out as much white energy as I can, watching as the energy spreads in a circle below me, forcing the dark smoke underground. When the smoke finally disappears, I see a vast void of black where the pond floor should be. So, this is the Hell Gate. Each one is unique, and we weren't completely sure what this one would look like, as it's never been documented. We knew where it was, based on Michael's research, but not what form it would take. Apparently, it's a black void. I find that to be a bit underwhelming, to be honest.

I push out more and more light energy and blood through the rune on my palm, watching as the ground around the empty black void closes in on itself. Finally, the void disappears as the ground connects with itself. The ground sizzles and a small pop gurgles out of where the center of the void used to be, before the marking indicating that an angelic seal has been locked appears as a soft white glow on the area of ground that the dark smoke had previously concealed.

I quickly swim back up to the surface of the water, desperate for air to fill my lungs. As soon as my head breaks through, I gasp desperately and allow my wings to propel me out of the water. I fly up to the ledge where Michael is waiting for me with a smile on his gorgeous face.

"I felt it close," he says. "Well done."

I smile back at him through my heaving breaths before stepping into him and wrapping my arms around his neck, letting my tired body rest against his for just a minute before starting the trek back to that ugly pink room in the bed and breakfast.

Chapter 18

BRIE

I've never been out of the country before. It figures that my first international trip would be to a Hell Gate because luck, right?! Mine is down the toilet for sure. When we returned to the bed and breakfast, Raphael was nowhere to be seen, but there was a note on the bed written in pink ink. It said he couldn't stomach so much gaudy décor, but would be trailing our energy signatures in a higher plane, so he would be able to arrive quickly whenever Michael calls him. I guess he figured the potential need for more healing wasn't as pressing as keeping his eyes from permanently seeing everything in shades of pink. Michael and I packed up quickly and slipped out of the bed and breakfast unseen, hoping to avoid additional hugs. I did feel a bit guilty about not saying goodbye to Cara though, so I left her a sweet note saying that we loved the room and unfortunately had to leave for more adventures, but would recommend her accommodations to our friends and leave a positive review online. I felt it was the least I could do, since she had been so welcoming.

Now, we're in Iceland about to hike up the side of an active volcano. Yep, you heard that right. An active volcano...because where else would one put a Hell Gate if not inside an active volcano? Mount Hekla is located in the southern portion of Iceland and is one of the most unpredictable volcanos in Iceland. Locals nicknamed Hekla the "Gateway to Hell" in the Middle Ages, but I doubt the residents currently living nearby realize just how accurate their ancestors were in coining that nickname. Although Hekla is known to be quite active, and provides little warning prior to eruptions, it has become quite the tourist destination. Are the views really worth the risk of ending up in the middle of a volcanic eruption? I wouldn't think any views could be that good, but what do I know?

It's been a pretty long bout of traveling since we left the forest in Massachusetts, which is hopefully no longer quite so cursed now that the Hell Gate there has been sealed. We had to drive an hour and a half to Boston Logan International Airport to catch our flight here. Then, the flight into Keflavik International Airport here in Iceland was a bit over five hours, which wasn't too bad considering it's about the same distance as a flight from California to New York. Michael had arranged for us to rent a four-wheel drive vehicle when we arrived, since the roads are hard near Hekla. After we picked that up, it was another three-hour drive from Keflavik to Hekla, not including our brief stop in Reykjavik for supplies. Add in the extra time we had getting into and out of both airports and, all in all, we'd been traveling for over twelve hours straight. The good news is that we left Massachusetts early in the day, so I was able to get a full night's sleep before we had to embark on our venture up the side of the volcano.

The hiking trail that runs most of the way to the summit took us a bit over three hours and then we shifted into mountaineering, which is why I am currently breathless, sweaty but also cold, and hanging off the side of the volcano by my ice axe. On the plus side, I now know what an ice axe is and can confidently say that I can use one well enough to stop myself from tumbling down an entire mountainside. I only tumbled like twenty feet before I was able to lodge my ice axe into the mountainside well enough to stop my downward trajectory. And bonus, I didn't even impale myself with it during the tumbling! That is a win for sure. Though I will say that the one arm currently attached to the ice axe is getting a bit fatigued, so the whole accidentally stabbing myself with my own ice axe thing isn't outside the realm of possibilities just yet. Don't count your chickens before they hatch and all that.

With a heave, I manage to swing my other arm up and grasp the ice axe with both hands instead of just the one. My body is still kind of dangling in the breeze, but I can see Michael picking his way down the mountainside toward me, so at least I know help is on the way. It would be nice if he could just fly down to me or if I could use my own wings to right myself and just fly up to the crater rim, but since it's daytime and there are other hikers and climbers around, we're not allowed to risk that kind of exposure. Even when the alternative puts my life at risk, subsequently endangering the future of all humankind if I die before sealing all of the Hell Gates. Most of the time, it's really hard being one of the good guys. Just saying.

I kick my feet a bit, trying to find purchase on this particularly steep area of the volcano's flank, but my toes can't get a good grip and all I end up doing is tiring my arms more, as I challenge the little balance I've managed to obtain hanging from the ice axe.

"Don't bother hurrying or anything," I call up to Michael.

He doesn't respond, but I see him glance past me toward the right. I turn my head to see what could possibly have diverted his attention from his soulmate—his word—who is literally hanging off the side of a mountain, and catch a few guys further down the mountain with their cameras out videoing my situation. I try to twist for a better look, but I guess I turn my shoulders a little too much and my right hand slips off the ice axe, causing my body to swing a bit with the momentum, and I once again find myself dangling by just one arm. Well, at least it's the other arm than it was before. This arm is less tired.

"Shiznits," I mutter, just as Michael calls down to me. "Try not to make things worse please."

"Will do boss," I call back, and start singing *I Will Survive* to myself to pass the time.

"Are you singing?" Michael asks incredulously as he gets closer.

"I was bored," I say after I've finished the verse I was in the middle of. "Plus, it felt relevant."

Michael chuckles and shakes his head, reaching out a hand to grasp my dangling right arm and hauling me up until my crampons can find a good grip on slightly less sloped ground.

"Are you ok?" Michael asks with concern in his voice.

"I'm great," I say with a big smile. "Also, I think we should agree that just counted as my arm workout for the next six weeks. A month at the very least."

"I don't think it works that way," Michael replies with a soft smile as he starts climbing up the mountainside again.

"I'm pretty sure it could work that way if you wanted it to," I retort, following him with a bit more care this time around.

It's not too long before we finally reach the crater rim. I warily look up at the cloud cover that has constantly hovered above the volcano since our arrival before turning to Michael.

"You said the Gate is inside the volcano?" I check.

"Yes, that is what we believe," Michael answers confidently.

"Soooo, how am I supposed to seal it, do you think? Like, do I just hover my hand over the opening or put my hand on the rim?" I probably should have asked these questions before we arrived, but it honestly didn't occur to me until I was standing here looking directly into the mouth of the volcano.

"Do what feels right," Michael answers. "I believe your intuition will guide you in how the Gate should be sealed."

Well, that was a non-answer if I ever heard one. Oh well, I take a small knife out of my pack, remove the glove from my left hand, and start carving the sealing rune into the flesh of my palm. Holding my hand out over the mouth of the volcano, I infuse my body with the pure, bright white angel light and channel it down into the crater through the rune. My blood drips from the rune, mixing with the angel light as it disappears into the depths of the crater just as the ground begins to shake. I notice dark shapes flying around frantically inside the crater, trying to escape being sucked into the depths of the volcano as a vortex of air pulls more blood from my hand. The vortex also pulls the dark shapes down into an abyss I cannot see, until none remain. A deep popping sound echoes up from far beneath us and I no longer feel the suction of the vortex pulling on my skin or my blood. For just a moment, everything is still, and I know the Gate has been sealed.

"That felt too easy," I say to Michael as I step away from the edge of the rim, but I spoke too soon, because just as the words leave my mouth, the ground starts shaking again. The shaking that occurred earlier was a slow, rolling rumble of the ground that I would call a tumbler in California. The shaking that's happening now is a violent, spasming type of earthquake I've never experienced before. The rumbles from beneath us are sharp and angry, with destructive groans, booms, bangs, and crashes. I look down at the ground, almost expecting it to split open right beneath my feet.

"We need to go. Now," Michael yells with urgency, and I am all over it.

We scramble to get down the mountain as quickly as possible while behind us, a plume of ash blankets the sky, concealing the light that had penetrated the cloud cover and causing a blackout which makes the day as dark as night. The ground continues to shake violently, and I hear a loud whistling noise as our surroundings light up in an orange glow. I turn back toward the mouth of the volcano as a massive, glowing red rock is hurled out of it. The rock hurtles through the air, crashing against the mountainside a bit further down from us to our left, before rolling even further down the mountain, melting snow and ice so a small stream of steaming water flows downward in its wake.

"Frick," I whisper, absolutely terrified as more lava bombs and projectile fragments explode from the mouth of the volcano and whistle through the air.

The melting snow and ice slows us down as we continue to scramble down the side of the volcano as quickly as we can.

Another huge boulder shoots from the mouth of the volcano and hurtles toward us, coming so close to landing on us that I have to hurl myself to the ground to avoid it. I can feel my skin searing from the extreme heat in the milliseconds before it slams into the ground in front of us and rolls further down the mountain. I stagger back up to my feet, a little disoriented, and Michael grabs my hand to hurry me along again.

We finally get back to the end of the hiking trail and remove our crampons as fast as possible before running down the hiking trail. A loud crack sounds and the ground actually does split open beneath my feet as a new fissure opens right along the path. Lava pours over the ground behind us, chasing our steps as a fire fountain explodes to our left. We veer right to avoid it, sprinting along the uneven terrain to get to safety. Ash covers us both from head to toe and my lungs start to reject the high levels of carcinogens in the air as we near the base of Hekla. I continue to sprint despite the searing pain in my chest, knowing that slowing down could mean death.

As we reach the rental SUV, I send up a little prayer of thanks that the tires haven't melted, nor was the SUV stolen by people scrambling to get away from the volcano earlier. I jump in the passenger side and barely have my door closed before Michael guns it and we are peeling away from the volcano. I slide into the door a few times as Michael swerves the SUV around craters and projectiles. We speed past the pastures that I saw on the way in. What were once beautiful vibrant green pastures are now gray, ash-covered wastelands. The wild horses, cattle, and sheep have fled, and I can only hope they find someplace safe and will be unharmed, though I know that hope isn't so realistic. Even if the poor animals can survive the heat, lava, and projectiles, the high levels of fluorine in the tephra will poison them. With that sobering thought, I allow myself a moment to mourn the innocent victims in this battle against the darkness—and then, I get angry. And you know what they say, Hell hath no fury like a woman scorned.

Chapter 19

MICHAEL

B rie has had a tempestuous, yet contemplative expression on her beautiful face since we sped away from Mount Hekla in the midst of its eruption. Even now, close to seven hours later, when I steal another glance at her I see that she's emanating a fierce determination, with anger simmering just under the surface, fueling her newfound determination. I can almost feel the feral energy brewing within her.

"All flights into and out of Iceland have been canceled due to the eruption. Officials tell us that all airports are now closed and will remain closed until further notice. Although it is not known when flights will resume, previous aviation disruptions from volcanic eruptions lead us to expect it to be about one week," a newscaster reports from the radio station I'm tuned into.

Brie glances over at me but doesn't say anything, still lost in her own thoughts and processing the events we just experienced. Sabriel has always been this way during difficult times. She takes everything in as it occurs, but doesn't react until she's had time to process everything after the fact. It's a skill that's extremely valuable in battle, and one of the main attributes that allowed her to rise to such a high rank in the Angelic Army.

I pull into the parking lot of a hotel near Akureyri International Airport. I've brought us about as far from Hekla as one can get while still in Icelandic territory. My hope is that when the airports do reopen, all international flights will be diverted to this airport, and we'll be able to make a quick exit from Iceland.

I park the SUV in a space near the entrance before entering the hotel and approaching the reception desk. At first glance, the hotel seems adequate. It's decorated in a modern style and has both a restaurant and a bar off to the side of the reception area, as well as a lounge area with several armchairs and couches. Standing behind the reception desk is a young man who appears to be in his early twenties, his eyes locked onto a tablet that he has propped up in front of him.

"Hello," I greet, alerting him to my presence since he's so consumed with his tablet.

The young man tears his eyes away from the tablet with great reluctance and looks up at me. His mouth falls open, his eyes widen, and his color pales as he takes me in.

"W-were you... You... Did you come from Hekla?" he stutters, disbelief and horror threaded into the cadence of his words.

"Yes," I answer shortly, wanting to get Brie into a room quickly so she can shower and rest. We only stopped once during the drive up here, and it was just a quick stop to top up the fuel and use the restroom. I feel crusty with all the ash and dirt covering me. She's more sensitive to it than I am, so I can only imagine how much it's bothering her.

"It... Wow. I've been watching the news broadcast since it started," the man says, turning his tablet so I can see the news stream he has playing on it. "They say it was a particularly violent eruption, with barely any warning."

"Yes, it was. Do you have a suite available?" I ask, trying to hurry things along.

"Oh, no sir. We don't have suites in this hotel, but I do have one of our nicer rooms available," he answers.

"Good, I'll take that. Do you offer room service? And what about a spa or a fitness center?" I question, trying to think of anything that might help comfort Brie as she processes the day's events.

The receptionist shifts uncomfortably as he answers, "We don't have a spa or a gym, no. I'm sorry. We do have complimentary Wi-Fi, satellite TV, and a coffee maker in all of the rooms. Plus, you get a free welcome drink at the bar and complimentary breakfast at the restaurant in the morning. We don't really have room service, but since you've had a hard go of it today, I'll get you a restaurant menu to take to your room. If you call down here to the desk with your order, I'll get someone to bring it up to you."

"Thank you, I would truly appreciate that," I tell him, recognizing that he's going out of his way to help me. "My wife is waiting in the car and is quite traumatized by the day's events as I'm sure you can understand."

"Oh, that's horrible," he replies. "I'm sorry for both of you. I'll have the bar bring up your welcome drinks as well. The rooms are pretty nice. I hope it will help you both to recover from your ordeal. Here are your room keys. You're on the third floor. Elevators are right over there. I'll go get the menus from the restaurant and the bar while you get your luggage so you can take them up to the room with you."

"Thank you," I say again, taking the room keys and heading back out to the SUV.

I open the trunk to get our bags, leaning my head in so Brie can hear me. "We're going to be staying here until the airports reopen. It seems like a nice place. They have a restaurant and a bar, and there's a coffee maker in the room."

"Coffee?" she perks up, her head whipping around to look at me, ash scattering around the SUV from her rapid movement. "Alcohol and coffee? Spiked coffee?" she asks me hopefully, her whole face lighting up like a kid at Christmas.

"If that's what you want," I reply, glad to see a little bit of life returning to her demeanor.

"Yes, definitely," she says as she nods eagerly, sending more ash scattering throughout the SUV.

As we enter the hotel, Brie peers around at our surroundings inquisitively. The receptionist approaches me with the menus, glancing at Brie sympathetically. She looks tragically beautiful with the ash covering her hair and her clothes. Feminine and delicate, but with the strength of a warrior to have survived such an event and still maintain her natural poise. She is truly an awe-inspiring being. And judging by the receptionist's continued glances, I'm not the only one who thinks so.

"Let's find our room, sweetheart," I say gently.

The room is clean, with carpeted floors and wood furnishings. Brie makes a beeline toward the shower as soon as we're inside. I set our bags down and turn on the television to watch for any news updates. Once Brie has finished in the shower, I take my turn, watching as the dirt and ash swirls down the drain and contemplating the best way to spend the next few days. I feel like I haven't been as attentive to Brie's needs lately as I should have been, and I want to remedy that. I seem to recall there being a botanical garden nearby, and Brie has always loved being in nature, so maybe I can take her there on a date. Yes, a date would be perfect. That decided, I finish my shower feeling a bit more settled.

I walk back into the hotel room to find Brie lying on her stomach atop the bed, the restaurant menu in front of her and her phone pressed to her ear.

"I know, Cals, and I promise I'm trying to be safe. How was I supposed to know that the volcano would just happen to erupt right when I sealed the Hell Gate?" Brie says exasperatedly into the phone, and I can't help but smile at how cute she is.

"Well, it's not like I really have a choice, do I? Would you prefer I just let the darkness take over the Earth and no humans will be able to ascend to the angelic realm ever again, including you?" she asks, and I really wish I could hear Callie's side of the conversation as well.

"Mmmhmmm. That's what I thought," Brie says smugly, glancing at me as I sit down on the edge of the bed and pretend to watch the television.

"Listen, I should go," Brie tells Callie with a hint of disappointment in her voice. "I'm pretty hungry and want to gorge myself with coffee, alcohol, and cake after dinner, before falling into a sleep that lasts at least three days. Plus, Michael is shamelessly listening to our conversation while he pretends to watch TV."

I bark out a laugh at her calling me out so easily and she rewards me with a coy smile.

"I will, Cals. And I miss you so much." There's a small pause, and then she says, "Love you too. Bye."

Brie pulls the phone from her ear and doesn't manage to conceal the little sigh that slips past her lips, showing that the distance from Callie has been more difficult for her than she's let on.

"Callie says hi," she tells me.

I smile. "That was nice of her. How is she doing?"

"She's good. Worried about us, but otherwise good."

"I'm glad to hear that. Have you decided what you want for dinner?"

"Yes!" Brie exclaims, and then proceeds to list off five different menu items, even though there's no way she can eat that much. Still, whatever she wants, I will give her.

Sharing a hotel room with Brie for the past five days without having an active mission to distract us has been torture. She's so perfect. Every little expression she makes, her quirks and mannerisms, even her sarcasm—every piece of her simply strengthens my love for her. I've desperately wanted to hold her in my arms and kiss her fervently more times than I can count over the past five days, but I was worried I'd be moving too fast for her, or that she doesn't feel the same way about me as I feel about her. I love her soul in all its forms, and I know who she is at the very core of her being. I've known her for millennia, and whether she's Sabriel or Brienna, it's still her. I know her, but she has no memories of me before I appeared in her living room only months ago. She doesn't know me and, honestly, I have no idea how she feels about me, so I'm trying to take things slow. I don't want to make her feel uncomfortable by professing my love for her right off the bat. I know she reacted well when I kissed her in Massachusetts, but she had almost just died. What if she accepted my affections because she wanted to feel alive again rather than any reason pertaining to feelings for me?

According to the news reports, the airport nearby will be reopening tomorrow. I booked us on one of the first flights out. With that knowledge, I feel like my time to make a move is ending. As soon as we board that plane, our downtime ends. We're back to mission after mission, barely having time to recover before we'll need to head to the next one. I'm not naïve about how dangerous our task is, and I almost feel like there's an hourglass, with sand running out, above my head. Our tasks are on a timer, and if we don't complete them in time, not only will the Earthly realm fall to the darkness, but the darkness could launch an attack on the angelic realm as well. So, if I'm going to have time to tell Brie how I feel about her, to show her how much I love her, without her being bone weary from a mission, now would be the time to do it. And yet, I can't bring myself to be that candid with her yet. I'm scared. I'm scared that she'll reject me, scared that I'll ruin things between us by showing her the depths of my feelings for her. Just scared.

My declaration of love will have to wait. When all this is over, I'll court her properly. Take her on dates and show her that I respect her before I take liberties. I know it seems old-fashioned, but she deserves a proper courtship, and there's no opportunity for such things right now. After she's sealed all the Gates, we'll make new memories here on Earth and she will fall in love with me again, even before I restore her memories. I know she will, but only when she can get to know me without all the stress of what she's currently facing. Then, when I'm certain she's ready for our relationship to progress, I will kiss her as though my life depends on it and tell her that I've loved her all along, as Brienna and as Sabriel. I will pledge my soul to her as I have done countless times in the past, and we will return to the angelic realm as two halves of a whole. Until then, I will offer her support, compassion, and comfort, and I will keep hidden my undying devotion to her. I couldn't stomach scaring her off. I'd be risking losing my soulmate forever.

Chapter 20

BRIE

Our next destination is Saint Patrick's Purgatory in Ireland. Michael informed me that he booked spots for both of us on one of their One Day Retreats, and we managed to make it to the pick-up point just as the first ferry of the day was arriving. There are a decent number of pilgrims in line to board the ferry as we take our places at the end of the line. Although the retreat doesn't officially commence until after 10am, most people want to arrive as early as they can to enjoy the island a bit beforehand.

The ferry ride is only around 10 minutes long. The air is chilly and damp, but we expected as much and are bundled up in warm, rainproof outerwear. The lake waters are still this morning and appear to be a slate gray, reflecting the storm clouds looming overhead more than the blue sky they conceal. Station Island itself is breathtaking. The grass is a vibrant green and the sprawling cathedral is awe-inspiring, the stone contrasting beautifully against the greenery and the mountains in the distance.

As soon as we step off the ferry, we are greeted warmly and offered a warm drink and scones. I know it probably won't be of the best quality, but my ears perk up as soon as I hear the word "coffee". Sign me up one hundred percent. Yes, please. Liquid gold, my friends. I give a little happy sigh as the first warm sip hits my tongue; Michael gives an "I can't believe she's more focused on coffee than our mission" sigh in response. It makes me all warm and fuzzy inside that I can interpret his sighs now. I've always wanted to be close enough to someone to have silent conversations, and that's what this feels like. Also, priorities man! Seriously.

Michael, who had been daintily sipping his tea, leans into me and whispers, "Once everyone gathers in the Basilica, we need to look for alternate exits that will take us further into the building. The original structures have been rebuilt several times to cover the cave entrance, but I'm confident there will be a way to access it through the Basilica. We'll need to slip through whatever exit we find while everyone else heads outside."

I nod in agreement and whisper back to him, "Do you have any idea what we'll encounter this time?"

Michael looks thoughtful for a moment. "I've read that the cave entrance is quite small. You'll probably have to go in alone, but once you're inside I don't know what you will encounter. I'm sorry."

He truly does look regretful that he can't help me more than finding the entrance, but I understand, and I don't blame him for not knowing more. No person has entered the cave in centuries, and I'm guessing that an angel has never gone in there, so how could he know what's down there? At least I have my coffee to put me in the right mindset—though I wish I had one of my mugs.

Michael catches me frowning down at the coffee cup and gives me an exasperated look.

"Are you really pouting right now because you don't have one of your own coffee mugs?" he whispers incredulously.

I keep my face perfectly blank as I respond very seriously, "This trip has really been stifling my self-expression. It's been very hard on me."

He rolls his eyes at me, but I can also see the little smirk turning up the corner of his mouth and I let loose a smile of my own. Our moment of levity is short-lived, however, as everyone is beckoned into the Basilica. The Basilica has an octagonal design and is mostly plain inside, other than the large stained-glass windows depicting the apostles. The pews are numerous and wooden, well-worn but still in good condition. At the very front stands an altar made of white Carrara marble, on which are arranged sacred objects sculpted in bronze. Directly behind the altar stands a large wooden cross that looks to be around 6 feet high. It's all very impressive, despite the lack of adornments.

Michael and I sit at the end of one of the pews on the right side of the Basilica and toward the back. We both start surreptitiously peering at the walls surrounding us to try to find a different exit than the one we entered through. The most obvious exit for us to use is through an archway to the left of the altar that the priest must enter and exit through. Hopefully it can take us into the heart of the building and isn't simply a single stand-alone room. I tap Michael's arm gently and tilt my head toward the archway, silently asking if that will be our plan. He glances around, double checking to make sure we didn't miss a better option, before nodding his head in approval. We have our exit point. Game time.

When the prayers end, we make our way toward the altar, pretending that we are trying to speak with the priest. Once we are certain that he is adequately distracted by some of the pilgrims vying for his attention and blessings, Michael and I slip through the archway as stealthily as possible. No one shouts after us, so we probably weren't seen, but we still need to move on from this area as quickly as possible in case we were. The room we've slipped into is small, still plain and unpretentious, likely a staging area for the priest, but it has another door that opens up to a long hallway. Perfect. This is exactly what we needed.

We hurry down the hallway, trying door handles, and peeking around the doors when they do open, until we find one with stairs leading down. The stairwell smells musty, and the stairs are covered in a thick layer of dust, indicating that these stairs aren't used very often. There's no light in here, so I put out my hand palm up and picture the pure white color of angel light until a small ball of it appears above my palm to light our way. Hopefully now I won't trip down the stairs.

When I reach the bottom of the stairs, I glance around quickly. The space is small, only about 5 feet by 5 feet. The floor is simply dirt—not dirt covering the floor, just dirt with no other flooring underneath. The walls are made of thick, gray stone and it all feels a bit suffocating. There is no other door down here, only the thick stone walls, but the level of malevolence I feel seeping out of the wall directly in front of me tells me that I'm where I need to be. Michael steps around me and removes the glamour making his angelic sword invisible. He proceeds to unsheathe it from its scabbard on his back. As soon as his hand makes contact with the hilt of the sword, the blade starts glowing with a dim angel light. He hands me his coat, knowing that the arduous task before him would overheat him if he kept the coat on. I marvel at both the beauty of the sword and the vision of masculine perfection that Michael embodies as he starts cutting into the stone wall in front of us with his angelic sword. It's no easy feat. Though the angel light coupled with the indestructibility of the sword are able to cut through stone, it's about as easy as trying to cut a ribeye with a butter knife. I watch as Michael's muscles flex beneath the fabric of his shirt, appreciating how much work he puts into maintaining those muscles all so that he can protect those under his care. I could seriously just stand here and watch him work all day, but I know I have my own job to do here, so I try not to let my mind become too entranced.

Little by little, the stone crumbles away from the wall until we're standing in front of a few feet of empty space cushioning another stone wall with a barred wooden door. The wooden door looks old and slightly rotted. There are beams of wood nailed across it to each of the doorposts, barring entry, and large metal chains anchored to the walls in front of the wood beams. Basically, a big "Do not enter" sign with flashing lights and everything. But of course our sole purpose in coming here was to pass through this door, so Michael just slices his sword through the chains and the wooden beams, allowing us access to the old, rotting door.

When Michael said earlier that the entrance is small, he wasn't exaggerating. The door is only about 2 feet wide and 3 feet high. There is absolutely no way that Michael could make it through that door. If we knew that there was a large space on the other side of the door, he could simply dematerialize to pass through it and re-solidify his body on the other side of it. But if an angel tries to solidify their body into a solid object, like a short ceiling or narrow walls in this case, they could be seriously injured or stuck in a half-materialized state permanently. Needless to say, that's not an outcome we can risk, so I'll be going in alone.

I remove my jacket and hand it to Michael. Once I do, we open the small door and I have to contort my body just to step through the doorframe sideways. Even then, my bum still rubs the rotting wood of the doorframe and I'm a little grossed out that I accidentally touched it.

Immediately on the other side of the door are six rotted wooden steps going downward. The wood of these steps is far more rotten than the wood of the door and there's no way I can put my weight on them without them collapsing underneath me. They're all already sunken in with large holes and broken wood in various places. I cast my angel light out before me to see where the stairs end up, and barely hold in the groan that wants to escape my throat. Normally, I might be able to jump down, since there are only six stairs and Michael put me through all that horrendous torture he referred to as agility training, but the space here is the same size as the door, so I can't jump without slamming my body into the ceiling. I could maybe try to dive forward, but the stairs end in a tunnel that looks to have a ceiling even lower than the one I'm currently crouched under. How did anyone fit down here at all before the entrance was barred?

I look down, examining everything and trying to figure out how I can get down to the tunnel. I guess I'll also need to figure out how to get back up, but that's a problem for future Brie. The sides of the stairs where they meet the wall look a lot more solid than the centers. Maybe I could use the walls as leverage and somehow shimmy down the sides of the stairs? Eh, worth a shot. I spread my legs wide so the outer sides of my feet are pressed up tightly against each of the side walls. Then, I bend forward so that my hands are directly in front of my feet, pressed right up against each wall. I proceed to walk my hands forward, testing the strength of the wood where my hands will step before putting my weight down there, until I'm in a plank position. I try not to picture myself crashing forward and landing on my head as I carefully plank-walk down the outer edges of the stairs, until both my hands and my feet are on solid dirt again. I never thought I'd be thankful for all those ab workouts Michael put me through, but here we are, alive and in one piece thanks to planks!

I drop my knees to the ground and kneel in the tunnel, my head nearly brushing the ceiling as I do, and cast my angel light out in front of me again. The tunnel feels still, but also like it's the edge of a precipice for something I definitely don't want to encounter. I crawl forward hesitantly, waiting with bated breath for whatever evil I will encounter here. It's been too quiet so far. Too easy. That makes me nervous. My muscles are poised to react at any moment as I continue to crawl forward, but still nothing comes. I can see that there's a turn in the tunnel up ahead, and that's when I hear it: hissing. It starts faintly, but the closer I get to the turn in the tunnel, the louder the hissing becomes. My breath hitches in my chest and I have a mini panic attack. My palms are sweating as I continue to slowly crawl forward on the dirt covered ground, my mind racing through a catalogue of everything and anything that could make such a hissing sound.

I pause just before I reach the turn in the tunnel and try to take a calming breath. It's not very calming if I'm being honest, but at least I tried. Ok, Brie, head in the game. I remove my short sword from the scabbard draped across my back. It's a bit hard to do in the small space, but I manage, and the blade lights up with dim angel light as my skin makes contact with the hilt. I take another breath and rest the pommel of my short sword against the dirt floor to continue crawling forward, careful not to let the blade too close to me as I do. When I reach the turn in the tunnel, I hold my breath and peek around the corner to determine what horror awaits me, and a horror it is. Snakes. So many snakes.

Even before I learned that snakes are deceitful agents from the eighth circle of Hell, I was always disgusted by the scaly reptiles. And now, I'm faced with hordes of the evil creatures. They are slithering and writhing over each other, covering every inch of the tunnel, probably a few layers deep. It's like my worst nightmare come to life. I quickly pull my head back and force myself to breathe. My whole body is shaking with terror. The adrenaline of the fear I'm experiencing is urging me toward flight rather than fight in this instance, but I have to find the Gate and seal it. Turning back is not an option, no matter how much I wish it was.

Chapter 21

BRIE

Steeling my spine as much as is possible in a tunnel that only allows you to kneel, I crawl forward quickly and mentally ready myself for the snakes. I visualize a gray light covering every inch of my body and feel my shield fall into place as the energy wraps around my skin like a warm blanket plated with armor. As soon as I clear the corner, the snakes all turn to look at me as one writhing unit and hiss venomously before launching themselves in my direction.

I channel some of my nature-based energy through the hand I have pressing flat to the ground, and a dark green glow emits dimly from my palm before the dirt floor in front of me collapses in on itself in waves, burying masses of the snakes underground with each wave. The snakes that manage to avoid being dragged beneath the dirt floor lunge at me and I swipe at them with my sword. My aim is not very good, with my attention split between the sword, my energy manipulation tactic, and my shield, but the snakes are cautious enough that swiping at them with the sharp blade keeps them from making contact with me—at least for a while. I can feel my energy starting to deplete. As I'll need a good supply of energy to seal the Hell Gate, I reluctantly cut off the energy I was channeling through the ground and pull a knife from a sheath on my hip.

There look to be around fifty snakes left, all still slithering toward me and hissing. They're even more enraged now, from having to actively work to escape being buried alive. The ones closest to me lunge viciously and I parry their attacks with my sword and knife. I swipe and slice, injuring each one, but not able to make many killing blows. They're too fast and too intelligent. Several come at me at once, right as my shield flickers, and I panic as I try to keep them away from me. My sword deals a killing blow to one, and my knife injures another, but the third dodges my weapons and latches onto my arm. I can feel its poisonous venom the moment it enters my veins. It starts as a slow burn, but quickly the site of the bite feels as though I'm being burned from the inside out, and as the venom spreads, the burning does as well.

I cut the snake in half with my sword, still battling other snakes as they keep coming at me, while my body is thrumming with an internal fire. The intensity of the pain starts to blur my vision, which is incredibly unhelpful when you're trying to battle a bunch of snakes with a short sword and a knife. Just saying. I lose feeling in the arm that was bitten and sway a bit on my knees. I can't give in to the pain though. I still have work to do, and failure is not an option. My shield is completely gone now, but I need to save my energy for the Hell Gate, and hopefully I'll have some left over for self-healing as well. Fingers crossed on that one.

I'm down to the last ten snakes, slicing and stabbing like my life depends on it—which it kind of does. My vision is now alternating between blurred and going out completely, but I keep my wits about me as much as possible, forcing myself to stay conscious and using my other senses to compensate for the loss of my vision. When the air finally stills and there isn't a hiss to be heard, my vision goes out completely and my head swims. My body is completely on fire and it's hard for me to tell if I'm even able to move anymore. I draw the tiniest bit of healing out of my magic—just enough to make sure that the poison doesn't make it to my heart and that I can see again—and force my body to move forward amongst the carcasses of the dead snakes. The dirt floor is wet with their blood, and it coats my waterproof pants as I drag my limbs forward in an army crawl. At least I'm still alive.

As I near the end of the tunnel, the black swirl of a portal appears on the wall in front of me. It grows as I get closer to it, the center filling with images of blood, and death, and torture. Graphic and gruesome. With the snake venom still in my bloodstream, the images within the portal penetrate my mind. Hallucinations, filled with seductive deception meant to lure me toward acts of evil, weave their way through my consciousness. I fall in and out of them, a form of torture in itself, for who knows how long. It could be minutes or hours. Every time I come out of it, it takes me time to realize that it was a hallucination and to remember where I am and what I'm supposed to be doing.

Finally, I manage to regain enough of my consciousness to swipe the short sword across my palm, drawing blood. I fall into another hallucination, but the wound is still bleeding when I once again recover, and I swipe the short sword across my palm again for the next line of the angelic rune for closure before falling into another hallucination. This cycle repeats until I've finished carving the rune into my palm, the blood loss helping a bit with the effects of the venom. I then drag my numb arm up my body to press my palm against the wall. I fill my body with the bright white energy that I need to channel through the rune to close the Gate, and push it out with all that I have. I push and push, my blood dripping into the portal more slowly than I need it to. The portal shrinks ever so slowly and I'm sure I've fallen into another hallucination when suddenly a face appears in the center of the portal looking directly at me. My eyes meet the man's angry green ones, and he sneers at me before his arm shoots through the center of the portal, his hand wrapping around my throat and squeezing until I can't breathe.

I don't remove my bleeding hand from the wall. I just push more and more light magic through the rune in my palm, hoping that the portal will close before I run out of oxygen. I had been close to passing out from the pain of the venom even before the man grabbed my throat, and the lack of oxygen right now is really compounding that problem. With barely any breath left in my lungs, the portal closes enough that the man has to release my throat and pull his arm back through, so he doesn't risk losing it. I gasp for air, and just before the portal closes with its little pop, I hear a whispered, "I'll see you again soon Sabriel." Then I pass out.

I regain consciousness as a loud groaning sound echoes throughout the compact tunnel and the ground rumbles minutely. I'm feeling much better than I was before I lost consciousness, my healing ability slowly but surely counteracting the snake venom as my energy naturally replenishes itself. I'm still not back to normal by any means, but my vision is clear and my limbs have regained feeling, so I consider it a win. The groaning noise starts again and a smattering of dirt cascades from the tunnel ceiling above me. I sheath my short sword, which had fallen to the ground beside me, and start crawling back toward the entrance of the tunnel. Michael had told me that the ferry off the island is scheduled to leave at 4pm, and I have no idea how long I was passed out for, so I need to get a move on.

The ground continues to rumble, the waves of it becoming more and more violent, and more dirt falls from the ceiling and the walls. Then, suddenly, it's no longer just a smattering of dirt falling, but the tunnel collapsing in on itself. Chunks of the ceiling come down, threatening to bury me alive the same way I buried the snakes earlier. Karma really is a bitch sometimes. I crawl faster, my hands and knees landing on snake guts and gore as I retreat through the site of our battle, but I can't slow down to be more careful of where I place my hands since the tunnel is literally collapsing behind me.

"Seriously?" I call out to the empty tunnel. "Did I break a mirror or something?"

I scurry around the turn as fast as I can and reach the other stretch of tunnel. My hands are once again sweating, and the adrenaline of trying to move so quickly, combined with the energy my body had to replenish and is now using to continue healing my body from the snake venom, is making my limbs quake more intensely than the tunnel is. I'm shaking so badly I can barely hold myself up. The part of the tunnel that I just exited collapses in on itself completely, a plume of dust blowing past me, clouding my visibility, and suffocating my lungs. The ground isn't rumbling anymore though, and the groaning sounds have subsided. When the dust clears, I cough a few times and look back to see a solid wall of dirt where the turn in the tunnel used to be. I breathe out a sigh of relief and continue crawling toward the entrance of the tunnel, this time at a normal speed. Finally, I near the end of the tunnel and look up at those terrible, rotted stairs, silently cursing their existence.

Ok, maybe not so silently. "I hate you," I tell the stairs, giving them one of my best glares

They don't respond of course, but Michael must hear my voice because he calls down, "Brie, are you ok?"

"Peachy." I reply dryly, still eyeing the stairs.

Michael tries to poke his head through the small door at the top of the stairs, but he's so broad and tall that he can only fit his head and one shoulder through while kneeling on the other side and doing a side bend. He reaches his arm out toward me and a small ball of angel light appears above his palm, illuminating the space. He sucks in a breath at my appearance. "Oh, Brie," he whispers sadly, his eyes filled with concern. "Do you need Raphael?"

I know he wishes he could protect me from all of this and seal the Gates himself, but it's simply not possible. It doesn't bother me. This mission is one that I chose to accept, and I'm secure in my decision, but Michael feels guilty that he can't take this burden from me, and that guilt eats at him. The regret and sense of helplessness shows clearly on his face.

"I'm fine," I tell him. "I just need to figure out the best way to get up these stupid stairs."

The corner of Michael's mouth turns up at the disdain in my tone.

I decide the best course of action is to plank-walk back up the stairs, just as I did coming down them, so I walk my hands out in front of me, one pressed against each wall, until I'm in a plank position. Then, I plank-walk up the stairs, which is admittedly much harder than walking down them, especially considering my still trembling arms. When I get close enough that I can reach Michael's outstretched hand, I grab it and he helps to haul me the rest of the way up and through the small doorway. Finally, once I'm safely back in the small room in which we found the entrance to the cave, I collapse onto the dirt floor, not even caring about the dirt and dust since I'm already so gross. This day has been too long and I'm pretty sure I want to sleep for the next three days at least.

"Let's get you cleaned up," Michael says as he peers down at me sprawled out in the dirt. "The ferry leaves in about two hours, and we don't want to scare any of the pilgrims."

I scoff, then groan as he helps me to my feet. We make our way to a private bathroom that we'd previously discovered behind one of the nearby doors in the hallway. Michael is quite stealthy in making his way toward the bathroom, but I look like death warmed over and am moving as gracefully as a zombie, while dripping snake blood and guts in a trail behind me as bits and pieces slide down my waterproof pants. The one bonus to that phenomenon is that my pants should be easy enough to clean into a presentable state, since the blood and guts haven't dried on the pants for the most part. I use a full stack of paper towels to wipe down my pants, and it's probably the second most disgusting experience of my life, bested only by the actual crawling through their blood and guts part. I do, however, manage to get my pants into a state where they shouldn't irreparably traumatize anyone.

I can't do anything about my shirt, but my jacket will cover it well enough. While not nearly as bad as my pants, there are intermittent blood spatters across my torso from the sword fight.

My hair is a different story, the golden blonde strands dyed a motley tomato red from absorbing the blood spatters. I duck my head under the tap in the sink and use the hand soap to try to wash the blood out. It feels like it takes forever, and I run out of soap in the process, but when the water finally runs clear again, I turn off the tap, pull my head back up and wring out the rest of the excess water in my hair. The thought of pulling my hair back into a ponytail with the hair tie I had in earlier is repulsive, so I leave my hair down to air dry and hope that the pilgrims either won't notice how wet it is or will attribute the dampness to the moisture in the air from the lake. Finally looking fully presentable, I leave the bathroom. Michael eyes me over before giving me a nod and silently taking my hand in his, showing his support and giving me a modicum of comfort without being too overbearing. I appreciate it. The warm, fuzzy feeling in my chest that only he can instigate makes an appearance. Although I'm still majorly exhausted, I remind myself to remember this moment and the feelings his simple gestures give me. I think holding onto these moments might be just the thing that gets me through the rest of this awful ordeal—and whatever evil might come after.

Chapter 22

MICHAEL

Brie had been in the tunnel underneath St. Patrick's Purgatory for hours before I heard her sweet voice sassing out an "I hate you" to goodness knows what. I had been in a complete panic for most of that time and was cursing the fact that my body was too big to fit through the tiny tunnel. Don't get me wrong, I trust Brie completely and know that she's tough and can handle herself with competence, but not knowing what she might face in the tunnel, combined with how long she was gone nearly sent me over the edge. If I could have seen that she was alright, I would have been fine. The not knowing was a special form of torture. Then, I poked my head through the tiny door and felt like I was looking at one of my worst nightmares. Brie was covered in blood and her whole body was trembling. I didn't know if any of the blood covering her from head to toe was her own, and it terrified me.

When Brie told me she was fine, the relief was overwhelming, but when she reappeared after cleaning up in the bathroom, I noticed how pale and lackluster her skin was, and that she had bruises around her neck and small puncture wounds dotting her left arm. I knew she would want some time to process whatever happened in the tunnel, so I just nodded to her and held her hand as we left the island.

We're now back in our hotel suite. I was ready to debrief as soon as we arrived and had the privacy to talk openly, but Brie kept muttering about how she "desperately needed a shower" and that she felt "tainted by grossness," so I gave her the time to do what she needed. Unfortunately for me, what she apparently needed was the longest shower in the history of humankind. I honestly cannot understand how anyone could stay in the shower for as long as she did. Finally, she emerges from the bathroom dressed in tiny shorts and an oversized tee-shirt, her skin red from being scrubbed so hard and the puncture wounds sealed by her natural healing ability, though a ghost of the bruising on her neck is still visible.

Brie drags herself over to the couch I'm already occupying and collapses down onto the soft cushions, fatigue infusing every movement. She lets out a huff of air, tilts her head back, and closes her eyes as I sit here stupidly, marveling at her beauty. Regardless of whether her appearance is that of Sabriel or Brienna, the beauty of her soul will always shine through her visage, and that beauty is absolutely breathtaking. It never ceases to amaze me.

"Brie, love," I start, finally gaining some semblance of rationality back. "I know you're tired, but we need to debrief while everything is still fresh in your mind. Details will fade over time and some of them may be important."

"Debrief..." she echoes tiredly, not even cracking an eye open.

"Brie..." I try again.

"Hmmmm?" she hums, even less alert than she was a few seconds ago.

"Why don't I make you some coffee, love?" And at this, her eyes pop open.

"Coffee?" she asks excitedly, her fatigue visibly draining away as her whole face lights up at the idea. "Yes, please," she answers with a dreamy smile that tells me she's already fantasizing about drinking the coffee I haven't even made yet.

I find Brie's coffee addiction incredibly entertaining. Sabriel always enjoyed tea, and I find this version of her, with such a quirky coffee dependency, endearing. I walk over to the little coffee bar in our suite and start preparing a cup for her in just the way she likes. Turning around, I stop short when I see a frown on her gorgeous face instead of the dreamy smile that I expected. Her gaze seems to be focused on the disposable cup in my hand as she grumbles to herself. Striding to the couch, I can finally make out what she's saying, and I have to rub one hand over my mouth to keep from laughing at her.

"It's fine," she grumbles. "The coffee will taste just as good in a paper cup as it does in one of my mugs. It's not like the words improve the taste. Inspirational sayings are only psychological, they don't actually affect the coffee itself. Maybe if I just write something on the cup, it will have the same effect as one of my mugs. No, but I can't do that. The coffee is already in the cup, and I don't have a marker anyway. Pen just wouldn't be the same. It's really ok, I don't need a quote—I only need the coffee. That's fine. This is fine."

Brie suddenly realizes that I can hear her little pep talk to herself, and her cheeks darken in an adorable blush of embarrassment.

"Thank you," she says, trying to pretend nothing is out of the ordinary. "Nectar of the gods, right here," she exclaims with a cheeky little smile that makes me want to kiss the heck out of her.

"I'm glad you're happy," I tell her honestly, "but we really do need to complete your debrief now."

"Ok," she replies with a little sigh as she holds the coffee cup in both hands, smelling the steam wafting out of it before proceeding to give me a rundown of everything that happened during those harrowing hours that we were apart.

"Tell me more about this man you saw through the portal," I say once she's finished her summary. "What color hair did he have? What shape was his face? What did his voice sound like when he spoke to you?"

I already have my suspicions on who it was that had the audacity to press his hand to my soulmate's throat, but I need confirmation.

"You're focusing on the wrong part of the story," Brie exclaims, throwing her hands up like she's exasperated with me. "Did you not hear about the snakes, Michael? So many snakes!" she says emphatically, and with a whole-body shudder of revulsion.

"I did hear that part, and I'm sorry that you had to face off with something that you're so afraid of. I know you have never been fond of reptiles, but I do need you to tell me more about the man you saw," I reply firmly.

She gives me such a side-eye that I feel I've done something unforgivable, but she does answer my request.

"I don't know. It was all so fast and overwhelming. I mostly remember his eyes. They were a deep, moss green color. Kind of dull, but there was so much anger in them. Not at all gem-like. I think he had lightish hair, but I don't know if it was a light brown or a dirty blonde. Honestly, I was too focused on his eyes, because they were so unsettling. His skin was light too, not sickly, but like he hadn't been in the sun for a while."

That's enough of a description for me, I guess. I can't fault Brie for being so focused on his eyes, given her ability to see the truth of a soul in this way. She's subconsciously conditioned herself to focus on a being's eyes. Even when she was unaware of her power, her subconscious knew that gauging a person's soul through their eyes could keep her safe. It's also why she would find his eyes unsettling. They mirror his soul. And that knowledge in itself confirms my initial suspicions, because the only being in the universe with the power to unsettle Brie is a man that I once considered family. He wasn't made of the same energy as me like Gabriel was, but I considered him a brother just the same. I still do, if I'm being honest with myself. Feelings like that don't just disappear, but his feelings toward me have evolved and warped since his fall. What was once an overpowering love turned to hate because, in his mind, I abandoned him. In his mind, I'm no longer his brother. In his mind, I've become his nemesis.

"So do you know who the dude was?" Brie asks nonchalantly. "I know I didn't give you much to go on."

"Yes," I respond, "I'm almost certain you just became reacquainted with Lucifer."

Brie's jaw drops and she stares at me dumbfounded for a moment before sucking in a breath and shakily asking, "Lucifer, as in The Devil?"

"Yes," I state shortly. "Why don't you go get some sleep. I know you're tired, and I need to revise our plan a bit. Now that Lucifer has threatened you directly, it would be foolish for us to go to each Gate in order based on proximity. We won't be able to avoid him at the last Gate or two, but until then we need to bounce around a bit. I prefer you have as little contact with him as possible, so we need to make it harder for him to predict which Gate we'll be going to. I don't know how far he would go to prevent you from closing all of the Gates, and your wellbeing is not something I'm willing to risk."

Brie nods and gives me a peck on the cheek before disappearing into the bedroom, leaving me to my thoughts. Like most of us, the humans have given my brother many names over the millennia—Lucifer, Satan, Plouton, Mephistopheles, Shaytan, and Mara, among others. Our history is complicated, but I've never stopped caring for him or hoping that his soul could lighten. It's been many years since Lucifer and I last spoke, and I know I'm partly to blame for some of the blackness in his soul because of it. I simply could not facilitate his selfishness any longer. It tore a part of me into pieces when I stopped reaching out to him regularly, but it was something I needed to do for my own health and light. The more I tried to help Lucifer see the error of his ways and guide him toward the light, the more my own light dimmed, until eventually I had to decide: maintain my relationship with Lucifer and fall myself; or cut off contact and stay in the light. Gabriel, Raphael, and Uriel intervened when they saw how close I was to falling and how my relationship with Lucifer was destroying me, but Lucifer didn't care that I was trying to preserve my own light. All he saw was abandonment, and I've never fully forgiven myself for that.

A pang of despair encompasses my chest and I let my head fall into my hands for just a moment. I try to never allow myself to show weakness around Brie. With Sabriel, it was different. She was so strong that we would each hold the other up when needed, but since Sabriel's soul entered Brienna's body, she's become far more fragile. She needs my strength more than Sabriel ever did, so I can't let myself be weak. For her, I need to be strong. Maybe once this is over and Sabriel recovers her memories, things will go back to how they were, but for now, I need to change to accommodate how she has changed. Our relationship now is harder because of it, but I don't love her any less. She's still my soulmate, and always will be regardless of what form she takes or what traumas she carries.

With that thought, I raise myself off the couch and walk over to the bedroom door, cracking it open just enough to see that she's sprawled in the center of the bed sleeping soundly. Trying not to disturb her, I close the door soundlessly before moving over to the dining table and spreading out the pile of notes on our travel plans and each of the Hell Gates. It shouldn't be too much work to reorder where we are going, but rebooking our accommodations and transportation at each locale will be a chore.

Just as I get into my flow and am making good progress on the necessary changes, there's a light knock on the main door of the suite. I check the peephole to see Raphael bouncing on his toes in the hallway with a huge grin on his face. Man, I love this guy. I really do. I open the door quickly with a finger to my lips, telling him to be quiet, since he likes to make boisterous entrances. Raphael nods and gives me a big hug as he enters.

"How did it go?" he asks, his face falling when I sigh. "That good, huh?"

"Lucifer appeared on the Hell side of the portal while Brie was closing it," I explain. "He tried to strangle her."

"No!" Raphael gasps in disbelief. "He used to love Brie. She was like a sister to him. Even after you cut off contact with him, Sabriel still talked with Luc every week without fail up until she was sent here. Even when we were out on missions, she would always find a way to get in touch with him and check up on him. How could he do that to her?"

"I didn't know that," I admit. "I knew he was confiding in her before his fall, but I didn't know they were in contact after that. Even when I was still talking to him, he never said anything about being in contact with her too. Right after it happened, she admitted that she felt guilty she couldn't prevent his fall, but I shut down the conversation. It was too painful for me at the time, and I refused to talk about him with anyone. You remember how devastated I was. I wouldn't talk to you about it either."

"I remember," Raphael says quietly, rubbing at his chest. "That was a dark time for all of us and you took it the hardest, I think. Brie was actually the one who asked us to intervene eventually. She saw that you were close to falling, but every time she tried to talk to you about the path you were on, you would shut her down, so she begged us to knock some sense into you before it was too late. That girl loves you more deeply and purely than any love I've ever seen. From what I understand, she was transparent with Lucifer about what happened when you cut off contact with him. She told him it was necessary and that if he needed someone to blame, it should be her and not you. Since they stayed in contact all that time since, I assumed he understood and didn't hold it against either of you."

"I didn't know any of this," I say, shaking my head.

"How could you?" Raphael replies sadly. "Any time she tried to talk to you about him, you would leave the room. Eventually, she stopped trying to bring the topic up."

"I guess I can't fault her for that," I respond, feeling like I failed her in those moments. I do remember Sabriel trying to talk to me about Lucifer many times, and Raphael wasn't wrong when he said I would get up and leave the room every time. I didn't feel like I could handle even hearing his name most days, let alone have an entire conversation about him or what had happened between us. I may be an angel, but I'm not perfect. I strive to be as virtuous and noble as any being can be, but we all have our flaws. Now, one of mine is coming back to haunt me and putting Brie in danger. I will make up for it in any way I can, and above all, I will keep Brie safe no matter what comes our way. Lucifer may have been a brother to me, but Sabriel is my everything and I will choose her every time.

Chapter 23

BRIE

I can't pretend that I wasn't happy to leave Ireland when the time came. Ireland had always been on my top ten list of countries I wanted to visit, but everything that happened in the tunnels on the island was more than a little traumatic. I'd be lying if I said I wasn't still having nightmares about snakes. I'm hoping the physical distance will help, even if the memories remain. It's not like I can wipe those moments from my brain. Believe me, I asked. Since my old angel self's memories were removed or locked or whatever, shouldn't Michael have been able to remove these memories? Or at the very least, modify them somehow so they don't affect me so strongly. Unfortunately, he said it wasn't possible to do while I'm in a human body. He said something about my brain matter turning to mush, though his explanation was much more scientific and technically advanced. Oh well. I tried.

"Brie, did you hear what I just said?" Michael's smooth voice cuts into my thoughts. Speak of the devil—or the angel, I guess. Let's not speak of the devil. Ever.

"Brie?" Michael says again.

"Oh, um, no. I was lost in my thoughts. Sorry, could you repeat it?" I respond, my cheeks flaming.

"I said we're getting closer to the Ploutonion so you may want to take out your portable gas analyzer. We need to start watching the levels of carbon dioxide before we go into the cave, so we start using the self-contained breathing apparatus before the levels become too dangerous, but not so soon that we're wasting minutes of oxygen that we may need."

"Right. Yeah, I'll do that," I say, pausing amongst the ruins of Hieropolis to remove the small, handheld device from its case. I power it on and stare blankly as the little screen lights up, before noticing Michael watching me with concern.

"I'm fine," I tell him, resuming my trek toward the Plutonium shrine.

"It's ok if you're not," Michael replies soothingly, gently massaging the back of my neck. I don't know how he has the coordination to do that and walk at the same time, but it feels so good I never want him to stop. Seriously, my eyes are about to roll into the back of my head as the tension I've been holding there releases. "I'm here if you want to talk about anything," he continues, not pushing but offering.

"I'm really ok," I affirm. "Just processing everything."

He gives me a warm smile and removes his hand from my neck. I definitely pout a bit at that, but a girl can't be too greedy, so I don't demand he put his hand back and continue. Even though I really, really want to. As we get closer to the Plutonium shrine,

I can finally make out more details of the statue erected atop. The statue is of a man with a round face framed by curly hair and a curly beard. His mouth appears small, and his eyes are large in proportion. He almost looks kindly as he sits next to...wait, is that a three-headed dog? It totally is. I vaguely remember something from Greek mythology about a three-headed dog named Cerberus that guarded the underworld, so this must be a depiction of Cerberus. The statue doesn't make him look intimidating or vicious. He just looks like a good, three-headed puppers sitting nicely. I tilt my head to each side, then side-eye Michael.

"What?" he asks, strangely in-tune with my intentions when I haven't even voiced anything.

"I thought Lucifer was the big man downstairs, but Pluto was considered the God of the Underworld, as well as Hades, so I'm confused as to the hierarchy or whatever. Did Pluto and Hades really exist, and if they did, but now Lucifer is in charge, what happened to them?"

"The Archangels, those of us that were the original angels, have gone by many names throughout history. Some civilizations labeled us as deities, though we did not encourage it. They saw or heard of our vast powers and abilities and labeled us as they wanted. We do not intervene in such matters. Pluto, Hades, Lucifer—they are all names for the same being," Michael explains.

"So that statue is supposed to be the same dude that I met in Ireland? It looks nothing like him!" I exclaim, pointing to the depiction of Pluto atop the Plutonium shrine.

"Well, the sculptor wasn't very good. It's likely the statue was sculpted based on a hand-drawn portrait that was itself based on only a vague description or an imagined appearance." Michael chuckles, though I can see the sadness in his eyes. He's been troubled since I told him about Lucifer grabbing my throat at the last Gate. "But also, Lucifer can glamour his whole being. He can appear to humans with whatever visage he desires, so it's entirely possible he chose to look like that at one point in time and it was memorialized."

"What about the dog? Does he really have a three-headed dog?" I ask, both excited and wary of the prospect.

"He does actually," Michael answers warmly. "Lucifer found Cerberus when Cerberus was a newborn pup. The three heads was a birth defect, and the corrupted human that had bred his parents abandoned the poor puppy. Removed him from his mother and left him to die. Lucifer found him and brought him back to the underworld with him. Lucifer said he'd been wanting a companion, and even though Cerberus' soul would have transcended when he passed on, Lucifer didn't want Cerberus to suffer until then, so he took Cerberus home and raised him rather than leaving him to die like his evil breeder had."

"That's really sweet," I reply. "I wouldn't have expected that someone with so much hatred and anger in his soul could be that compassionate."

Sadness and soul-deep pain penetrate Michael's voice as he says, "I haven't spoken to Lucifer in a long time, but he used to be a good soul. He was misunderstood a lot, and completely bull-headed when he believed in something, but he always tried to do what he thought was right."

I'm saved from trying to muster up a response to that statement by a middle-aged man with dark features rushing toward us. He calls out in a thick Turkish accent, "Are you the scientists?"

"We are," Michael calls back.

The man quickens his steps even more until he reaches us, breathing heavily. "Welcome to Pluto's Gate," he says with a smile through his panting. "I'll unlock the fence for you to reach the entrance, but I can't go down with you, as you already know. I'll come back in two hours to let you back onto this side of the fence so you can leave. Is that enough time?"

"That's perfect," Michael replies. "We only have an hour of oxygen in our tanks, so we should be all finished and waiting for you here when you return."

"Good," the local says as he unlocks a portion of the fence and drags it open for us to pass through. "Good luck!"

"Thank you!" I call back to him as Michael and I start climbing down the boulders that form a natural wall between the entrance to the cave and the fence we just passed through. It's not a hard climb, and we're able to reach the arena floor that surrounds the entrance in minutes.

"Be careful where you step," Michael warns me, and I look down just in time to avoid stepping on the carcass of a small bird. I was so distracted with the scenery surrounding me that I didn't even notice the dozens of dead creatures surrounding the cave entrance. I really need to start focusing.

"They're attracted to the warm air and then suffocate from breathing such high levels of carbon dioxide," Michael explains, gesturing to the carcasses before us. "Sometimes, that which we find enticing is as deadly as it is desirable."

That statement seems pointed somehow, but I really don't want to get into it right now. "Maybe we should put our masks on now?" I ask instead, playing with the straps of the harness that holds the oxygen tank to my back.

Michael leans in to look at the screen of my portable gas analyzer. "Not yet," he answers. "We can wait until we're just inside the entrance of the cave."

I fidget a bit, uncomfortable with this type of danger. Especially since an early symptom of carbon dioxide poisoning is visions and I actually have visions in real life from my angelic abilities. How am I supposed to know if a vision is a real vision or a sign I'm going to die from inhaling too much carbon dioxide? I'll just try to hold my breath as much as possible until I have my full-face mask on and the oxygen flowing.

The bottom portion of the entrance to the cave is a wall made of stones, while the top portion is a stone arch. Michael boosts me up so I can plant my hands on the top of the wall portion of the entrance and haul myself through. Then, he vaults through the opening like it's not difficult in the slightest. We both put on our masks, and I feel much more relaxed knowing that the air I'm now breathing is safe.

The space we're in is extremely small. Michael is crowded into my back and nudges me forward gently, reminding me that our oxygen is limited so we need to hurry. The floor slopes gently downward, but the top half of the space is covered by another stone wall. I'm guessing they restored the entrance to the cave in this way to block a greater percentage of the toxic gasses from escaping into the surrounding area. I crouch down to crawl under the wall and am relieved to see that it truly is just a stone wall about a foot thick. I was worried that it might turn out to be the height of the ceiling and I'd end up crawling the length of the cave. My knees had enough damage after crawling so much in the last set of tunnels.

I turn on the flashlight that's built into the portable gas analyzer and continue forward, hearing Michael following closely behind. We soon reach an uneven drop in the ground, around three feet deep, and I jump down it into a large stone-roofed chamber. The middle of the chamber has a river of steaming water flowing through a deep fissure in the ground, cutting the space into two. The fissure is too wide to jump over, but the ceiling is high enough that we'll be able to fly over.

I allow my wings to unfurl from my back, careful not to dislodge my harness in the process, and sigh deeply at the feeling of relief. You never realize how much tension your body is holding until it releases, do you? Pushing off from the ground with my legs, I let my wings propel me further into the air and toward the fissure. At first, the kiss of steam that hits my body feels like the sharp sting of a papercut as I begin to drip sweat from the heat of it, but as I fly closer and closer to the center of the fissure, the heat from the steam encompasses my body like a boiling vat until it's burning my skin even through my clothing. I feel like I'm being boiled alive and scream in agony as my muscles clench up from the pain and I almost drop into the bubbling water below me. Gritting my teeth, I force my muscles back into motion despite the anguish it inflicts and clear the other edge of the fissure, crashing into the ground and convulsing from the pain of the third and fourth degree burns now covering my body.

The pain is like nothing I've ever experienced, and it takes all of my willpower not to break down and pray for death. I picture my green healing energy and let it permeate every cell in my body in an effort to speed up my natural healing, but the pain only gets worse as my exposed muscles knit themselves back together and layers of skin slough off before reforming in new, healthy layers. The pain begins to decrease and I twitch my fingers toward Michael, who is panting on the ground next to me. Although Michael was not gifted with the ability to heal others as Raphael and myself were, his self-healing ability is much faster and more efficient than mine is. I guess self-healing was deemed essential for the fiercest protector of the light when angelic abilities were dealt out. Regardless, I gently press the tips of my fingers into Michael's body and redirect my healing energy into him, to speed up his healing even further. Within minutes, Michael is healed enough to function again, and removes my hand from his newly healthy skin.

"Enough, Brie. I'm ok. You need to focus your healing energy on yourself," he says gently, though his voice is still rough from the steam burning his throat raw.

I don't outwardly acknowledge Michael's words, but I do heed them as I let the green healing energy once again infuse my own damaged cells until I'm able to move sufficiently again as well.

"I never really thought about how steam can burn before. Especially not through clothes. I mean, of course anything can burn you if it's hot enough, but I just never thought about it," I ramble while trying to regain my wits.

Michael looks at me in concern but doesn't respond. Instead, he simply asks if I'm ready to continue and reminds me that we have limited oxygen in our tanks. I quickly agree to continue, but am inwardly panicking about getting burned again on our way back, because we can't leave this awful cave without crossing that fissure again in the other direction. I can't imagine any sane being wouldn't have a panic attack over that prospect.

Beyond the chamber is another cave tunnel that curves steeply downward until it opens up into a natural grotto filled with more boiling water and scalding steam. My portable gas analyzer beeps, and I look down at it to see that the level of carbon dioxide is reading at ninety-one percent concentration. Looking back up, I pan the flashlight on the portable gas analyzer across the area between myself and the lip of the grotto. I'm keeping as much distance as possible to avoid being burned again, though I have accepted that getting burnt on the way back to the surface is inevitable. When my flashlight reaches the far edge of the wall on my right, I pause, noticing a large, oddly shaped something on the floor.

Creeping closer, I'm quickly distracted by a flickering in my periphery. I turn back toward the grotto to see the flickering glow penetrating through from the depths of the water. A second later, I realize that, beneath the noise of burbles and popping coming from the boiling water of the grotto, is a low growling noise. I turn back toward the edge of the wall in time to see the giant lump on the floor stretching and rising onto four legs, before its three heads all turn my way and its six glowing eyes freeze me in place. Looks like I'm about to meet Cerberus in real life...not in statue form.

Chapter 24

BRIE

Just as the statue representation of Pluto looks nothing like the real-life version of the man, the statue representation of Cerberus is far from accurate. The sculpture depicted Cerberus as lean and tall, similar to the build of a Doberman. In reality, Cerberus' build is more stocky—and therefore more intimidating. He looks like a giant Cane Corso, or a breed similar to that, with midnight black fur and reddish-brown eyes that seem to hold an inner light, giving off an eerie glow.

A rumble of a growl comes from one of Cerberus' three throats, and is then echoed by the other two, and I can actually see the vibrations in each of his three necks. I can practically see the thought bubbles above each of his heads with a repeating, "Guard, protect. Guard, protect," as he stares at me through the murky light of the grotto. Michael shifts slightly behind me and whispers, "Back away slowly, Brie." Cerberus becomes more aggressive as the soft tenor of Michael's voice pierces the silence, and he bares his teeth as his growls become louder.

"Brie!" Michael whispers with more urgency.

And me being me, well...I scoff. "None of that," I say to Cerberus in a firm voice, before slipping into a softer coo. "I know you're being such a good boy, protecting the Gate like your daddy told you to, aren't you?"

Cerberus stops growling and tilts his heads to the side like he's confused, while Michael hisses at me, "What are you doing? Back away!"

I turn my head to look over my shoulder at Michael and say lightly, "Don't be silly." Then I turn back to give Cerberus my full attention again.

"Cerberus is doing his job like a good boy, aren't you baby? You are, huh. You're such a good boy."

Cerberus starts to growl again, but it has less power this time, and sounds almost questioning. Still, I interrupt with a firm, "None of that, I said," before the growl has a chance to form fully, and he cuts it off abruptly. "Thank you, sweet boy," I praise. "I don't like it when you growl at me. It makes me feel sad. I just want to be your friend. I don't want us to be enemies. Don't you want to be friends?"

Cerberus takes a tentative step toward me and I hold out my hand, palm down, so he can scent me without getting too close.

"You do want to be friends!" I cheer, my genuine happiness permeating my words. "My name is Brie and this is Michael," I say, gesturing behind me.

Cerberus shifts his gaze to Michael and another growl forms, but once again cuts off abruptly when I give a firm, "Cerberus". Cerberus whines and ducks his heads, upset by my visible displeasure with him, but I reassure him quickly. He's only trying to make his owner proud, after all.

"It's ok, baby. I know you didn't mean it. Michael wants to be your friend too, he's just not so good at showing it."

Cerberus seems to accept that answer and inches a little closer. I see his nostrils flare as he tries to gain a whiff of my scent and I smile at him indulgently.

"I seem to remember reading that you like music. Would you mind if I sing to you a bit, Cerberus? I do like to sing, but I get nervous singing in front of people, and I think you would be the perfect audience for me."

Cerberus gives me a little tail wag, so I launch into "I'll Stand By You" by The Pretenders. Getting into the music playing in my head as I sing the lyrics, I sway to the music and close my eyes for a moment before I feel a soft head butt up against my thigh. Opening my eyes, I see that one of Cerberus' heads is indeed against my thigh, while another stares up at me with its mouth open and its tongue lolling out in happiness, and the third is glaring past me, toward Michael, with narrowed eyes. I dig my fingers into Cerberus' fur, petting both the head that is watching me and the one that bumped my thigh, as I continue to sing to him. By the time I finish the song, Cerberus is sitting in front of me, all three heads gazing up into my face as I pet each of his heads in turn.

"Do you want another song?" I ask Cerberus gently.

All three heads give happy little yips in response.

"Ok, let's do something a little more upbeat this time. You can dance with me," I tell Cerberus as I rack my brain for an upbeat song other than "Who Let The Dogs Out?" I don't think he'd appreciate that one very much. I settle on "If You're Going Through Hell" by Rodney Atkins, launching into it with gusto and dancing along as Cerberus wags his tail so hard that his whole body wiggles with it. I go right along with it, adding in my own booty shakes. I even dance over to Michael, who has a full-on facepalm going on, and spin myself under his other arm as he stands rooted to the spot, his eyes glued to Cerberus. I let his arm flop back down after my spin when he doesn't move at all and dance back to Cerberus, who's now adding in little hops to match my energy. I'm breathing heavily when I finish the song, but my soul is filled with happiness and light as I smile at Cerberus and give him some love.

"Really?" I hear Michael intone lowly. "You're singing songs with references to Hell now? It's a bit sacrilegious, no?"

"It's just a song," I say flippantly. "Plus, I'm sure my little Cerberus misses his home. Don't you, baby? Do you miss your home, sweet boy?"

"Little..." Michael whispers in disbelief as Cerberus gives a little whine of confirmation along with the most tragically sad puppy dog eyes I've ever seen. And there's six of those tragically sad puppy dog eyes, so it's hits me in the heart with three times the power.

"I'm so sorry, sweet boy. You'll be home soon," I lament, but as I say the words, I can feel the frown forming on my face. Turning to Michael, I say, "Cerberus can get back home, right? Please tell me I didn't just make an empty promise."

"You did not," Michael assures me. "Cerberus can get back to the underworld through any of the open portals. He simply needs to swim though the water to the portal and he can be home."

"Won't he get burnt though?" I question nervously, biting my lip in concern. The water in the grotto is super-hot, and I don't want Cerberus to get hurt.

Michael gives me a soft smile and answers, "When Lucifer adopted Cerberus, he gifted Cerberus protection from toxic chemicals and heat equivalent to the strength of hellfire, since Hell has both and he didn't want Cerberus to get hurt. He also appealed to the divine spirit to allow Cerberus' soul to become immortal as our souls are, so Cerberus could be his companion for eternity."

"And the divine spirit granted his request?" I verify.

"Yes," Michael confirms.

Satisfied, I thank Michael for explaining all of that to me. Knowing that Cerberus wouldn't be hurt getting to or going through the portal is a relief.

"How about I give you one more song? I have to sit for this one though," I say to Cerberus, turning back to him before moving over toward the wall and plopping down next to it. Cerberus follows me over and lies down next to me, gently placing his heads in my lap and gazing up at me with invisible hearts in his eyes.

My hands immediately start petting Cerberus' heads again as I start to sing a slowed-down, sadder version of "Girl Who Didn't Care" by Tenille Townes. This song always hits me right in the feels. I get so lost in it that I don't realize Cerberus has fallen asleep until I finish the song and realize the grotto is filled with soft snores rather than silence. I gently move myself out from under him so as not to disturb him and stand up, shaking out my limbs as I do and remembering Michael and I are on limited oxygen—a fact I forgot while I was busy singing to Cerberus. Michael, on the other hand, definitely did not forget that fact.

"You need to close the portal now while he's sleeping," he says, pointing to the flickering glow peeking up at us through the murky water.

"But what about Cerberus?" I ask. "Will he be able to get back home if I close it while he's on this side of it."

"He'd need to get to one of the other Gates, but he'll be fine," Michael says dismissively.

"No," I state, walking over to where Cerberus is sleeping peacefully.

"Brie, what are you doing?" Michael hisses. "You need to close the Gate and we need to leave before our oxygen runs out!"

I crouch down next to Cerberus' back and gently stroke him while softly saying his name until one eye peeps open.

"Cerberus, baby. It's time for you to go home to your daddy, ok? Will you do that for me, sweet boy?"

Cerberus looks at me with drowsy eyes before lumbering up to his full height, licking my cheek—thankfully with just one of his tongues—and diving into the depths of the water. When I can no longer see his dark form against the reddish-orange glow, I carve the sigil for closure into my left palm and take a deep breath.

"This is going to hurt," I say, picturing the gray light of my shield and letting it encompass my arm before shoving that arm into the boiling water and pushing my light energy out into the water through the sigil.

"Why don't I have protection from heat?" I lament through gritted teeth as my skin burns quickly even with the shield in place. I force myself not to cry out from pain. My whole body starts to shake and I feel Michael's hands on my shoulders, steadying me. After what feels like a millennium, the flickering glow disappears from depths of the water, and Michael pulls me from the water and away from the edge. I try not to look at my arm, knowing it's burnt down to the bone, as I send as much healing energy as I have at the moment toward my arm. I can feel the ligaments, tendons, and muscles rebuilding themselves before the tightness of new skin alerts me that the process is almost complete. I'm happy that I'm healed and no longer in pain, but as I gauge my energy reserves, I worry that I might not have enough energy left to heal my body from the steam burns I will inevitably get on the way back out of this cave system.

Michael's panicked eyes meet mine as he asks, "Are you ok?" with a calm that belies his true emotion.

"I'm fine," I say. "Let's get going before we run out of air."

"You were great back there with Cerberus," Michael tells me as we make our way up the steep slope of the curving tunnel. "How did you know that would work?"

"I didn't," I tell him honestly. "But I could tell he had a good soul and was just trying to follow orders. Really all he wants is to be loved," I say with a shrug.

Michael smiles over at me. "I'm proud of you. Your compassion and empathy have always made you one of the strongest beings that I know."

"What about my sense of justice?" I tease.

"That too," Michael responds with an even wider smile and a sparkle in his eyes.

"I'm glad you're here with me," I tell him. "I don't think I could have made it through this one without you."

"You're stronger than you think," Michael responds.

I groan loudly as we arrive at the chamber holding the fissure and give myself a little mental pep talk, comprising equal parts of "I can do this" and "just get through it". Michael launches himself through the air before me, and I quickly follow before my logical brain has the opportunity to stop me. Like the last time, the steam isn't so bad at first, but quickly strengthens in intensity until I feel like I'm being boiled alive. I fly as fast as I can, trying my best to ignore the pain and power through, but falter about halfway when

I try to take a breath and come up short. Propelling myself through the scalding steam, I try to look at the gauge on my harness, but it's too fogged up for me to see anything. Cursing mentally, I hold my breath and focus solely on my wings until I crash into the ground, landing hard and rolling a few times.

I can see that Michael is already healing and I push my healing energy into my damaged body with as much force as I can muster, continuing to hold my breath though I know I will need air soon. As my body renews itself, the air in my lungs reaches its end. I try to suck in another breath, without success. I know the concentration of carbon dioxide is higher closer to the ground because it is heavier than oxygen, so without being healed nearly enough to even move, I launch myself back into the air and fly as close to the ceiling as I can get before sucking in a wheezing breath. I continue to focus on my healing energy until it too falters, fully depleted. My head lolls to the side as I fight to stay conscious with barely any energy left to sustain my lifeforce and not nearly enough oxygen in my bloodstream.

Michael flies up to me and looks at the gauge on my harness. I follow his gaze and see that it is indeed reading at zero. Without another thought, he quickly removes my mask and slides his own over my head. I gulp down oxygen and then motion for him to take it back. He shakes his head and I stare at him in terror as he refuses. I can't lose him. He has to make it out of here, and I can't carry him if he passes out or something. He can carry me, but I can't carry him.

"Take it back!" I yell to him, but he just shakes his head once again and starts descending to land in front of the opening to the chamber. I follow as quickly as possible, jumping up onto the ledge that makes up the ground of the tunnel which will lead us back to the entrance. Michael speed walks through the tunnel and I jog to keep up, sighing in relief when I see the stone wall that blocks the view of the outside. Ducking under it, I realize that this oxygen tank is now empty as well, but I don't panic, knowing we are already at the entrance. Michael is waiting for me so he can boost me up through the stone archway, and I quickly move to the side once I'm through to give Michael room to climb out as well. Removing the mask, I hold my breath a little longer until we are a bit further away from the entrance and then breathe deeply. My head swims a bit, but I know I'll be fine. Dodging the animal carcasses that still litter the area around the cave entrance, Michael and I make our way back toward the fence to leave. Thank goodness. If I never see another cave again, it will be too soon.

Chapter 25

BRIE

"Another cave?! You have got to be kidding me!" I groan. "What is it with Hell Gates and caves? Was Lucifer just completely unimaginative and like, 'Well, if it works for one, it will work for all of them'?"

"At least this time you get to travel by boat. That's a nice new experience for you," Michael states optimistically.

"I get seasick," I reply flatly, as my stomach flips uneasily for probably the twentieth time in the last five minutes. I palm the packet of Dramamine that I picked up at a drugstore as soon as I heard we would need to enter the Cape Matapan Caves by boat, and debate taking another of the little tablets.

"Can I at least put on some music as a distraction?" I ask Michael as I lean over the side of our little speedboat, watching Greece's coastline and aiming any potential seasickness toward the sea rather than the interior of the speedboat.

"Of course," Michael answers, then frowns as he glances at the packet I'm holding. "How many of those have you taken?"

"Three," I admit. "But they're not working," I explain, not wanting him to think I'm a secret druggie for popping too many Dramamine tablets.

"Brie," Michael admonishes, "you haven't given the medication enough time to start working yet. Why don't you lay off them for a bit and give them time to do their job. What if a side effect of taking too much is nausea? Then you'd be no better off than you are right now."

Ugh. Why does he always have to be so reasonable and logical. Like, yeah, I know I'm a hot mess most of the time, but does he have to be *so* perfect? It makes me seem worse in comparison. Slipping the half-used packet into the pocket of my shorts, I grab my phone off the seat next to me and connect it to the speedboat's sound system via Bluetooth, making sure to keep the volume low enough for Michael and I to still be able to talk.

The interior of the speedboat oozes luxury. It has a U-shaped couch up at the front, two captain's chairs, and then an L-shaped couch and a love seat, along with a small dining table at the back. The color scheme is all soft creams and tans. When I first saw it, I worried it might be too big to fit through the cave system, but Michael assured me it would be fine. If I weren't so nauseous right now, I would be savoring this experience. Never did I think I would ever be in a luxury speedboat on the coast of Greece, watching the gorgeous blue-green water brush up against the rocky coastline. Normally, it would be a dream come true. I mean, it's literally picture perfect. But alas, the nausea.

Breathing heavily, while keeping my lips firmly shut to avoid any accidents, I turn my gaze to the front of the boat as we approach the cave entrance. The water below looks gem-like and, in areas where the water meets a sandy shoreline rather than the rockface, it appears backlit. The waves gently rock the boat and I finally feel my nausea begin to abate as the medication kicks in. The entrance to the cave is darkly shadowed, a stark contrast to the brightness of the sun outside the cave, and the lack of light transforms the water from a light aquamarine hue into a dark sapphire. Still beautiful, but more stunning as opposed to awe-inspiring.

The mouth of the cave itself is embedded into the gray, salt-covered rockface just underneath the ruins of an ancient temple built to honor Poseidon. As we pass through the threshold, I remove my sunglasses and give my eyes a few seconds to adjust to the darkened interior, while Michael places a lantern on the couch at the bow of our boat. The cave itself seems to glow from within, regardless of the lantern. The cavern we are currently in has a blue glow illuminating the rocky structures surrounding us, as well as the stalactites hanging from the cave ceiling, but I can also see yellow and green illuminations in the caverns ahead of us. Michael steers the boat expertly as we float through tunnel after tunnel, past columns and through archways. I just take it all in, trying to absorb as much of our surroundings as possible.

As we get further into the cave system, I notice the stalactites changing from white to a honey color, and gradually darkening to a deep red, some with strips of black. The glow of the cave has also transformed into reds and oranges, with more numerous shadows stretching out in deeper, inkier shades of black. The stalactites protruding from the ceiling have become longer and more pointed, looming ominously, as though they are waiting to fall and spear us through. Overall, the feeling of the cave has gone from dazzling to fearsome.

Just as I have that thought, a screeching noise that reminds me of metal scraping against metal overwhelms the soft music playing through the speakers of our boat, bouncing off the walls of the cave to incapacitate our eardrums in surround sound. I even bring my hands up to my ears, feeling for the warm liquid thickness of blood, and am relieved not to find any dripping from either ear. The screeching noise disappears, although my ears are still ringing from it, and I look around, trying to find the cause as Michael continues to navigate the boat through the tunnels.

"I believe our hull scraped against a stalagmite hidden below the water," Michael tells me when he sees me swiveling my head every which way.

"Our hell?" I parrot, confused.

"Our *hull*—the bottom of the boat," Michael clarifies.

"Oh. Ok... That's bad, right?" I'm not sure why I ask, since I already know the answer. I mean, clearly it's not a good thing.

"I don't think there's anything to worry about," Michael replies confidently. Famous last words.

Only a few minutes pass before I suddenly feel water splash against my sandal-covered feet. Looking down, I realize that there's about a centimeter of water covering the floor of the boat.

"Ummm, Michael!" I call. "I think we're taking on water."

"What?" Michael says, even though I know he heard me, and I see him look down at his feet. "Heavens no!" he exclaims.

"Maybe it just splashed over the side or something," I say, though I seriously doubt that's the case. But, you know, positive manifestation and the law of attraction and all that. Maybe if I say it, it will become true.

Looking around, I'm dismayed that I can't find an ice bucket or a trash can anywhere. Instead, I end up grabbing a half-empty water bottle from one of the cup holders built into the small dining table and dump the remains of the water over the side of the boat. Now empty, I bend down and scoop the water bottle through the water inside the boat, which has risen to ankle height, and dump it out over the side again. I repeat this several times, but the water just keeps rising faster and faster. Unfortunately, my little water bottle isn't large enough to be effective—though honestly, I'm not sure if a larger vessel would have been effective either. It was worth a shot at least.

When the water reaches mid-calf, Michael calls out to me, "We'll need to swim the rest. Get ready to jump."

Like a bad movie, I slosh my way up to the front of the boat as it sinks rapidly and dive off of it into the cool water just as Little Big Town sings through the speakers about having fun jumping off their pontoon. As I swim freestyle away from the sinking boat, they continue with how much of a party it is. I swim far enough away from the boat to stop and turn around. Once I do, I watch the speedboat's final moments. The speakers garble out the last two words of the song's chorus before they cut out completely. The top of the speedboat slips beneath the inky water with a gurgle as a few bubbles pop along the surface where it's reached its final resting place.

Michael, who had jumped off the boat just after I did, is treading water next to me and looking completely unruffled by the events that just transpired. "At least you won't be nauseous anymore," he says easily, and I can't even try to hide my smile because that is a definite positive.

Michael and I swim through tunnel after tunnel, each becoming progressively darker and more sinister. I'm in much better shape than I was when Michael started training me for these trials, but I still have the physical limits of a human body that only started an intense exercise regime recently and I can already feel myself flagging. Michael notices that I've fallen further behind him and turns around to check on me while treading water.

"It shouldn't be much farther. I can feel the energy of the Gate already," he says.

I'm just about to reply when I notice a ripple in the water between us that doesn't synchronize with the water's natural flow. Distracted, I try to follow the ripple to its source. Just for a second, I think I see something moving beneath the surface of the water, but it's so quick, it could have been my imagination. I keep staring at the area between Michael and myself while continuing to tread water. Suddenly, I catch sight of another ripple a bit to the left of where the first ripple was.

"Michael..." I hiss urgently, "I don't think we're alone anymore. There's something moving in the water."

Michael immediately draws his sword from its permanent position in the scabbard on his back and scans the water. I silently lament the fact that I didn't have the foresight and soundness of mind to rescue my weapons bag from the boat before it sank. Now, the only weapons I have left are my metal chain belt with a spiked ball on the end (which looks hella cute with my shorts, by the way), the small blades hidden within my bracelet and necklace, the two daggers hidden in my hair, and another small knife hidden in a secret compartment sewn into my tank top. All small weapons, other than the belt. I would really prefer my short sword, or at the very least, my throwing stars. Oh well, we do what we can with what we have. That's life.

Unlooping the chain belt from around my waist, I wrap it firmly around my left hand, making sure the spiked ball is uninhibited in its movement. I then take out the small knife from my tank top, holding it in my right hand while also focusing on staying afloat. I don't know how deep the water here is, but considering it swallowed our boat whole a few passages ago, I don't want to risk finding out.

The dramatic sea beast takes forever to make its appearance and I'm getting really impatient because this whole time we're waiting for it, we're stuck treading water with only our legs and I'm getting pretty worn out. Doesn't this sea beast realize I need to conserve my energy to close the Gate? It's being seriously rude by drawing this out. I'm just about to say "Frick it" and start swimming again, regardless of the sea beast, when it finally makes its grand entrance and holy Heaven above, this thing is huge! It's like a sea snake on steroids. Black as night with depthless pits for eyes, the sea snake must be at least eight feet long and three feet in diameter. Its body could easily wrap around my own and crush me to death.

I look down at my pitiful chain, which may or may not be long enough to wrap around the sea snake's body, and the small dagger, which is approximately the length of my hand, and feel entirely outmatched and underprepared. At least Michael has his sword. Speaking of which, he swings the sword powerfully toward the gigantic sea snake's head, cleanly slicing it off from its body. I breathe a sigh of relief, but then gasp in horror as not one, but two heads grow back in its place.

"It's not a snake, it's a hydra," Michael calls over to me.

"What does that mean?!" I yell back, my voice echoing through the tunnel we're in and bouncing back to me in multiples.

"When you cut off any of its heads, two more grow back in its place," Michael responds.

"Well, I can see that," I respond sarcastically. "But how do we kill it?"

"When Heracles fought the Lernean Hydra during his twelve labors, he and his nephew found that cauterizing the wound before the new heads grew in prevented them from growing at all. We need fire," Michael explains.

"How are we supposed to get fire when we're literally surrounded by water?" I remark, exasperated.

I barely finish my question when the massive hydra, now with two heads, decides to focus his energy on attacking me. I'm not sure why. Michael is obviously the bigger threat here. Maybe the hydra figures it's easier to get rid of the weaker one first. Regardless, both heads strike at me faster than my eyes can track, and it is pure luck that I slam one of the heads to the side with my spiked ball and stab the other head in one of its eyes with my knife. When the snake rears that head back, my knife pulls free from its eye socket and I quickly stab the other eye, rendering that head blind. The other head is hissing at me and trying to strike at me from the side while I'm distracted, but I turn just in time to slam it with my chain and the spiked ball again. The snake tips to the side, off balance from my strike before disappearing under the water, which is arguably worse. Thankfully, I'm already expecting the attack from beneath the water and have my knees pulled up to my chest, so when the hydra tries to strike at me from below, I catch the movement in time to slam my feet down onto both heads.

The hydra reappears above the surface of the water and Michael pummels the pommel of his sword into one of the heads while I wrap my chain around the other and pull it tight, holding the head immobile. I send up a silent thanks that the chain is actually long enough to wrap around the hydra's head. Unfortunately, I have to also wrap my legs around the hydra's body so that I'm not flung around in the air. The slimy, rough texture of its skin is something that I know I will have nightmares about. Hanging onto the hydra and my chain as it tries desperately to dislodge me, I yell to Michael, "If I use angel light on my chain, would it work as a substitute for fire?"

"I don't know," Michael replies solemnly. "Anything is worth trying though. We're not going to get out of this otherwise. I can't seem to knock the thing unconscious no matter how hard I hit it."

Taking a deep breath and trying to calm my racing heart, I picture a vibrant red energy in my mind's eye. I think of passion and courage as I let the red energy flow through my body and into the metal chain I'm still holding around the hydra's neck.

"Michael, now!" I call, and he quickly pivots to swing the sword just above my chain, severing one of the hydra's heads.

My chain nearly slips off in the process, but I quickly slide it atop the wound and pull it across the bloody area while simultaneously pushing as much bright red energy into the chain as possible.

"It worked!" Michael breathes, and I'm about to switch my focus to the hydra's remaining head when I see movement in my peripheral vision. I turn my head just in time to see the hydra latch onto my thigh and I scream in pain as its venom assaults my nervous system. You'd think the snake bites I endured in Ireland would have given me some immunity to snake venom, or at least some resistance, but as my vision wavers and pain overtakes my every cell, I know that's not the case. I just hope I'll survive it again this time.

Chapter 26

BRIE

Despite the poison currently demolishing my body from the inside out, I can't allow myself to rest or lose consciousness, because we still have another head to deal with. A head that is still firmly latched onto my leg and tossing me around like a rag doll. I accidentally lose my grip on my knife with all the jostling, but thankfully it doesn't hit Michael as it flies through the air and disappears beneath the water. Meanwhile, Michael is scrambling around, trying to gain control of the beast's movements, but he's at a disadvantage, since water isn't his natural environment like it is the hydra's.

Ok, Brie. You can do this. Just hold yourself together for a little bit longer. You got this. I use the confidence my mini pep talk instills to retrieve one of the daggers hidden in my hair and stab it into the side of the hydra's head. In reaction, the hydra finally releases its grip on my thigh and I'm able to swing myself on top of it using the dagger embedded in the side of its head as a hand grip. Like before, I throw the chain around it to use as leverage so it can't throw me off. I try to picture the pure red energy that I did before, but I keep losing my focus as the pain of the venom dances through my body in waves.

Steeling my resolve and making a Herculean effort to block out everything other than the red energy, I refocus and feed the energy into my chain. It's not as bright or vivid as it was before, but I'm hoping it will still do the job. I grit out "Michael", but I'm not sure if he can hear me. Nevertheless, he swings his sword, severing the hydra's head, and I slide the chain across the wound, singeing it shut. The hydra's body slumps beneath me, and I almost fall into the path of its lifeless body as it plummets into the depths below. Luckily, I manage to both avoid being crushed by it and to jump off of it just in time to avoid taking the trip down with it.

Task complete, the exhaustion of my body's battle with the venom tries to take control, but I know I can't let it, so I desperately picture the soft green color of healing energy in my mind and let it flow throughout my body until I'm breathing heavily from exertion. Michael swims over to me and takes the chain out of my hands before looping it securely around his ankle and handing the end back to me.

"You've been through enough for now. Let your body rest until we get through these last few tunnels. I'll swim; you just hang on," Michael tells me softly, his large hand tenderly cupping my chin and his thumb gently caressing my cheek.

"Thank you," I tell him gratefully. And I mean it. These little considerations he has for me make me fall a little more in love with him every day.

As he told me to, I hang onto the end of the chain while Michael swims us through the remaining tunnels with powerful strokes. In almost no time, we end up reaching a rocky beach sloping gently up from the water and I let go of the chain, allowing Michael to unloop it from around his ankle. We make our way up the rocky beach, me mostly hobbling my way up and occasionally stumbling into Michael as he keeps a steadying hand on my arm.

As we continue across the terrain, which has now leveled out, the light within the cave grows and I catch sight of a glittering archway directly in front of us. At first, I think I'm hallucinating, but the archway doesn't waver, and its appearance doesn't distort in any way as time goes by. The closer I get, the more the archway seems to sparkle from the dim glow of the cave. I can see how this sight could easily lure someone in. It's quite beautiful, and not at all what one would expect a gateway to Hell to look like. At the base of the archway, leaning against the sparkling rock, is a gleaming lyre. I bend down to brush my fingers against it and am immediately sucked into a vision.

The vision is brief. I'm pulled out of it almost as soon as I enter it, but I do get to see a man dressed in ancient garb playing his lyre for a sleepy Cerberus. From the short glimpse I got, the man seemed very talented and played his lyre with a special kind of reverence, while Cerberus was cute as ever. Gosh, I miss that dog. He was so sweet, and we had such fun together. I hope I'll get to see him again.

Coming back to reality, I unhook my bracelet from around my wrist and use the tiny blade hidden within it to carve the sigil for closure into the skin of my left palm. I picture the bright white angel light that I need to push through my palm, noting how little energy I have left for this, and place my palm against the sparkling rock of the archway. My blood coats the rock beneath my palm and both the blood and my angel light are absorbed into the archway. The glittering quality of the rock starts to dampen, telling me that the portal is closing, when a form rushes into view in the distance on the other side of the archway. As the form rushes closer, I realize it's Lucifer.

He looks a bit panicked at first, but quickly covers the panicked expression with one of sleazy arrogance as he slows his strides. Just before the glimmer of the archway flickers out permanently, Lucifer opens his arms wide and says with a sneer, "Ah, Michael, my long, lost brother. So, we meet again." Then, as the Gate's seal is complete, Lucifer disappears, and all we see on the other side of the archway is the wall of dark rock behind it.

Turning to Michael, I decide to ignore the whole Lucifer issue and just ask, "So, how do we get out of here with no boat?"

Michael looks down at me with such fondness on his face, and pulls me into a comforting hug, whispering, "First, you need to rest."

I'm awoken by terse whispering, though it takes my brain a minute to recognize the voices and make out their words. Michael and I had sat with our backs against the dormant archway to rest, and I must have accidentally fallen asleep on his shoulder, considering there's a very muscular shoulder beneath my ear and a crick in my neck.

"But I don't understand why you didn't just rent a speedboat," Michael whispers, exasperated.

"Rowing is good for the health. It will be a nice workout for you. We have to make sure you stay in top notch shape. Plus, look what happened to the last speedboat you brought in here. Do you really want poor Brie to suffer a repeat of that? It must have been terrifying for her to have to literally jump off a sinking ship," the second voice whispers back.

I recognize the voice, but I can't place it, so I drag my eyelids open and sleepily glance around. "Raphael!" I exclaim, though it comes out groggily. "What are you doing here?"

"I came to rescue you, bestie," Raphael replies cheerily. "Michael called me," he says, tapping his temple. Then he cheekily adds, "Since your official knight in shining armor failed you, I, of course, had to step in to save the day and show him how it's done. I hope you'll share with Gabriel how strong, confident, and majestic I look while doing so."

I can't help but laugh as I seriously reply, "Of course. I will give Gabriel a full report on your magnificence."

Raphael winks at me and gives me a huge smile.

"How does that work, by the way? The calling each other thing," I ask.

"We can tap into each other's energy and basically send up a flare with our location when any of us needs help," Michael explains.

"Can all of you tap into my energy?" I ask, remembering how Michael would visit me energetically before he was able to reveal himself to me in physical form.

"Michael can since he's your soulmate, but the rest of us can't," Raphael answers. "It's really only a gift shared between the archangels or soulmates. It has to do with the frequency of a soul's light energy and a whole bunch of scientific things that would take way too long to explain."

"Hmmm…" I hum.

Michael rubs a small circle on my back as I sit forward to stretch, before standing up and we all make our way back across the rocky ground toward the water. It's then that I see the bright yellow rowboat at the edge of the rocky shoreline and their previous whispers make more sense.

"Isn't it great?!" Raphael exclaims as he bounces up to the rowboat with enthusiasm.

My response is to call "Nose goes!" along with a loud "Not it!" as I quickly place my finger on the tip of my nose. I'm not sure what it is about Raphael, maybe his genuine enthusiasm or his childlike nature, but he definitely brings out my inner child when we're together. It's liberating.

Raphael, catching onto what I'm doing faster than Michael, follows my "Not it!" with his own and presses his finger to the tip of his nose as well. Michael gives an indulgent smile to us both as he mutters, "We all know I was going to end up being the one rowing anyway." Raphael and I burst into laughter as I lean into Michael and, standing up on my tiptoes, give him a kiss on the cheek.

When Raphael gets his laughter under control, he manages, "You know we love you, brother, but you are the big boss of the Angelic Army for a reason, and part of that reason is your physical prowess. We all know you're the most qualified to row this boat. Plus, I rowed it all the way here and I'm tired now."

"Whine a little more, why don't you?" Michael lightheartedly teases Raphael, and we all climb into the bright yellow rowboat, which appears to seat four.

Michael takes up the two wooden oars as Raphael and I sit next to each other on the bench behind him. At least the rowboat doesn't feel rickety. That's a relief.

"How are you doing, Brie? Really? Not the polite, 'I'm fine' answer," Raphael asks me.

"It's been a bit rough," I answer honestly. "I know Sabriel was some badass angel, but I'm just not. I'm rather mediocre as a human, but I'm expected to do all these exceptional things and I feel like at some point, they're going to get the best of me. I'll either fail or become so damaged by the experiences that it will destroy who I am."

I can tell Michael is listening to our conversation as he rows the boat, and I'm impressed that he's giving us the illusion of privacy rather than interjecting to try to comfort me. Another tick in the "Things that make me love him a little more" box. I'm really sunk when it comes to him.

Raphael breaks into my thoughts, responding, "You may not have the memories of Sabriel's experiences, but you still have the same soul, and that soul is so incredibly strong and filled with the brightest light. That soul is what gave Sabriel her strength to become a badass angel. You have the same strength, whether you realize it or not. I know we've thrown you into the deep end with the whole business of sealing the Hell Gates, but there is no doubt in my mind that you will not only succeed, but come out the other side a stronger and more confident version of yourself. This won't break you, Brie. It will compel you to reinforce your foundation and you'll end up stronger for it."

"Maybe," I relent, "But right now I feel fragile from all of this. I'm having nightmares almost every night from the stuff I've experienced in this journey, and I was already pretty broken to begin with."

Raphael wraps his long arms around me, hugging me tightly, and says, "You're the strongest person I know. You've never been broken. You've only ever been remarkable."

"Thank you, Raf," I whisper back to him as we disentangle from the hug.

There's a long silence as we're all lost in our own thoughts until Michael breaks in, "I agree, Brie. What Raphael said is true. You've never been broken. You were sent here with no memories, and powers that you didn't understand seeping into your human life. You thought you were broken because it made you different from the other humans. But in reality, it shows how exceptional you are. You're unique, one-of-a-kind in the best way possible. Literally heavenly. That's not someone who's broken."

"Thank you, Michael," I say as my heart flutters a bit in my chest and Raphael gives me a huge grin before he gestures between Michael and myself emphatically, then gives a thumbs up and makes kissy faces. I roll my eyes at him, but can't help the smile that breaks through at his antics.

"So," Raphael starts, "would you like to hear the story of how I procured this beautiful vessel?"

"Oh, this will be good," Michael mutters at the same time I respond, "Definitely," and Raphael launches into his story with gusto. I listen and sneak glimpses of Michael's powerful back muscles flexing with each stroke of the oars.

Chapter 27

BRIE

I'm perched on one of the armchairs in our hotel room, impatiently waiting for my call to connect. I was able to pick up a new phone at the airport when we arrived here in Japan, after my last one sank with our speedboat in Greece. This whole journey, I've tried to check in with Callie before and after each trip to a Hell Gate, so she doesn't worry too much. Also, because I miss her. Callie is the best friend I could have ever dreamed of finding, and maintaining our friendship, no matter the distance between us or the craziness going on in my life, is incredibly important to me.

The call finally connects, and I start rambling before she can even say hello. "Callie, oh my gosh, I miss you so much! I have to tell you about Greece—we were going through these caves and our boat sank and it took my phone down with it so I'm sorry I didn't call sooner. How's everything at the shop?"

I pause, waiting for her to give an enthusiastic greeting of her own, but there's only the sound of breathing on the other end of the line.

"Callie?" I ask, wondering if maybe she butt-answered or something. I check the call info, seeing that it's still connected. I wait another beat and am about to hang up and try again when my phone beeps, alerting me that Callie wants to switch to a video call. I accept, of course, happy for the chance to see her beautiful face, even if it's just through the phone. The call switches to video, and I can see my own face smiling in the box at the bottom corner of the screen, but the rest of the screen is black, and I notice her mic is off too.

"Callie, you're on mute," I say, waiting for her to turn her mic and video on.

It's a little odd. Callie has never entered a video call with her video off. I'm always greeted by her smiling face, even when she's in the middle of something when she picks up. I'm about to say her name again and ask her if everything's ok, when the video finally switches on.

It's not Callie's face that greets me.

The man on the other side of the call gives me a smarmy smile, as he swipes his greasy, dirty blonde hair back from his face in a way that I think is meant to be attractive, but just makes my cringe. His face is gaunt, and he has dark circles under his eyes, complimenting his sallow skin tone. He looks vaguely familiar, but I can't place him. I'm parting my lips to ask where Callie is and why he has her phone, when he unmutes his side of the call. There's some muffled shouting in the background and my body stiffens, just as the man says, "Hello, Bri-ennnnna, did you miss me?"

That voice, the off-putting way he says my name, it triggers a memory. I remember my name being said in that same way at the beginning of a bad date that I walked out of months ago. What was his name? I don't remember. Charles, Champ? Something with a "ch" I think. What is he doing with Callie's phone?

"Um, who are you again?" I ask, hoping that playing dumb will be a good tactic for information gathering. Also, I just really don't remember his name or anything about him. I simply remember that it was a terrible start of a date, and I was super creeped-out by him.

"Oh, Brienna," he sing-songs awkwardly. I think maybe he was attempting to purr my name but didn't quite know how to do it. "No need to play coy, sweetheart. I know how memorable I am."

He grins broadly, and I bite my lip to hold in my retort of "I really don't remember you though." Instead, I reply, "Oh, you got me. Of course, I remember you, um, Ch—Cham—Charlie! Mind telling me why you have my friend's phone?"

Anger flashes across the man's eyes as I fumble over his name, and he spits, "Chad! My name is Chad, you stupid girl. I knew you were faulty when you walked out of our date." He takes a deep breath, before continuing, "And I tracked down your little friend because I heard some rumblings among the darkened souls that some silly girl was traipsing from Hell Gate to Hell Gate, sealing them. It didn't take long for me to find your identity. What a coincidence that we had already met. And an angelic soul, huh? It was well hidden. If I'd known what you were when we met, I would have killed you then. But perhaps now is better. And since I couldn't get to you, with you flying from country to country, I thought I'd make sure you felt the need to come to me. I'm certain that if I'm the one to kill you and stop you from sealing the Gates,

I will finally gain Lucifer's attention. He will reward me greatly, and I will become royalty amongst the demons. All I need is for you to die and all my dreams come true."

Ok, so I'm just going to say it now—dude's totally crazy. Like, one-way train to crazy town crazy. I'm so glad I walked out of that date. I'm also really worried about Callie now though. If this whack job found my best friend...I really hope she's ok.

"Where is Callie?" I ask, my voice hard.

"Oh, yes, I almost forgot," Chad answers casually, flipping the view of the camera around. The camera is now focused on Callie. She's tied to a chair and gagged. She struggles as he walks closer to her. She manages to dislodge the gag from her mouth and shouts, "Don't come, Brie! Stay where you are and focus on sealing the Gates! It's more important!"

The phone clatters to the ground and I hear a loud smack, before the gag is reaffixed in my best friend's mouth and her words become muffled again. Chad picks the phone back up and turns the camera so it's once again facing his ugly mug. His smile falters a moment as he takes in Michael, who is now standing behind me, leaning over my shoulder to peer at the phone as well.

Chad recomposes himself, saying, "Yes, of course you have a man with you. A foolish woman could never accomplish what you have been credited with. I couldn't figure out how one little girl could have sealed even one of the Gates, but now I realize you're simply the tool, wielded by a man. It makes so much more sense now. Regardless, you will come back to Los Angeles in person, within the next four hours, and trade yourself for your friend, or your friend will die in your place. Better hurry, Bri-ennnnna."

And before I can so much as tell him that it's literally impossible for me to get there in four hours, he ends the call. The flight alone would take more than double that amount of time. With shaking fingers, I text Callie's phone, explaining that the flight takes longer than four hours and begging him to give me a day instead. His response is, "I'm sure you can find a way to make it happen."

I look up at Michael with tears in my eyes and ask, "It's physically impossible. What am I supposed to do? Should we call the police?"

Michael's expression is pensive as he answers, "You can't travel that distance in four hours, but my brothers and I can. We will arrange a rescue party and extract Callista from her current situation."

Exactly three hours and seven minutes later, Michael messages me that he, Raphael, and Gabriel have just arrived back on the Earthly plane, this time in Los Angeles. They stopped at a gas station near the address Chad sent to buy burner phones, and should be arriving at the storage unit that the address matches up to in about nine minutes.

I feel like these nine minutes are the longest nine minutes of my life as I pace back and forth across the span of the hotel room. My hands are shaking, and my stomach is in knots as I pray to the divine spirit to keep both Callie and the archangels safe and unharmed. The plan is for Michael, Raphael, and Gabriel to enter the storage unit fully glamoured. Raphael will free Callie, heal her if necessary, and get her to safety, while Michael and Gabriel cut down any of her captors who resist letting her go. They are operating on the assumption that Chad will have some amount of backup with him.

I check the time again as I continue to pace the room, and then startle as my phone rings with a video call from Callie's number. Gulping, I answer the call.

Chad's face comes into view, and he looks irate, though his voice is calm as he tsks at me. "Oh, Brienna," he says patronizingly. "I told you the deal. You for your friend. You should have known better than to have that man and his buddies come instead."

Chad rotates his chair so I can see a bunch of monitors behind him. On several of the screens are different views of Michael, Raphael, and Gabriel battling at least twenty men and women, but I can't find Callie amongst them. Maybe Raphael already brought her to safety and then went back in to help the other two?

"Did you really think I would be foolish enough to give you the address where my hostage is? No, you silly girl, that address was supposed to be a drop point. You show up, my men take you, they leave your friend there later if you cooperate. You see, this is why you should leave the decision-making to the men. You are far too stupid to understand how these things work," Chad chastises me.

I don't think I'm too stupid to realize his plan. I think I'm simply not deranged like he is, but I keep my thoughts to myself so as not to make the situation worse.

"I'm sorry," I try. "As I explained in my message, it would take me at least twelve hours to get to Los Angeles. Please forgive my foolishness. I was simply desperate. I'm sure you can understand how a woman might lose her head in matters such as these," I say, playing into his sexism, hoping he won't condemn Callie for our attempt to rescue her.

"Well, yes. There's not much sense in you to begin with, so I can see how you'd lose all sense when faced with something that makes you emotional," Chad answers, and hope bubbles up in my chest. "Be that as it may, your four hours is running out, and you're clearly not on your way here." The bubble of hope in my chest pops and Chad maneuvers the camera once again, so it is now pointing at Callie, still tied to the same chair as she was before.

Chad walks toward her, and she looks up toward the ceiling to keep the tears that have been pooling in her eyes from falling. She's so brave, my Callie.

"No, Chad, no! Please don't do this. I'll come, I will!" I beg.

"You're too late," Chad replies emotionlessly before a gun comes into view of the camera and he shoots Callie in the center of her forehead at point-blank range.

"No!" I wail, falling to my knees in absolute devastation. Not Callie, not Callie. She was my light, my sunshine. How could he kill her? Why? Her death had no purpose. Why not just leave her alive? This is all my fault. I'm the reason she's dead. If I had just gotten on a plane instead of sending the guys in, maybe she would still be alive. This is my fault.

"Maybe now you'll be too broken to seal the other Hell Gates. Lucifer may still reward me after all," Chad's voice penetrates the buzzing in my ears. He's laughing now. The evil piece of garbage just killed my best friend, and he's laughing.

I grapple for the phone, bringing it up to my eyes so he can see the fury and hatred they now hold, and yell, "I will kill you! I will hunt you down and kill you for this! I will kill you slowly and painfully, and you will beg me to show you mercy, but I will not! You will beg for Hell when I get my hands on you!"

And I mean it with my whole being. Those words are a promise, not only to him, but also to myself.

Michael appears in the room only minutes later. He sits on the floor next to me and bundles me into his arms.

"She's dead," I whisper. "He killed her."

"I'm sorry," Michael replies. "I failed you, and I will never forgive myself for that, but I want you to know that Callie will be ok. Death is not the end. Her soul is that of a phoenix—when bad things happen to her, her soul becomes stronger. With this death, her soul will only radiate even more light, and she will either return to the Earthly plane with even more radiance than before or she will ascend to the heavenly plane. Her soul is uncorrupted, she is light through and through. It's part of why you two were attracted to each other so strongly and became such close friends. She will not suffer in death, I promise you."

Michael's words of comfort bring me little relief as I grieve the loss of my best friend. I don't blame Michael for failing to save Callie. The fault of her death belongs solely to Chad. I will seal the remaining Hell Gates as I have promised to do, but as soon as the last one is sealed, I will enact my revenge on Chad and fulfill this new promise I just made. I am an angel of vengeance, after all.

MICHAEL

Despite what humans commonly believe, angelic beings are not infallible. We do make mistakes and we do have flaws. We are also more self-aware than the light souls that inhabit the Earthly plane, however, and work to stymie our flaws and improve our souls every minute of every day. We are not infallible, but we are ever-improving.

I had been confident in our plan to save Callie. I've planned a hundred and one such missions in my eons of leading the Angelic Army, a few of which were extractions of innocent souls held captive in the depths of Hell. Successful extractions. If I could achieve success in saving captive souls from the depths of Hell, how could I possibly fail in extracting a single hostage on the Earthly plane? Failure was inconceivable. And yet, fail I did. I failed in what was my most important mission to date. My most important mission because my failure destroyed my soulmate. The devastating effects of my failure ripped her apart and tore her best friend from this world. They will meet again, of that I have no doubt, but until then, my beautiful Brie suffers because I have failed her. I shouldn't have failed her. That never should have been even a remote possibility, but I see now that I was overconfident. I underestimated the demon because his dark soul inhabits the Earthly plane and has not yet descended into Hell. That was a mistake on my part. A fatal mistake.

I glance at Brie as the bus pulls to a stop in front of the entrance to Chinoike Jigoku. Outwardly, her face is emotionless as she walks down the aisle of the bus and disembarks, and her energy feels hollow, as though her soul abandoned her body when Callista lost her life, but I can also see the glint in her eyes that tells me she is simply compartmentalizing the trauma until her passion for righteous vengeance can come out to play. My majestically strong soulmate will soon be on a warpath, and I will be right by her side through it all.

I descend the last step onto the pavement, the bus driver asking me if we're sure we want to get off here and making sure I realize that the attraction closed a few hours ago. I thank him for his concern and tell him we're just meeting a friend nearby, waving him off as the bus pulls away. Although the Blood Hell Pond is closed for the night, there is no security present to reinforce the closure, so Brie and I walk right into the small park that surrounds the hot spring.

We follow the path along to the plaza area without exchanging words. Brie has barely said anything since Callista's death. I know she needs to process the events that transpired, so I've tried to respect her silence, giving her the space and quiet she needs for her internal reflections. It's hard though, seeing the woman for whom I breathe dealing with this kind of pain. I know she'll bounce back from the loss and return to herself eventually, but it still hurts to see her this way. Especially knowing that my failure contributed to it.

The plan was to infiltrate the storage unit fully glamoured, so none of the occupants would see us. Raphael would find Callista and bring her to safety while Gabriel and I revealed ourselves and cut down our opponents should they attack us. Gabriel and I revealed ourselves as planned, not realizing that Callista was being held in a different location. By the time we realized, we couldn't easily extract ourselves from the battles that we were engaged in, we had to finish them out. And once we did, the demon had already murdered Callista. I felt Brie's pain, felt her heart shatter the moment it happened, and I went to her as quickly as I was able, but I was too late. In retrospect, we shouldn't have revealed ourselves until we knew that Callista was there. It was a costly mistake, and one I won't make again.

I let Brie take the lead as we walk toward the hot spring. The water is a murky reddish orange, bubbling and steaming. There is a low metal fence separating its small bank from the plaza, which Brie hops with ease. She kneels down on the small bank. As she does so, her hand touches one of the large rocks that borders the pond, and she freezes, her eyes clouding over in a vision.

I move to stand behind her, placing my hands on her shoulders to ensure she doesn't accidentally fall into the hot spring when she comes back to herself. I'll only have to wait a few minutes for her to reemerge from her vision. Regardless of how much time seems to pass for her within the vision, they never take more than a minute or two on this side of things. It's a convenient loophole that time works differently within the vision than it does outside the vision. It wouldn't be very inconspicuous if she were to randomly freeze in place for hours when out in public amongst the humans. It wouldn't be safe for her either.

Brie's pallor becomes more and more concerning as the vision progresses, until she emerges from her vision looking completely ashen and a little green. She immediately leans forward and vomits into the hot spring, before closing her eyes and taking a moment to recompose herself. I'm well aware of Chinoike Jigoku's grizzly history. The pond has existed for over thirteen hundred years, and it was previously used to torture prisoners, to boil them alive, usually until death. I can only imagine how horrifying the scene was that Brie just witnessed. More often than not, her visions are a burden rather than a gift.

I rub slow circles on Brie's back, lending her what little comfort I can. I know it's not even close to sufficient given everything she's been through since her selfless decision to sacrifice her memories and come down to the Earthly plane, but I'm trying. How can one comfort one's soulmate in these types of situations? I'm not sure it's really possible. Yet still I try.

Regulating her breathing to keep the composure she's regained, Brie pulls one of her smaller knives out of its sheath and carves the rune for closure into her left palm. I feel sick every time she does this, knowing the pain it causes her. She breathes in slowly, muttering a short prayer beneath her breath, and presses her hand to the rock that gave her a vision only moments ago. The hot spring emits a loud groaning sound, and the water starts boiling more violently, bubbles popping along the surface, their droplets burning us as they splash out of the pond's boundaries. I see Brie gritting her teeth against the physical pain as she pushes more of her light energy into the rock. A few seconds later, it becomes clear to me that red-tinted shale is forming in the depths of the pond and rising to the surface of the water. More and more slabs of shale are formed from the red clay at the bottom of the hot spring, until the hot spring no longer exists, and the area of the pond is now a pond of rock, no water to be seen. The Gate has officially been sealed.

I breathe a sigh of relief at another Gate being sealed. It means we are one step closer to finishing this mission, returning to the heavenly plane, and restoring Brie's memories. I long for that day with every particle of my being, for the peace it will bring her to have her memories back.

Brie removes her hand from the rock she had channeled her light energy into, and I watch her as she closes her eyes to focus on her healing energy, her burns healing before my eyes. She then stands and gives me a ghost of a smile. It's barely perceptible and doesn't reach her eyes, but it's the first smile she's had since Callista's passing. I'm grateful for it. It means she's processing her loss and coming back to herself. It means she's healed more than just the physical burns. Some part of her will sweep her pain under the rug, conceal it until she can take action against those who perpetrated the injustice of Callista's murder, but another part of her will continue to process the events and her feelings on them in the background of her mind. It may take a while, and she won't truly be whole again until she and Callista reunite, but in time, she'll be able to focus more on the good memories they shared than on her loss.

"Ready?" she asks me.

I nod and reach for her hand as we head back toward the road to catch a bus back to our hotel. She doesn't say anything more, but she squeezes my hand briefly, and I know that's her way of letting me know she'll be ok.

Chapter 29

BRIE

Houska Castle, one of the Czech nation's greatest contributions to world culture, one of the best preserved castles from the Early Gothic architectural period, and known gateway to Hell. Legend holds that it was built to keep "something that must not be named" from escaping into this world. Unfortunately—or fortunately, depending on how you look at things—these early records don't mean the "He who must not be named" we all know and love to loathe. Nope, they meant demons. Fun, right?!

Michael and I are walking along the road that runs from our current bed and breakfast to Houska Castle just as the sun begins to rise. We're about thirty miles north of Prague, in a remote area of the countryside. The road is paved and there is grass on both sides of it. It's pretty here and peaceful, even though I still feel as if a rain cloud is hovering over my head. We pass a restaurant and a pub, both closed since it's so early in the morning. I know this is the calm before the storm, since there will inevitably be some sort of mayhem when we get to the castle, but that knowledge makes me cherish this peacefulness that much more. Michael trails his hand up my back, massaging my neck a bit as he smiles over at me, and I just want to melt as I give him a dazed smile back. It's hard to smile these days, but the mini-massage feels so good, and I love these little things he's started doing to show me that he's here with me and he cares, so I'm able to muster up a small one.

As we get closer to the castle, the trees become more numerous and it feels like we're in a forest by the time we reach the castle gates. The castle's caretaker has already opened the gates for us and welcomes us in, before leaving us to ourselves once we're in the entry courtyard. The castle looms above us. It's made of a light-colored stone with a green roof. Windows line the exterior, indicating the castle is at least four stories high in some parts. It's not at all the dark, ominous building that I had expected it to be.

Once inside, we find a unique variety of rooms, from a pink sitting room with a full grand piano that Michael claims gives him "traumatic flashbacks of the Pepto Bismol room," to a hunting lodge style room covered with animal and skull mounts. There's also a stairway with demonic art lining the wall, and we frequently come across glorifications of demonic symbols. It's quite disturbing to be honest, but nothing overtly dangerous or indicative of a Hell Gate so far.

"We should make our way down to the chapel," Michael says. "I think that will be our best bet, since that room specifically is said to have been built atop the entrance of the pit."

"Sounds like a good plan," I respond, side-eyeing Michael and trying not to let my tempered glee show on my face as I casually say, "You know, I did some of my own reading on Houska Castle before coming here. It seems you forgot to give me a few key details during our mission prep."

"Did I now?" Michael asks as he looks at me skeptically.

"For example," I continue innocently, "did you know that the chapel here was dedicated to the archangel Michael?"

Michael blushes all the way to his ears before mumbling, "I had heard something of the sort. But it's not really related to the mission, so there wasn't any need to mention it."

Michael smiles sheepishly as my laughter escapes. It comes out sounding a little sad and hollow, even though I don't mean for it to be. Michael is so darn humble, and I think messing with him like this has become one of my favorite pastimes. I also think he secretly enjoys it as well, and he clearly knows I don't mean it in a mean-spirited way. I'm especially certain of that when he proceeds to wrap his arm around my shoulders, pulling me into his body and planting a kiss on my temple before gracing me with his full, breathtaking smile. I smile back at him, a little more genuinely this time, and give him a saucy little wink as he lets go of my shoulder only to interlace our fingers instead.

The chapel is relatively small, but with an impressively high ceiling and several large windows. Both the walls and the floor are made of thick stone, and while the room is relatively plain at first glance, upon further inspection, I find that it's filled with a strange mix of pagan and Christian iconography. Although several aspects of traditional Christian iconography are thought to have been adapted from or influenced by pagan iconography, it is incredibly rare to find the two mixed amongst each other as they are here. I'm so distracted by the wall art that I startle when a muted wail of anguish penetrates the stone floor and echoes around the small space. Michael and I glance at each other before we both kneel down on the floor. I press one ear to the cold stone as Michael starts knocking on various spots along the floor, searching for a place where the stone may be thinner. Suddenly, another wail of anguish assaults my hearing, and with my ear directly against the cold stone floor, I can also make out a woman's voice crying, "Help me!" My body stiffens with anger on behalf of this poor tortured soul, and with the devastating knowledge that I can't help her. At least not yet.

I rise from my position on the floor and look over to Michael. "Do we break through the floor?" I ask him.

"No. The stone is too thick. We need to find another way to access the pit."

I sigh. Of course it can't be that easy. We've been through most of the rooms in the castle already, because we wanted to chance to explore it out of pure fascination before getting into the mess of closing a Hell Gate, so really all we have left to look at is the interior courtyard and the woods surrounding the castle. And the cellar, which is the deepest part of the castle, was built with the thickest walls, and is sometimes referred to as "Satan's Office". I'm super excited to go down there—not.

We leave the chapel and head over to the cellar. It's a small room, smaller even than the chapel. The air is musty and oppressive, and the stone floor is covered by a thick layer of dirt. In contrast to the chapel, this room contains very little light, and when a chill runs up my spine, I nearly jump out of my skin.

Michael is tapping on the floor again, looking for weak spots, and with every tap a cloud of dirt mixes with the air, making the room feel more and more caustic. Thankfully, it doesn't take long for Michael to determine that the stone in this room is too thick as well. He gestures for me to ascend the stairs, and just as I take the first few steps up, a muffled scratching noise fills the room. I trip over my feet in response and reach out to grab the handrail to steady myself, but as soon as my fingers touch it, I'm thrown into a vision.

The cellar looks much like it did in the present, but there is a man on his knees in the center of the room holding a thick, parchment-filled book with a black leather cover. He is surrounded by black candles arranged in a circle, all of them aflame. The man has wild black hair and appears frail and unkempt, his clothes hanging loosely off his frame, as though he has lost a substantial amount of weight in a short amount of time. His back is to me so I am unable to see his features, but I can hear him muttering to himself under his breath like a madman. He gives off the energy of someone who is completely unhinged, and a tingle of apprehension roils in my gut. Slowly, he opens the thick book to a page marked by a black leather bookmark attached to the book's cover and gently removes the bookmark, letting it hang down from the book by its attachment where it sways slowly like an eerie pendulum, foreshadowing a dark deed yet to come.

The man raises his voice. It comes out clear and strong, despite his frail appearance, as he chants a summoning spell from the book before him.

"Satani of the darkness, hear me now! Satani of the darkness, hear me now! Satani of the darkness, hear me now! I summon thee and thine Misophaes to breach the veil between light and dark.

Come to me thy demons and flood this world with a blackness that could only be imagined. I summon thee, as thy faithful servant to do thy bidding, in the darkness that you will bring. Infuse me with thine dark power, and together we will wage war upon the bearers of light, snuffing out the flames of those who bring good unto the Earthly realm. I summon thee! I summon thee! I sum—"

The man's chant is cut off as the door behind me bursts open violently. He turns to see who has entered, his concentration on the summoning spell wavering and the candle flames dimming as the magic of the spell dissipates before reaching its completion.

"No!" he yells as he realizes the energy of his spell has been lost. He rises from his knees, standing in the middle of his spell circle, and raises one arm so that his palm is facing the two hunters that had burst through the door and are now standing at its threshold.

One of the hunters shouts, "Black magic practitioner, you have brought destruction and darkness to our town that must be avenged!" Before the man can harm the hunters with the dark magic now flowing out of his outstretched palm, the hunter raises his rifle and shoots the man in the heart, his magic cutting off abruptly. I watch as he crumbles to the floor, seemingly in slow motion. The hunters descend the stairs, checking that the man is dead, before hauling him out of the room by his limp arms.

I come back to myself as bright sapphire eyes stare down at me in concern and a strong hand gently steadies me through a soft grip on my elbow.

"Are you ok?" Michael asks.

"Yes, it was just a vision. A warlock was trying to summon demons here, but he was murdered before the spell could be completed."

"It's good that the spell was unsuccessful, but both events likely left a residue of dark energy in this space. I will cleanse the room before we move on. Otherwise, the dark energy here could contaminate visitors even after the Hell Gate is sealed."

I nod and pull a small bundle of rosemary and a lighter out of the little backpack I brought with me. I figure the room could use a fresh start rather than just a general energetic cleansing. I hand both to Michael, who lights the bundle of rosemary and waves it in a circle above his head while murmuring a short prayer about cleansing the energy of a space and restoring harmony. When he's finished, he places the bundle of rosemary on the ground in the center of the room and leaves it there, walking over to me and gesturing up the stairs. Regardless of the cleansing, I'm still careful not to touch the handrail again. I do not want to be pulled into another vision right now. Or preferably ever. Especially since they rarely seem to be visions of joy or contentment.

The interior courtyard of Houska Castle is quite large, with a stone floor and two stories of balconies overlooking it. In the center is a depressed square that looks like it may have been a shallow pool of some sort, but what really draws my attention is the area near one of the corners that contains a tree trunk pedestal with an old-timey phone on it. On one side of the pedestal is a wooden door that matches many of the other wooden doors branching off of the courtyard, but next to this particular door is a barred window, which strikes me as unusual because none of the other windows appear to be barred. On the other side of the pedestal is another wooden door, but this one is half the height of the other doors and looks like one you might see for a laundry chute. The discontinuity between this corner of the courtyard and the rest of it is a big red flag to me, so I make my way over there.

I peak in the barred window first. The curtains are hanging closed on in its interior, though, so I pass it to open the little door and see where that leads me. I kneel down and reach for the little latch, placing my other hand on the tree trunk for stability, and accidentally brushing the old rotary phone atop it with my fingers. Bad decision, Brie. Bad decision. I guess I jinxed myself earlier when I sent my request for no more visions out into the universe, because I'm immediately sucked into yet another vision. Lucky me.

A man stands just in front of what is now a table, positioned in the same place that the tree stump is in the present. He's an intimidating looking man, probably around mid-forties, with a menacing presence and dead, black eyes. He's wearing a military uniform that reminds me of old photos I've seen of German officers during World War II. The jacket and pants are a greenish gray, adorned with a black belt and tall black boots that reach just under the knee. On the collar of his jacket are patches with two leaves, and on his shoulders, silvery braided looking straps with two yellow sunbursts in each. Beneath the jacket he wears a white dress shirt with a black tie. His cap has a stiff bill, with an eagle above a swastika in the center near the top and a creepy looking metal skull just below. He's holding the handset of a rotary phone to his ear and gives a grunt of acknowledgement, before placing the handset back in its cradle, taking a few steps away from the table, and turning to face the primary entrance to the courtyard from the castle.

The man stands so still it's unsettling. His face has absolutely no expression, and doesn't so much as twitch for several minutes. If he weren't standing upright, I might think he was a corpse with how still he is. It seems unnatural almost. Finally, another officer appears in the large doorway and motions for the three men trailing behind him to line up along the wall in front of where the first officer is still standing. These men are clearly not officers, but they are wearing military uniforms as well, just that of a lower ranking. Their uniforms contain fewer and more basic adornments. The second officer shouts gruffly at the three men, urging them to move faster, and they quicken their steps in response. They form a line in front of the first officer, standing at attention in front of the wall as expected.

The first officer still has absolutely no expression on his face, or anything other than blankness in his eyes as he says, "You were tasked with creating a supernatural army to advance our cause, at the very least a powerful supernatural weapon that could be used to our advantage. You were ordered to find a method of granting our soldiers immortality, to secure the future of our superior blood and ensure that racially invaluable blood is destroyed, removed from this world completely. This order came from Reichsfuhrer-SS Heinrich Himmler himself. You have not carried out a single one of the orders you were given. You have failed. Those who have failed are no longer useful to the cause and must be executed to prevent the contamination of our blood."

Before any of the men can even process his final words, the officer pulls out a pistol and shoots the first man between the eyes. The action reminds me of how Callie was murdered, and I flinch, but I still continue to observe the events that transpired here. The second man in the line is immobile with shock as blood spatters across the side of his face, and he is quickly executed as well, but the third man started sprinting toward the door as soon as the first shot rang out. He only lasts seconds longer before the second officer shoots him in the head as well, and he crashes to the hard ground mid-stride.

The first officer walks over to the second officer casually, seemingly without a care in the world, and as though he hasn't just murdered three people in cold blood. He says tonelessly to the second officer, "We have been ordered to dispose of the bodies and prepare for our next assignments." And that's it—three lives lost, and not a flicker of remorse between the two of them.

I once again resurface in the present, Michael's clear blue eyes focused on me with an intensity that threatens to burn me from the inside out. His face is a mixture of concern and relief, likely worried that having two visions in such a short time span is taxing me too much.

"I'm ok," I reassure him. Then I grumble, "Flipping Nazis. They really were the worst of humanity."

Some days it's really hard not to curse. Today is one of those days.

"They were," he agrees. "I'm sorry this area is hard on you. There is a lot of history here, and many evil deeds that have left their psychic residue. I hope you won't have too many more visions before we are able to find the Gate and seal it."

"More?!" I sputter. "You think there will be more?!"

My voice has risen to a slightly hysterical pitch, but I think it's pretty understandable given the circumstances. I mean, seriously, how many murders can a girl watch before she ends up in a mental institution? That is not a path I want to go down, or even close to something I would want to find out. No, siree. I am perfectly content to keep my sanity intact, thank you very much. Or what's left of it anyhow.

I let out a small sigh of exhaustion before asking, "Do we need to clear the dark energy from this area too?"

"No," Michael responds solemnly. "Smudging won't be effective since it's open air. The dark energy will have to dissipate naturally over time, and through acts of kindness and compassion performed in this spot."

I let out another small sigh, trying to chase away my pessimistic thought that it's unlikely the energy will ever dissipate if that's the case, considering the current state of the world. Oh well. I reach again for the little door that I was intending to investigate before the vision. It creaks open, but it's just a small storage space, likely meant for grain or something similar.

"I guess we should head outside then," I say to Michael as I relatch the door and stand up. Pins and needles shoot through my legs from the rush of blood after kneeling motionless for so long, and I suck in a breath to try to temper the small pains before forcing myself to start walking. I'm a bit unsteady at first, but as my legs regain feeling, my gait returns to normal and I block out the feeling of defeated weariness that's trying to penetrate not only my being, but also my soul. And just as I'm about to reach the main doors to leave the courtyard, a dead bird plummets from the sky and crashes to the hard stone ground right in front of my feet.

Chapter 30

BRIE

Other than a stone cross marking a gravesite on the side of the castle, there's nothing of note immediately outside the castle, so Michael and I venture into the surrounding forest. We quickly come across a stone statue, but it's so eroded from both age and the elements, that it's hard to determine what the statue depicts. It somewhat resembles a hooded figure carrying something within their cloak, and I shudder to think of the implications of a statue depicting a cloaked figure with their hood obscuring their features. Perhaps it was meant to symbolize some sort of dark guardian, but that is the best-case scenario of all the options whirling around in my thoughts.

Michael catches me inspecting the statue and whispers, "It's a monument of Ludmila of Bohemia. She's a Czech saint who was murdered in 921. She was strangled to death with her veil."

"Well, that's not morbid at all," I state dryly.

Honestly, it's not quite as menacing as I was imagining, but it's still not anything even close to the sunshine and rainbows type of story I would have preferred. As we trek further and further into the trees, I start seeing movement in my periphery, but anytime I turn my head, there's no one there and no movement evident. The feeling of the woods is sinister and filled with ominous gloom. Leaves cover the forest floor and crunch around our feet as we move, echoing amongst the trees and cascading back to us in a symphony of dread.

Eventually, we come across a cave at the base of a tall, gnarled old tree. The roots of the tree twist around the rocky entrance of the cave like snakes slithering among prey, patiently waiting for the best opportunity to strike. The closer we get to the entrance of the cave, the warmer the air becomes, until I'm removing my coat as a drop of sweat rolls down my spine. Unfortunately, I stupidly decided to remove my coat while still walking down the sloping path that leads to the entrance of the cave, rather than stopping like a smart person would have done, and my feet slip on the slick leaves beneath me until I find myself falling forward. I reach out to grab onto the rocks and tree roots beside me to steady myself and am immediately sucked into yet another vision. Frick my life.

A mousy looking man wearing a hunter green, knee-length tunic with reddish cloth tights and black, pointed shoes, and several burly guards dressed similarly but in poorer quality cloths, escort several prisoners toward me. The prisoners, wearing only rags in the frigid winter air, are shackled at their wrists and ankles, making it hard for them to traverse the unforgiving forest floor.

"Faster!" the mousy looking man snarls at the prisoners. "The Duke is waiting!"

They come to a halt a few feet away from my position and the mousy man bows deeply while looking at a point beyond me. I whirl around as I hear the mousy man say in an overly saccharine tone, "Your Grace," and see another man standing just beyond my position near the entrance to the cave. The newest man, the duke, is dressed in finer clothes than the mousy looking man. His tunic is long, reaching just above his ankles, and is an elegant blue rimmed with gold. He nods at the mousy man and directs his reply to the prisoners.

"Gentlemen, you are all here because you have been found guilty of crimes punishable by execution. I, however, am a benevolent man who believes one can earn redemption through one's actions. We have had several reports lately from villagers who live nearby about these woods and a deep pit that has opened over yonder. The villagers claim the woods are haunted. They see shadow figures and ghosts. They claim that they have seen winged creatures with the bodies of animals and the heads of humans flying out of a pit with no bottom. So, to you, I offer redemption. Any man who is willing to be lowered into the pit, and will tell us what he sees and how deep the pit runs, will receive a full pardon for his crimes and will be released to return to his family before nightfall."

The prisoners exchange hopeful glances before voicing their assent one by one.

"Good," the duke responds. "You, boy, in the front. You will go down first. Follow me."

The duke leads the prisoners, the guards, and the mousy man in the direction of where Houska Castle stands in the present day—though in the time of the vision, it has not yet been built. I walk alongside them and examine the young man who was chosen to be lowered into the pit first. He looks to be in his early 20's. His complexion is ruddy, and his cheeks are sprinkled with freckles.

He is fairly thin, but not thin enough to look malnourished. He has copper brown hair and a pointed noise, with light brown eyes.

As we walk farther, I start to see the pit that the duke referenced earlier. It's larger than I had imagined and has a malevolent feel permeating the air surrounding it. I notice that there are no sounds of wildlife here, as one of the guards produces a long rope and ties it around the first prisoner's legs and waist like a harness, while another guard unlocks the prisoner's shackles. Once complete, the prisoner walks to the edge of the pit, before briefly turning around to glance at the duke, giving me another glimpse of his youthful face.

The guards all take hold of the rope and start lowering the prisoner down into the pit. Several minutes go by, the duke occasionally calling down to the prisoner and asking him what he sees. Each time he responds, "It's all blackness." But then, he doesn't respond. The duke calls down again, asking the prisoner what he sees, and this time an ear-splitting scream of terror is his response before he gives a panicked yell, "Pull me up! Pull me up! No, lord almighty, save me!" followed by more terror-filled screams. The guards pull the prisoner back up as fast as they can. When he tumbles over the lip of the pit, he's muttering to himself in a terrified whisper, alternating between prayers and nonsensical noises. But that's not all. The young man who went into the pit now looks like a completely different person. His skin is so pale it is nearly translucent. His once copper brown hair is now completely white, with not a strand of color to be seen, and his skin no longer holds the smooth elasticity of youth—it is brittle and wrinkled, aged like leather, as though it were sucked dry of all moisture.

The other prisoners start backing away from the pit quickly, stumbling over each other in a bid to distance themselves from encountering the same fate, as the duke whispers, "What did you see?" But the prisoner doesn't respond to the question, muttering his prayers and unintelligible sounds until suddenly his hands grasp at his heart as though he's trying to keep the beating organ inside his chest and he falls to the ground, completely lifeless, claimed by death from the horrors he just witnessed.

The duke gasps and declares, "This is a pit of evil. It must be sealed in immediately!"

This time, when I come to, I'm not greeted by Michael's blue orbs. Instead, I'm lying on my back in the leaves covering the slope of the cave entrance, staring at the sky. Deciding to play things cool on the off chance Michael didn't notice me just fall on my ass while walking down a slope that's not even steep enough to be considered a hill, I just brush off my tush, stand up like nothing happened, and continue my descent.

As I step into the cave, I look around the dark, cavernous space. It's more expansive than I imagined from the outside. I whip around as I see movement out of the corner of my eye again, but there's still nothing there. Only darkness and shadows, though a chill runs down my spine as I remember the duke's words about the local villagers seeing shadow figures in the woods. When I reach the center of the space, I see some gaps in the rock on my left side. One of the gaps runs laterally, and wouldn't be high enough to even army crawl through, but the other gap is an opening that is roughly the same dimensions as a doorframe. Bingo.

Michael walks over to the door-sized aperture in the cave wall and extends his angel light out into the dark passageway that extends from it. The passageway looks deep, continuing far past the light's range of illumination and extending into blackness. We cautiously make our way down the passageway, the scenery unchanging for the longest time. Just as I'm starting to feel bored, we encounter a fork in the tunnel.

"Which way?" I ask Michael, hoping he has some sort of angel intuition or built-in cave tunnel GPS that I'm not aware of to make our journey easier. Unfortunately, he just shrugs in response.

"Let's try left."

We take that branch of the cave system, and it gently slopes downward, while continuously widening, until we're walking through an expansive cavern. Despite the increasing size of the space we're traversing, the temperature also becomes increasingly warm. I find that to be quite odd. I'd expect that normally, the larger spaces would be colder rather than warmer. I'm lost in thought about the possible reasons for the temperature disparity when I suddenly hear a noise. It sounds like a low groan mixed with a growl. It's not a sound I've ever heard before and that instantly puts me on alert. Ahead of me, Michael also reacts to the sound, his body freezing mid-stride as his muscles go taught in anticipation of battle. Slowly, he turns his head in my direction and hisses, "Dragons."

"What?!" I squeak, my voice hitting an octave that I didn't even know was possible in my vocal range. "Dragons? You've never said anything about dragons. I thought they were a myth. Are you kidding me right now? How the heck are we supposed to fight dragons? How do they even..."

Michael holds up a hand to cut off my terrified rambling just as another groan-growl echoes through the large cavern.

"The dragons on this plane are humans infected by darkness, with a propensity for spewing vitriolic, hate-filled speech from their mouths. Their words burn their victims like fire—that's where the mythological representation comes from. They covet rare items and hoard what they feel is valuable. They will probably have rare weapons to fight us with. They are extremely protective of what they claim as theirs, volatile, and violent, but they are still human. Lucifer must have called them here to protect the Hell Gate. I don't know how many there will be, and we will need to fight hard, but we *can* get through them to seal the Gate."

"Assuming the Gate is even on this branch of the fork," I retort bitterly.

Michael doesn't say anything in response, taking the high road by ignoring my childish outburst, which makes me feel both embarrassed and ashamed that I lashed out at him at all.

"I'm sorry," I apologize. "You didn't deserve for me to lash out at you like that when you're just explaining the situation. None of this is your fault, and I shouldn't be directing my anger toward you in any way."

Michael nods in acceptance and closes the distance between us, giving me a soft kiss on my temple and a reassuring squeeze before unsheathing his sword in preparation for our impending battle with however many dragons Lucifer brought here. I unsheathe my new short sword as well, and quickly create a protective shield with my energy that should block out the negative energy their words might throw at me.

"Aim for a knockout rather than a killing blow," Michael tells me. "They may be infected with darkness to an irredeemable extent, but they are still human."

"I'm cool with not killing people, don't get me wrong," I say. "But won't their darkness infect others and exacerbate the imbalance between the darkness and light on Earth?"

"It will, and we'll have to deal with that after all the Gates are sealed. But for now, we need to focus on sealing the Gates. We'll fix the imbalance in the right way once that's taken care of," Michael responds solemnly.

Am I heartless for thinking Michael may be making a mistake with that decision? I'm no mass murderer, but anytime the hero of a book, TV show, or movie shows compassion and leaves the villain alive, it always comes back to bite them in the butt, and I always end up thinking how stupid they were to not take care of the problem when they had the chance. How many lives could have been saved if they had just killed the villain instead of trying to take the high road? I don't want to be that foolish person and have to deal with the repercussions of such a mistake later, but I do respect Michael's decisions and it is the right thing to do morally, even if it's not the smart thing to do.

We inch forward purposefully, poised to defend ourselves at any moment, when I see a glint of light reflecting back to me through the darkness ahead before numerous burly men and Amazonian women come charging toward us. I can only just make out their figures through the blackness of the cavern, but Michael's angel light glances off of metal and gemstones in their weapons, casting some additional light to help our visibility.

As the dragons overwhelm us with their numbers, I jump into battle. Swinging and stabbing, throwing punches and kicks like my life depends on it because, well, it kind of does. I battle against almost every type of medieval weapon one could imagine. There are men and women swinging clubs and maces, swords, flails, battle axes, spears and glaives. One dude even has a war hammer, which is something I never thought I'd see. And all of the weapons have precious gemstones embedded in them, so I guess dragons really do like shiny things.

I slash and whirl, blocking as much as possible, but there must be at least thirty of these massive, strong beings surrounding me, all with the sole purpose of killing me so I can't seal any more Hell Gates. The one thing I have to my advantage is that, since I'm much smaller than them, I'm also able to move much faster, especially when low to the ground. I use this advantage as much as possible, taking them out at their knees or calves, where they have more trouble reaching me. Little by little, the crowd surrounding me starts to diminish, but my endurance is diminishing as well, so my survival isn't guaranteed at this point. I can only hope that Michael is still ok and fighting as well. I lost sight of him when we were initially swarmed.

I notice many of the dragons flagging. They may be brutal and strong, but the stronger the flame, the faster it will burn out, and their flames are burning out extremely quickly, which is definitely a good thing for me. I'm still swooping low more often than not, but also occasionally having to jump so I can gift someone unconsciousness in the form of a pommel blow to the head. The only way I have enough strength for such a feat is with the downward momentum from a jump assisting me, because these dragons are no joke. They are strong and brutal. I'm more than a little banged up when Michael battles his way through the remaining dragons to fight at my side. He's much better at this than I am, which makes sense, but also makes me feel like I need to work harder to compensate. Together, we take down the remaining dragons, but not without taking too many hits ourselves. By the time it ends, I'm favoring one leg, and I had to switch to fighting primarily with my left hand because my right was hit with a club at some point. I think several of my ribs are broken, and there's a good possibility I punctured a lung, because my breaths are wheezing out of me and I don't feel like I can get enough air in, even when my heart rate finally returns to normal.

Michael is in better shape than I am, but there are some nasty bruises on his skin that are healing before my eyes. I close my eyes and picture my healing energy flowing throughout every cell in my body. It's taking a lot of energy out of me, but I can feel my breathing improve and my ribs knitting themselves back together and into proper alignment. I flex my hand a few times, checking that the bones have reformed and everything seems healed enough to be functional. Opening my eyes, I check on Michael again to find he's already watching me. I nod that I'm ok and extend my arm in front of me in an "after you" gesture.

"Shall we?" I ask primly.

Michael nods and resumes walking in the original direction we were headed in. It's only a few minutes until we come to the edge of a massive underground pit.

"Do you think I can seal it from here?" I ask Michael, hoping luck will be on my side for once and I won't have to go down into the pit.

"I doubt it will work, but there's no harm in trying, as long as you have enough energy left to do it again if it doesn't work," Michael responds.

I take stock of my energy levels and figure, since I'm not at dying level yet, I'll have enough energy if I need to do the thing twice. Removing a small pocketknife from an interior pocket in my coat, I carve the closure sigil into my hand and press my palm to the ground, right at the lip of the pit. My blood mixes with the soiled earth beneath my hand and I push bright, white angelic energy out through my palm where it connects to the ground, but nothing happens. In my head, I had thought that maybe the ground would start to close in around the pit or something, but nope. There's nothing. No response whatsoever.

Seeing the same thing, Michael softly tells me, "You'll need to fly into it."

I nod with a frown, having come to the same conclusion. Slowly, I let my wings stretch themselves to their full span and take a steadying breath before launching myself toward the center of the pit and diving down into it. For the longest time, all I see is blackness. No light is penetrating the darkness clouding the interior of the pit. But as I get closer and closer to the bottom, light starts to seep through, and what looks like a window or a television screen grows larger and brighter the closer I get to it, until I'm close enough that I can actually see what it is and what's going on inside it. In that moment, I know why the young prisoner's hair turned white. I've now realized that this transparent film I'm looking through is not only the Gate but also a window to Hell, and what I see on the other side of it is more traumatic than a human brain can handle.

The Hell version of demons have human-looking souls chained to various surfaces and are torturing them in gruesome acts of violence. The souls wail in pain and agony, tormented beyond imagination. Tears stream down my cheeks. I wish I could turn my eyes away from the horror. Instead, I press my hand against the transparent Gate and push the white angel light out through my palm. The window darkens until it becomes completely opaque, and as I feel the seal on the Gate lock with a tremor of finality, I send a promise to those tortured souls that I will try to save them. Somehow.

Chapter 31

BRIE

The SUV jostles me harshly as we traverse the dirt road that will lead us into the nature reserve. Michael pulls up to the guardhouse and rolls down his window, aiming a professional smile at the sour-looking guard.

"Park's closed," she barks at us before Michael can greet her.

"Ah, yes," Michael replies, reaching into the cup holder and pulling out the laminated badges he somehow procured, holding them up for the guard's perusal. "We're the archaeologists from the World Archaeological Society. We've come to examine the closed portion of the Actun Tunichil Muknal Caves and analyze some of the artifacts there that have not yet been dated."

"Oh," the guard grunts. "Welcome to Belize," she continues, not sounding welcoming at all. "Your guide is finishing up a tour. Said he'd meet you in the parking lot."

"Great! Thank you," Michael responds cheerily, in stark contrast to the guard's gruffness.

Michael pulls away from the guardhouse and our SUV bumps along the rocky road toward the parking lot. My seatbelt strains against my shoulder each time he drives over a particularly large rock or hits a divot in the dirt. Needless to say, it's not the most pleasant of drives, but despite my physical discomfort, I can't help but marvel at the lush greenery enveloping the road on both sides. The trees, bushes, and brush cover so many different hues of green that I feel like I can see the entire spectrum in a single glance. It's truly magnificent.

We reach the parking lot just as the last remaining van is pulling out, signaling that all the tour groups have left for the day. A lone man stands at the trailhead, watching as Michael parks the van and we both step out. Michael heads straight toward the man while I grab our backpacks and helmets from the rear. I join them just a minute later, handing Michael his pack and helmet before greeting our guide. He eyes our packs for a moment, shifting from foot to foot nervously.

"Hi, I'm Mateo. Welcome to Tapir Mountain Nature Reserve. I've never been a guide for archaeologists before, so this is exciting for me. I'm glad to guide you through the reserve and into the cave. Tourists aren't allowed to bring anything into the cave, but I know you need some special tools for the scientific part, so you're approved to bring in what you need. Just be careful with them. I guess I don't need to tell you that though, since you're professionals."

"Of course," Michael reassures him. "We understand how fragile and precious the relics are. That's why we do what we do."

"Good to hear. Your packs are waterproof?" Mateo asks.

"Yes, and everything inside is individually wrapped in waterproof bags as well," I answer.

"Good, good. And you're not wearing any bug spray, sunscreen, perfumes, or lotions?" Mateo checks.

"No, we're not," Michael replies.

"Ok. Well, let's get on with it then," Mateo says, turning away from the parking lot and leading us down the dirt trail into the jungle.

We're only about five minutes into our trek when the dirt trail ends in wooden stairs that go down into a river. There's a rope crossing the span of the river's width and Mateo directs us to hold onto it as we wade through the river to pick up the trail on the other side. I gasp at the shock of the cold when the water first hits me, but continue to wade into it without delay. The water rises to the height of my chest once I've cleared the stairs, and I can feel myself shivering as a pull myself along the rope to reach the other side. My clothes are heavy as I climb out of the water and onto the riverbank, but the warm air is a welcome comfort after the chill of the water. Still, it takes me several minutes to stop shivering as I trudge along the trail in my wet clothes.

The hike to the cave takes around forty-five minutes overall, and we cross several shallow streams and two additional rivers along the way. It takes some athleticism, but it's not overwhelmingly strenuous as far as hikes go. Wet, but not strenuous.

"Wow!" I murmur in awe as I catch my first glimpse of the cave entrance.

The mouth of the cave is shaped like an hourglass, and there's a shimmering stream of gem-like aquamarine and turquois water flowing through the bottom portion, making it seem like something out of a fairytale. Surrounding the hourglass opening, growing right out of the nearly vertical cliff-face, are shrubs in deep shades of green, and the boulders surrounding the stream are covered in light green moss. The beauty this scene embodies is truly spectacular, and I briefly wonder how something so beautiful could survive so close to a Hell Gate.

After I've had a few minutes to marvel at the absolute beauty in front of me, Mateo directs us to wade into the stream and turn on our headlamps as we approach the cave mouth. As he leads us, I can see him sink down into the water inside the cave as soon as he crosses the threshold of the entrance. I'm careful of my footing as the ground sinks lower beneath my feet and I find myself having to swim across the cavern. When we reach the other side, Michael helps me climb up the slippery boulders, so we can continue further into the cave. I turn back for a moment before I leave the cavern, to take in the view of the entrance from its other side. It's just as beautiful as the view from the exterior was, with the sunlight piercing through the hourglass entrance, illuminating the gem-like water so I can see the silhouettes of the fish that swim in its depths, and stalactites hanging down in the center of the cavern ceiling like a chandelier.

As we continue through what Mateo has said is the lower portion of the cave, we are constantly moving against the flow of water. For most of the journey, the water only comes up to my knees or ankles, but in some portions, I again find myself swimming. The cave is generally quite wide, though I do encounter two sections that I need to squeeze through. At one point, with water up to my shoulders and my feet unable to reach the ground, I have to squeeze my head and neck through a tiny space between two boulders that is only about a centimeter wider than my helmet, and I'm almost certain I'm going to end up stuck.

Luckily, I managed the tight squeeze and came out the other side with my head still attached to my body.

Eventually, we get to an area covered by massive boulders that we need to free climb, and my muscles are shaking from fatigue by the time I reach the next section of the cave, in which the fading rays of sunlight stream through a round opening above us. Droplets of water pitter patter against our helmets as Mateo explains that the opening above us was caused by a sinkhole that collapsed the jungle floor.

We continue through to the next chamber of the cave, once again walking through knee-deep water. This chamber is absolutely covered in stalactites and stalagmites. Calcium formations completely cover the walls of the chamber, and it almost looks like we're encased by hard-packed snow. If it weren't for the stark difference in smell, I'd feel as though I were inside a quinzee. The calcium formations lessen little by little as we continue along, until we reach another section of intimidating boulders.

Mateo explains that we are ascending into the upper portion of the cave now and we will need to remove our shoes. Once Michael helps me past the final boulder and onto the ledge for the upper portion of the cave, I pull a bag containing socks out of my pack and swap my water shoes for the dry socks. As soon as I pull them on, the dampness on my feet penetrates the material of the socks so they are not so dry anymore. Can I just say that wet socks are the worst? They really are.

Socks in place and shoes put away, I move further into the chamber and glance around in horror at the ancient Mayan artifacts, bones, and skulls scattered throughout the chamber. My heart squeezes in my chest as I see the skull of an infant tucked into a crevice in one of the walls, and I'm very careful not to touch anything. If there was ever a time to avoid having a vision of a place's traumatic history, it would be now.

"You can reach the unexplored portion of the cave by squeezing through that crevice there," Mateo says, pointing to a thin crack in the back wall that's barely visible through the shadows obscuring that particular area of the chamber. "I will leave you to your work and come back to collect you a few hours before dawn."

"Perfect," Michael replies. "Thank you for showing us to the area."

As Mateo leaves us, I head over to the gap in the wall and start to squeeze through it sideways, solid limestone both in front of and behind me. It takes me several minutes to clear the wall of rock surrounding me, but I eventually free myself from the small gap and find myself in another chamber. The floor of the chamber slopes steeply downward and is littered with bones and skulls. I step carefully, so as not to crush any of the thousand-year-old skeletons, and make my way down the slope, Michael following closely behind me. We soon reach a collection of boulders that we will need to climb down. As I bend to sit, placing my hand on the topmost boulder for stability, I'm sucked into the vision that I was hoping to avoid.

A group of men and women roughly pull three others through the chamber I'd just traversed. Their three victims are bound and gagged, though the woman continually tries to talk through her gag. The bound woman and the bound man each appear to be in their mid-thirties, while the bound teenager with them appears to be only about fifteen. As the group approaches the section of large boulders, they push the boy. He's just about to tumble down the cascade of boulders before him when the bound man lurches forward, dislodging himself from his captors' grips, and throwing himself in front of the boy, cushioning his fall as much as he can, as they tumble down the rocks together. The woman cries out, seemingly begging the group to spare the boy, but her pleas fall on deaf ears and the group pushes her down the boulders as well.

The group then follows their captives, carefully climbing down the cascade of boulders without urgency. I carefully follow behind them. When I arrive at the bottom, I see that the bound man and the boy are crouched over the woman's still form sprawled out at the bottom of the boulders, her neck bent at an unnatural angle. The boy is now crying as he tries to gently nudge the woman, who must have been his mother, with his knee. The bound man, his father, is visibly distressed and looks torn between comforting his son and mourning his wife. The group of captors looks down at the deceased woman dispassionately, before one of the men toward the front of the group speaks.

"Bring her body. The gods will still accept her blood as long as it remains warm," he orders the group, and they pick up her corpse, towing it along with them and their two remaining captives, who are now overwhelmed by grief.

I follow the group through the next cavern for a few minutes more until they pause before an altar carved from the natural cave formations. The altar is quite large, and it's surrounded by broken pottery. The leader of the group points at the woman's corpse and motions for the group members holding her to place her body on the altar. The two group members unceremoniously dump her corpse on the altar before moving back to stand with the rest of the group. The bound man and his bound son are now hysterical, trying to shout through their gags.

The leader ignores them, approaching the woman's body and picking up a bone awl that had been laying among the broken pottery. Before I can even process what's about to happen, the man stabs the woman's corpse through first one ear, then the other. As her blood starts flowing out of her ears and onto the altar, her son starts gagging. The group members remove his gag, so he won't choke on his own vomit. As the boy purges the meager contents of his stomach, the group's leader opens the woman's mouth. Tugging out her tongue, he stabs the bone awl through it. He then moves to her cheeks, arms, and legs, stabbing each viciously, multiple times until she is covered in blood and unrecognizable. Satisfied with the harm his inner monster has inflicted on the woman's corpse, the leader motions to his group to move her off the altar and place her son on it instead.

Two of the group members grab the woman's corpse and throw it toward the wall of the chamber, showing a complete lack of respect for her remains. The boy is then forcibly thrown onto the still-wet blood of his mother covering the altar, as the leader watches his father's reaction with an evil gleam in his eye. It's clear that the leader is taking pleasure in the father's suffering, intentionally prolonging his suffering by making him watch the desecration of his wife's corpse and his son's torture before his own begins. I look away as the teenage boy screams in pain, his mother's torture mimicked on his own body while he is still alive and conscious. When the boy's bloodletting has concluded, the leader walks over to the side of the cavern and picks up a wooden club that had been lying on the ground. He returns to the moaning teenage boy and smashes his head with the club, crushing the boy's skull. As the boy's moans abate and his body slackens, he is thrown to the side as well, his body landing partially on top of his mother's.

I'm internally begging for this horrible vision to end when the leader's dark, malicious gaze falls on his last victim yet again. The bound man is catatonic after watching the immense suffering of his wife and son. It's almost as if his brain has shut off, and I'm secretly hoping that it has so he doesn't continue to suffer through his own violent end.

"Change his binds so that his hands are in front of his body. He will sprinkle the sacrificial blood around this sanctuary," the leader orders.

The man's hands are released, then rebound in front of his body and he is dragged toward the altar. His bound hands are forced into the slick blood of his wife and son and then he is dragged around the cavern as the blood drips from his hands onto the ground. The cavern is vast, and the group returns the man to the altar many times, forcing him to feel the blood of his loved ones each time. Finally, what seems like hours later, the circle around the cavern has been completed.

"Now, we will perform a ritual reenactment of a ballgame to offer the gods entertainment alongside our offerings," the leader says with a menacing smirk.

The man's body is forced into a ball and more binds are added to secure his position before the group proceeds to kick, hit, and bounce his body along the ground of the chamber. It's a vicious beating, causing irreparable damage to the man's limbs, spine, and skull, but somehow he remains conscious when the group finishes.

"And now," the leader remarks, as though he's presenting the winner of a contest, "unbind all but his hands and place him on the altar."

The group does as they were commanded, then the leader proceeds to skin the man alive as the group watches without remorse or comment. And all I can do is pray that his soul finds peace after his passing.

Chapter 32

BRIE

I'm released from the vision when the group leaves the cavern and I come back to the here and now still primed to climb down the cascade of large boulders. I feel Michael's hands on my shoulders, steadying me and ensuring that I didn't fall while consumed by my vision. He must sense that I'm back in the present, because he lets go of my shoulders, asking if I'm ok. I know that I should tell him that I am, but instead I just keep staring down the cascade of boulders, remembering how the man threw himself in front of his son to take the brunt of the injuries from the harsh bumps on the fall down. I guess if I'm being honest with myself, I'm not ok. Physically, I'm uninjured, but psychologically, I just witnessed a scene that no being should be forced to watch. I just saw one of the darkest parts of humanity's history and it affected me deeply, so I can't tell Michael that I'm ok if I'm being honest with him. I'll have to shove this terrible memory into a small box in the corner of my mind to process later and continue on with our mission, but I won't lie to him and tell him that

I'm ok when I'm really not. So, I don't. Instead, I say, "Let's just keep going," and I start climbing carefully down the cascade of boulders, trying not to fall.

When I reach the bottom, I glance at the place where the woman had landed in my vision, her neck broken and her life stolen. There's no visible indication of what transpired in this specific spot so many years ago, but I can feel a darkness that grows more intense the closer we get to our destination. Evil has permeated even the dirt beneath our feet. Michael and I walk through the cavern in the echo of the group's footsteps, and I barely hold in a whimper of distress when I see the now dust-covered altar. Then, looking toward the wall of the cavern where the bodies of both the mother and son were discarded like trash, I'm even more horrified to see their skeletons preserved and calcified, glittering like crystal in the low light of our headlamps in exactly the same position they had originally landed over a thousand years ago.

Michael follows my gaze and understanding crosses his features.

"I'm sorry you had to bear witness to such an atrocity," he says, compassion emanating from each word.

I simply nod silently, willing myself not to cry for their suffering and the injustice of it all.

We continue through the cavern hastily, though careful not to disturb any of the artifacts or sacrificial remains. And there are many. Too many. Though for me, I'd consider even just one to be too many. Even so, we don't see just one. We see hundreds. Hundreds of skulls, hundreds of calcified skeletons from victims of all ages. The remains of the babies hit me the hardest. What kind of monster could kill an infant? Not that killing someone of an older age is any better, but you get what I'm saying.

After the cavern of terrors, we reach another passageway that slopes downward and then curves to the left sharply, so I can't see where it leads. As I get closer to the curve in the passage, however, the silence that had been surrounding us diminishes, replaced by a slight burbling, faint hissing, and some scuttling noises. I slow my pace and brace for whatever could be causing such noises, knowing that whatever it is, it won't be anything good. Sure enough, I round the curve and am struck stupid by the sight before me.

The passageway opens up into another large space, but instead of bones and relics, this space is packed with scorpions. There must be thousands of them in this cavern, and past the masses of deadly tormentors from the ninth circle of Hell, is a red river. It burbles and pops as it flows from some unknown source through cracks in the rocky walls of the cavern. The viscous liquid drips down the rocky walls and over boulders, leaving red stains on the rock in its wake. It appears slightly thicker than water and fills the air with the scent of iron as it falls into the river channel. I watch the deep red colored liquid splash over the side of the channel, staining the dirt as it settles, and I feel sick, because I'm pretty sure the red liquid is blood. I'm staring at a river of blood.

I bend over and start retching as my mind finally catches up to the sight before me, but the microscopic vibrations in the ground created by my violent dry heaving seems to alert the scorpions to our presence. They turn toward Michael and me and start scuttling toward us, their claws snapping and their stingers whipping back and forth in agitation. The scorpions aren't very fast, which is a good thing for us, but the sheer number of them will overwhelm us quickly regardless.

"We need to stab through their exoskeleton," Michael whispers to me, trying to keep his voice low so it doesn't cause more vibrations for the scorpions to pick up on.

"There are too many of them. We can't stab them all one at a time. There are thousands of them. It's impractical," I whisper back, even though I don't think the whispering is really necessary at this point. I mean, they already know we're here and are scuttling toward us in attack mode, so would more vibrations really matter? I think not.

"Do you have a better idea?" Michael asks, and despite how it comes out, I know he's not being facetious or flippant in asking such a question. He genuinely hopes that I will have a better idea.

I don't, but I remember when some ants infiltrated my apartment a few years ago and I looked up natural remedies for the problem. I'd found a list of a bunch of natural substances that were supposed to repel or kill the ants, and after trying three or four of them, one of the remedies finally worked. With that thought in mind, I reach into my pack and bring out my pouch of herbs and essential oils. I bring out my knife as well, of course, in case the natural route doesn't go well, and I end up having to spend the next four hours stabbing the little things one at a time.

I dump the contents of my pouch onto the ground, looking through them as quickly as possible, while simultaneously keeping an eye on the deadly little critters that are just starting to get within stabbing distance. I seem to recall cinnamon being on the list of ant repellants, so I open my little bottle of cinnamon oil and shake it toward the scorpion closest to me. The scorpion appears unfazed by the cinnamon oil, so I stab it with my knife instead and move onto the next bottle. Lemon is commonly used in cleaning agents, so that's my next choice. Opening the bottle and flinging it toward the approaching scorpions as I did before, I'm dismayed to find that once again, there is no reaction, although this time I need to stab three of my potential tormentors before moving on to the next bottle.

Seven bottles later and I am overrun by scorpions. I'm stabbing as many as possible with my left hand as I continue trying to find a more effective solution with my right. The scorpions cling to my clothes with their little claws and try to penetrate them with their stingers. One of the scorpions manages to reach my bare hand as I'm opening the next bottle of essential oil. The sharp pain of its venomous sting causes me to drop the bottle. The cap falls off and a drop spills out. Immediately, like a scene out of a movie, all of the scorpions near the bottle turn tail and scuttle away from it. Bingo, we have a winner.

I pick up the bottle and fling the oil it contains on both myself and Michael. The scorpions that were gripping onto our clothing release their grip and scuttle away from us, just as the others had scuttled away from the bottle when it dripped onto the ground. My vision blurs slightly as the venom from the sting on my hand spreads throughout my body, so I focus on my healing energy and push it toward the rapidly spreading venom in my bloodstream, while simultaneously dousing both myself and Michael with more of the oil.

It takes a few minutes, but I feel the exact moment when my healing energy has pushed the last of the venom out of my system and breathe a sigh of relief. Looking down at the little bottle in my hand, I read the label to find out which essential oil turned out to be our saving grace. Cedarwood oil. I am so thankful that it was in my pouch, and I make a mental note to find a store that carries it and buy at least five more bottles before we head to our next destination. Just in case. Gathering the rest of my supplies back into the pouch, I keep the bottle of cedarwood oil in my hand, ready for use at a moment's notice.

Michael and I walk cautiously toward the river of blood, and thankfully all of the scorpions are now giving us a wide berth as we do. The riverbank curves, so that the middle of the riverbank protrudes further than the ends. Whereas the ends of the river appear quite narrow, the middle seems fairly wide. I only give the riverbank a cursory glance to determine that, however, because my true focus is on how we're going to get across the darn thing, since the ceiling is too low for us to fly over it. I look for a bridge or some sort of path along the length of it, but I don't see anything that could help us traverse it.

"Do you think there's a way to get to the other side without having to wade through it?" I ask Michael, shuddering at the prospect of having to wade through a river of blood.

"I don't think we'll need to get to the other side," Michael says cryptically, before pointing to the center of the river and continuing, "I think the Gate is right there."

Confused, I look to where he's pointing and see a whirlpool in the middle of the river. Now, I'm sure you're wondering how I could have missed a whirlpool spinning around in the middle of the river, but in all honesty, I've been avoiding looking at all the blood since I first realized that it was blood. Now that I am actually looking at the river itself rather than just its banks, I notice that the blood from each side of the river appears to be draining into the whirlpool. Draining into Hell. That's grotesque. I don't even want to consider where such a large amount of blood is even coming from.

Sighing, I turn to Michael. "I have to go in there, don't I?"

"Yes," he replies, not mincing words.

"Well, great," I say sarcastically.

For a moment, I wonder if maybe I can get away with not cutting the rune for closure into my hand this time. I mean, there's so much blood already, I shouldn't have to add my own to the mix, right? Wrong. Because then I remember that the blood used in sealing the Gate can't be contaminated by darkness and needs to come from the same source as the light energy used in the sealing ritual. I really can't catch a break. And now, I have to wade into a river of blood from unknown sources with an open wound. That really doesn't seem safe. It's certainly not sanitary. I better not get any bloodborne illnesses from this. I guess I should add "Take a broad-spectrum antibiotic" to my to-do list as well. I'll put it just above buying more bottles of the cedarwood oil.

I debate for a moment which scenario is more gross: wearing clothes soaked in blood that's not my own or having more of my bare skin in contact with the blood. I think it's kind of a toss up, but ultimately decide that wearing blood-soaked clothes is just slightly more disgusting. Mind made up, I drop my pack at the edge of the river and pull my shirt up over my head, placing it on top of my pack so it doesn't get too much dirt on it. I have a change of clothes in my backpack, sealed tight in waterproof bags, but I'd rather save those for after we get out of the cave, and I can clean up more thoroughly in the nature reserve's bathroom.

Michael makes a choking sound, then attempts to mask it with a cough before asking, "What are you doing?"

"Stripping," I reply easily, reaching for the waistband of my yoga pants and shimmying them down my legs until I'm standing in only my bra and panties.

Michael gulps, then clears his throat, heat sparking in his eyes. "I can see that, but *why* are you stripping?"

"I don't want my clothes to be contaminated by the blood."

Michael barks out a laugh and I carve the closure sigil into my palm with my knife before wading into the blood-filled river. The blood is cold and sticky against my skin as I sink deeper and deeper into it. I'm only a few steps away from the riverbank when the slope I was walking down drops off abruptly and I fall into the blood. My head sinks under the surface and I flail my arms trying to propel myself up, but the current of the sinkhole continues to pull me down toward the Gate. I wasn't prepared for the fall, so I already feel short on air, but I tell myself that the faster I seal the Gate, the sooner I'll be able to breathe again. With that in mind, I picture my pure white angelic energy in my mind and push it down my arm and through the sigil on my hand, keeping my hand positioned toward the Gate as best as I can despite the spinning. The angel light bursts out of my palm, directing my blood toward the Gate and protecting it from mixing with the rest of the blood surrounding it.

I feel the whirlpool slowing, and a few beats later there's a pop and the whirlpool disappears completely. The river stills. I manage to swim up to the surface, gasping a breath of air as soon as I do. I direct my strokes toward the riverbank, where Michael stands watching, but before I'm able to make substantial progress toward him, I hear a roaring sound and the blood starts draining out of the riverbed through the cracks in the walls where it had originally entered the river. The flow of the river has seemingly reversed, and I'm caught in the violent current, being swept toward the rocky wall at a rapid pace as the level of the river falls. I'm slammed into the rocky wall on the left side of the cavern, but thankfully this end of the river is narrow enough that I'm able to climb over the boulders that line the wall. When I reach the edge of the channel, it now holds only half the volume of blood that it did when I entered, and continues to drain more of the blood with each second that passes. I slip a few times climbing over the slick boulders, but I do end up making it back onto solid ground.

Michael, who at some point rushed over to help me, is fussing over my wellbeing. It's sweet, but all I really want is a towel so I can wipe at least some of this blood off me. I assure him that I'm fine and start walking toward my backpack, which is still over near the middle of the riverbank. Unfortunately, it doesn't occur to me that the cedarwood oil was mostly on my clothes and that the blood either masks or washed off what little oil was on my skin, so the moment I step more than a pace away from Michael, the scorpions rush me like I'm the last sip of water in the Sahara Desert.

"Nope, nope, no sirree!" I squeal, quickly shuffling back to Michael and cowering by his side. "You will not make a meal out of me today. Not happening," I tell the scorpions firmly.

Michael looks down at me fondly and wraps an arm around my shoulders, seemingly unfazed by the blood that still covers every inch of my skin.

"You tell them," he says, pulling the bottle of cedarwood oil out of his pocket and handing it to me.

I douse myself in the oil, but still stay close to Michael's side as we walk back toward my pack. It's only then that he seems to realize I'm still in only my bra and panties, and he quickly removes his arm from around my shoulders so I can towel off. After I've wiped off as much of the blood as I can manage without a mirror or a shower, using water from my water bottle on my hair, I pull my clothes back on, refreshing the cedarwood oil on them as a precautionary measure. The bottle is almost empty now, but I think we should both be ok to leave without trouble as far as the oil situation is concerned.

Michael and I retrace our steps back to the chamber where Mateo, our guide, had left us. I don't know what time it is, but I hope we won't have to wait long for him to come back for us because the dried blood is itching against my skin, and I really want to go get that antibiotic. Thankfully, the wait isn't too long. Mateo doesn't even seem to notice that my blond hair is now colored in reds and pinks from the blood that the water from my bottle wasn't able to rinse away. Instead, he just tells us that we'll be passing through the chamber with the crystal prince on our way out, and asks if we're excited to see the crystallized skeleton. Excited isn't the word I would use. Honestly, I'm just hoping I don't have a vision of that murder too.

Chapter 33

BRIE

"This is a joke, right? This must be a joke," I rant. "A cave and a volcano, seriously? I swear, if this one erupts while we're here, I'm going to erupt right back."

"I think I'd like to see that," Michael replies cheekily.

There were no direct flights from Belize City to Nicaragua and I vetoed taking a seven-hour ferry ride followed by a twelve-hour bus ride that the most direct travel route would have required, because being seasick for seven hours straight sounded like a new kind of torture that I did not want to experience. As a result, we ended up flying from Belize City to Guatemala City, then from Guatemala City to San Salvador, then from San Salvador, we finally arrived in Managua and immediately caught a taxi from Managua to Masaya. The taxi driver was really nice, and the ride was only a half-hour long, which isn't bad at all, but add that to three one-hour flights and two three-hour layovers, and I'm sure you can understand why I'm a little grumpy. Now, I did know well in advance of arriving here that we were heading to an active volcano and that we would need to journey through a bunch of caves to get down to the crater floor, but it didn't really sink in until we hopped out of the taxi, and I found myself standing in front of a sign that says "VOLCAN MASAYA" in big, colorful letters.

To be honest, the prettiness of the sign just adds to my irritation. Like, shouldn't the sign for a volcano be imposing or ominous? I feel like a pretty sign is just luring people into a false sense of security, considering volcanos are pretty darn deadly. And now, I'm full-on scowling at the sign. I'll be the first to admit that my mood is somewhat off today. I've experienced my share of ups and downs, but I'm usually not quite this cranky. It almost seems like my subconscious knows something I don't.

Shaking away those thoughts, I rationalize that I'm just exhausted from all the travel and frustrated that we always seem to be trailing the darkness rather than getting ahead of it. Plus, I'm still coping with Callie's death, so it makes sense that I'm grumpier than I would normally be. Leaving the cheery sign behind, Michael and I make our way to the picturesque trails that run throughout the park. Despite my foul mood, I can admit that the scenery that surrounds us is quite breathtaking. In one direction, you can see a beautiful blue lake amongst lush greenery with a few hills in the distance, the currently setting sun casting the sky above in hues of pinks and blues. In another direction, you can look down into the brown, rocky depths of a volcanic crater as smoke obscures the sky and the red glow of a lava lake illuminates the dull rock at the bottom. The juxtaposition between the two only adds to the overall magnificence of the place.

Michael and I cross over to a trail that will take us to the network of lava tubes. The lava tubes will ultimately allow us access to the crater floor without having to rappel down into the crater, a two-hour climb, in darkness. The trail, along with the cave that serves as an entrance to the network of lava tubes, is technically closed to visitors due to safety concerns, but we figured closing the "Mouth of Hell" is slightly more important than following safety regulations. I mean, if we don't close the Gate, then the entire world will be a safety concern so...yeah.

The cave entrance is the largest we've encountered thus far and comprised of jagged gray and white rock. I take my helmet out of my pack and turn on the lamp that's built into it before securing the clip under my chin. There are a multitude of smooth, shallow steps carved into the natural rock, curving down into the belly of the cave, and I have to focus hard to make sure I don't misstep in the low lamplight. The steps continue down further than I expected they would, and when Michael and I have both reached the bottom, I take a moment to look around. I examine the walls to either side of me and the empty stretch of tunnel in front of me, before tilting my head back to look at the ceiling and gasping in horror. I was so busy watching my feet on the way down the stairs, I didn't notice the thousands of bats hanging from the ceiling. Yes, thousands. And like a scene out of my worst nightmare, as soon as the gasp slips past my lips, all of the gluttonous creatures from the third circle of Hell turn their beady little eyes on me. With a little shriek, I turn and run back up the stairs as fast as I can without slipping, but when I reach the top, I'm met by a coyote pacing in front of the cave entrance. It slowly turns toward me and cocks its head before baring its teeth. I slowly back down the stairs a little bit with my hands held up placatingly in front of me when the coyote crouches into an attack position and I consequently decide to give up on my escape.

As quickly as I can without slipping, I hurry back down the stairs, literally bumping into Michael who had seemingly been following me up, before breathlessly stumbling my way back into the bat nightmare. Glancing over my shoulder, I'm relieved to see that the coyote didn't decide to venture into the cave after me, though I guess if he had, I would have been bitten back when I was still near the top of the stairs. Instead, all I see coming down the stone steps is a bewildered Michael looking adorably perplexed. I take a moment to trace his facial features with my eyes, committing his strong jaw line and blazing blue eyes to memory, before I'm jolted back to reality by a rush of air blowing past me.

I look around again, cringing when I scan my gaze over all the bats hanging above me, but don't notice anything out of the ordinary until I look down at my feet. A squeal escapes me, and I jump away from the single, brave little bat that had landed right near my feet. As though my squeal were a call to arms, several more of the gluttonous creatures fly from their places on the ceiling, landing on ground around me. And then several more, and more after that, so many that I find myself completely surrounded, and they're all just staring up at me with their beady little eyes. They're paying no attention to Michael, and it baffles me for a moment before I realize Michael doesn't have blood. He's comprised of pure energy, so he doesn't have blood, but I do. Well, frick, these must be vampire bats.

It's almost as if the bats were waiting for me to figure that out, because as soon as that light bulb illuminates in my brain, that first little bat crawls toward me on all fours and then jumps and latches onto the sliver of skin at my ankle that's exposed, between where my sock ends and my yoga pants begin. Have you ever seen a bat crawl and jump? It's terrifying. This experience will live on in my nightmares for ages. I feel a small pinprick sensation as the bat's razor-sharp teeth pierce my skin, then a slimy dampness as its tongue starts to lap up my blood, the anticoagulant in its saliva preventing the wound from sealing over.

I don't know what to do at this point—should I try to shake it off, or would that aggravate the others? My decision is made for me when a bunch of the other bats surrounding me start running towards me and jumping onto various parts of my body. I feel their teeth penetrate through the thin material of my yoga pants and curse myself for not choosing to wear thicker clothing. More and more of the bats launch at me. I bring my arms up to cover my face as much as possible, trying to shake them off of me at the same time. Dear divine spirit, please don't let me die of blood loss in this terrible bat cave. I still have a Hell Gate to seal.

My thoughts, which had been mostly paralyzed temporarily from the terror of the events transpiring, come back online and I see Michael trying to swipe the bats off of me, too afraid of accidentally cutting me to attempt to use a blade. I, however, do not have the same reservations, but swiping at the bats with one of my knives would mean losing the protection I'd been giving my face. Is it worth it? I wish I had thought to put up an energetic protection barrier before the first bat latched on. Now, it's too late for it. I shake my whole body as much as possible, trying to make it hard for them to stay on me, but it's no use. As I lose more and more blood simply from the sheer number of bats lapping up my blood like it's a fine wine, I start feeling lightheaded. Ugh, please don't let me pass out surrounded by all of these blood-sucking bats. That seems like a recipe for disaster.

My sense of time becomes fragmented so I'm not sure how long has passed, when I notice the first bat has finally given up its grip on my ankle and is now a few feet away, regurgitating a portion of the blood it took from me. A few of the remaining bats rush over to the liquid and lap up the regurgitated blood from the ground. Now, my stomach is queasy to compliment the lightheadedness.

"Brie!" I look up through the gap in my arms to see Michael is shaking me. He must have been trying to get my attention for a while. When he sees that I'm finally looking at him, he says, "Run!"

"Run?" I parrot faintly.

"Yes, Brie, run," Michael says firmly, pulling on my elbow and moving forward, deeper into the cave system as he continues trying to bat away the bats.

I clumsily follow as he pulls me along. The bats that haven't fed yet follow me, like some sort of deranged conga line. I continue to lose blood, of course, since the bats can fly much faster than I can stumble along, but it makes the process somewhat harder for them at least. Michael lets his wings unfurl fully, and they illuminate with the glow of his innate angel light, but it doesn't deter the bats in the least. The call of my blood is apparently stronger than their aversion to light. Racking my brain, I unzip Michael's pack—which is conveniently right in front of me, since he's still dragging me along behind him—and remove one of the flares he has packed. Maybe fire will scare off the bats, even if light doesn't. It's not like we need to worry about the smoke, since we both have gas masks and goggles in our packs as well.

Reaching into one of the pouches on my belt, I retrieve a lighter and turn away from Michael to light the flare. It ignites with a crackle, and a bright red light further illuminates the lava vent as flame consumes the end of the flare. I wave it around between myself and the bats, but again, it only serves as a minor deterrent for the bats, and they fly around it or walk underneath to reach me. Exasperated, I reach into the different pouches on my belt, searching for anything that might help. I remove my bundle of sage, lighting it with the flare and letting the smell flow throughout the space with no effect. Then, I try a stick of palo santo. Still nothing. Dropping the flare, I throw acacia powder and allspice, rub aloe onto my skin, crush dried bay leaf in my hand and let it scatter across the ground. Still nothing. Then, I grab a eucalyptus leaf from my pouch and throw it into the flame from the flare. The smell of eucalyptus overwhelms me as it ignites, and the bats pause briefly in their attacks before fleeing back toward the cave entrance. Finally, I'm no longer being munched on and drained dry. The relief sweeps through me like a wave in the ocean, and then I pass out.

I come to feeling rejuvenated. My body must have replenished the blood that I lost to the bats while I was unconscious. I blink my eyes open and realize that I'm gazing up at a cave ceiling that is, thankfully, bat free. The ceiling is moving, though, which I find to be a bit odd, so I tilt my head to the side and realize Michael is carrying me. He must feel my movement, because he stops walking and smiles down at me.

"How are you feeling?" he asks with concern.

"I'm actually feeling surprisingly good," I answer, and quickly add, "I can walk, you can put me down."

He gently lowers me to my feet and says, "Take it easy, and let me know if you need a break, ok? No need to push things if you're feeling weak."

"I won't," I assure him, and we continue on our walk through the network of lava tubes toward the Santiago crater.

"Why didn't we prepare for bats? We should have looked up how to ward off bats before we came," I tell Michael.

"It's extremely rare for a bat to bite a human. They mainly try to find cattle, pigs, horses, or other similar animals, and I've never heard of so many targeting the same animal at once. I'm sorry you had to go through that, Brie, but it's not something I would have ever predicted happening. Lucifer must have influenced them somehow. That wasn't normal bat behavior," Michael consoles.

I simply growl "Lucifer" in response, my budding hatred of the fallen angel suffusing my tone.

We've only gone a short distance further when I catch movement in the shadows in front of us. Stopping, I catch Michael's arm.

"Did you see that?" I ask warily.

"See what?" Michael questions.

"I thought I saw movement in the shadows up ahead, but maybe I imagined it," I explain.

"I doubt you imagined it," Michael replies, straining to see whatever it was that I noticed earlier.

I peer in the same direction, glimpsing another barely-there movement that's so miniscule it could be a trick of the light. But then I also catch the glint of light reflecting off a metal blade, and that, I'm definitely not imagining.

"Blade!" I whisper sharply to Michael, and he unsheathes his sword in response.

I do the same with my short sword, gripping the hilt tightly and drawing comfort from the familiarity of it. Then, I hear a sudden, sharp intake of breath and my energy level falls dramatically.

"Vampire," Michael sighs unhappily.

"More bats?!" I whine, not at all looking forward to the prospect of dealing with the tiny terrors again. At least this time, I know how to get rid of them.

"No," Michael says lowly. "Not vampire bats, the human manifestation of the dark entities we refer to as vampires. In this form, they feed on their victims' energy."

"And...?" I prompt. I need to know what I'm dealing with before we start battling these things. I mean, I assume we'll be battling, given the blade the vampire is carrying. I highly doubt it's been waiting around in a dank cave, holding a bladed weapon, just to have a friendly chat.

"And that's it," Michael replies. "They don't move faster than humans nor are they stronger, but when your energy declines, as their victim, *you* move slower and feel weaker, so it seems like they are stronger and faster, though they are not. We'll engage them with our blades. Everything will be fine."

"Sure it will," I mutter pessimistically as I hear another sharp intake of breath and my energy levels plummet further. I feel like I'm ready for a nap, not a fight, but I drag myself into a fighting stance and ease forward nonetheless, Michael right by my side.

Chapter 34

BRIE

The vampire doesn't step out of the shadows to meet us. Instead, she waits for us to approach and as we do, I can see that she has a buddy with her. The two vampires are both tall, one is lankier than the other, but both display quite a thin build, similar to what you see from the top marathon runners. When we are merely a few feet away, the first one I noticed steps forward with her sword at the ready and a mocking smile on her face.

"Ah, Michael. Alas, we meet. Shall we parry?" the vampire says with feigned cordiality.

Michael gives a sharp dip of his chin and both vampires launch into ruthless attacks before I can even process it. Thankfully, my body reacts to the threat automatically and my arm automatically rises, blocking her downward slice effectively. Her eyes widen in surprise. Apparently, she expected me to be an easy kill. Haha, joke's on you, vamp. Luckily for me, her surprise causes her a miniscule hesitation, and I take advantage of the delay, moving from defense to offense with a sweep of my leg. She doesn't fall, but her balance falters and I slash at her ribcage, penetrating the skin with the edge of my blade before spinning away.

The vampire launches a brutal counterattack, and although I'm at a disadvantage with my shorter reach, I manage to hold my own against her. She stabs at me, and I evade the attack by dodging to the left, before lunging at her in response. She's too locked in her position, doesn't move out of the way of my blade quickly enough, and I spear her through the shoulder. She howls in both pain and frustration as I pull my blade free of her body, then dip low to swipe at her knee, spinning and kicking my leg out at the same time to knock her further off balance. The move works and she starts to tumble to the side. She realizes she can't stop herself from falling and reaches her left arm out to catch herself and soften the blow, as I dance away from her so she can't cut me on the way down.

Now on the ground and at a visible disadvantage, the vampire's eyes glow with a manic intensity in the low light and I can tell she's about to go for broke. Instead of giving her time to launch whatever attack she's currently envisioning, I take a running leap over her kneeling form, land behind her, and thrust my sword straight through the bone, muscle, and sinew of her neck. I feel her body slump and I pull my sword free. As she crumples to the ground, I pant from exhaustion and try not to mourn the loss of life, since this was clearly a kill or be killed situation. She wasn't a good person, and her darkness would have contaminated anything and anyone she came into contact with, but I'm sure someone cared about her. Maybe her mom. It had to be done, but that doesn't mean it has to be celebrated.

Forcing my eyes away from the form of the woman I just killed, I quickly find Michael's blue ones examining me carefully. He's leaning against the wall of the lava vent, arms crossed, sword already sheathed, his own opponent dispatched a few feet away from my own. He pushes off the wall and walks over to me, enveloping me in his strong arms, and I allow myself to melt into him and relax, if only for just a moment. This, in his arms, is the only place where I truly feel safe.

The hug only lasts a few seconds before we break apart, but it's enough to keep me from unraveling before Michael and I continue on our way. I'm just starting to feel like that sword fight was a little too easy, considering what Lucifer could throw our way, when I hear another sharp inhalation and my energy drops again. I stiffen, moving a few steps away from Michael and once again raising my sword as two more vampires step out of the depths of the shadows ahead of us.

There's no fake gentlemanly banter this time, the vampires launching into battle with gusto as soon as they are visible to us. I strike and lunge and swipe at the lanky man that is my opponent, and he stabs and pursues my retreats right back. We dance in a battle of blades, parrying and dodging each other. In this battle, we are evenly matched, and I struggle to gain the upper hand. Finally, though, I thrust my blade at just the right angle, causing my opponent to misjudge the location of the blade, and I manage to land a fatal blow. I look around to once again find that Michael has finished his fight before I finished mine, as expected, considering he's the leading warrior of the Angelic Army.

We continue on our way with less fanfare this time, only to be stopped by another pair of vampires as soon as we pass a bend in the tunnel. Then, again...and again...and again. Eight pairs of vampires later, and I understand that Lucifer's game is not for us to lose our swordfights. No, he knows that outcome is unlikely. His goal must be to deplete our energy to such an extreme that I won't have enough energy to seal this final Gate and Michael won't be able to loan me any energy either. His goal is probably to deplete our energy so drastically that the damage will be irreparable, and we will cease to exist completely. Angels are formed of light energy, so if that energy is depleted, just as when a human is drained of too much blood, we die. And we won't come back.

By the time we finish our tenth vampire face-off, I feel as though I can barely stand. I've been able to feel the heat growing within the tunnel, the roaring sound that was barely audible during our third fight has become exponentially louder, and the pungent odor of sulfur dioxide has become more pronounced, so I assume we must be close to reaching the crater floor.

I gently place my hand on Michael's arm before he can stride off toward our ultimate destination. "We need to rest before we continue. Give our energy stores some time to replenish," I reason, as I simultaneously look inside myself to see the last dimly glowing ember of my light energy flickering slowly, as if it could extinguish at any moment.

Michael sighs, then says, "You're right, we do. I just worry more could come, and we won't be as alert if we're resting."

"Maybe," I concede, "but at least we won't be dead because we let our energy burn out completely."

"True," he concedes, and we both sit with our backs against one of the walls of the lava vent. I rest my head on Michael's shoulder, and before I even realize that I'm falling asleep, I'm out.

I awaken some time later, praying that I didn't snore in my sleep. I don't think it's been too long since I fell asleep, but the stone wall Michael and I propped ourselves against hasn't been kind to my back. My head is still resting on Michael's shoulder, and I tilt it up slightly to examine him. His own head is tilted back against the hard rock of the wall behind us, and his eyes are closed, his lashes lush and dark against his porcelain skin. I can tell from his breathing that he's not sleeping, and he surely felt my movement against his shoulder when I tilted my head up to look at him, but he hasn't acknowledged that I'm awake yet, which I guess is good since I'm basically just staring at him like a total creeper right now.

I remove my head from its place on Michael's shoulders—yes, I've officially called dibs on that spot forevermore—and stretch my arms up above my head as I internally check in to see how much of my energy has replenished. It looks like I'm juiced up to about fifty percent capacity, which isn't terrible, but isn't great either. Michael finally stirs next to me as well, giving me a crooked smile as he stands and subsequently extends his arm to help me up as well.

We slowly walk toward the growing, red glow that indicates the exit from the lava tube system onto the crater floor, wary for additional attacks. Just as we begin to cross the threshold onto the crater floor, I hear the sound of rocks scraping against each other and jump back just in time to avoid the cascade of debris falling from above. The dust cloud created from the impact of the debris against the crater floor clogs my lungs, making me cough.

"We should wear our masks now anyway," Michael says, giving me a once over to make sure I'm ok.

I nod and pull the mask and goggles out of my pack. The masks have a special filter for the sulfur dioxide and the goggles will keep our eyes free of the sulfur as well. I unhook my helmet and brace it between my knees so that I can secure the mask and the goggles around my head, before readjusting my helmet as quickly as possible. I don't want to risk getting sneak attacked by vampires while the helmet is between my knees. Not that they've been very sneaky thus far, but you never know.

It seems that luck is on our side, even if only for the current moment, because the mini landslide that just occurred only created a small hill in front of the cave exit. It's small enough that we can just climb over it. I take a moment to send up a little ping of gratitude that we don't have to dig our way out. Once again, Michael and I move to exit the lava tube system, this time with no surprises. We carefully pick our way over the debris hill and walk out onto the crater floor, distancing ourselves from the walls and the prospect of more falling debris. The crater floor is much rockier than I expected it to be, and I have to watch my foot placement carefully as we walk, so I don't accidentally twist an ankle.

There are several large boulders scattered around the area as well, and as we get closer to the lava lake, I think I catch glimpses of movement behind several of the boulders. I reach my arm out to stop Michael and I watch several of the boulders carefully, searching for additional signs of movement. I stand stock still as I glance around at each of the boulders, the roaring, bubbling, and popping of the lava filling my ears. Just as I'm about to write off the movement I thought I saw as a trick of light from the flickering glow of the lava, a wiry woman stands up from behind one of the boulders.

"Well, ladies and gents, I do believe we've been spotted. No point in hiding anymore," she shouts with her arms spread wide as though she's a ringmaster, presenting to an audience at the circus.

And with her words, eight other vampires rise from behind the other boulders. Nine against two isn't so great, especially when they can literally suck our energy out of us, but the good news is that I caught the twitches of movement in time to prevent us from being surrounded. They'd obviously been trying to ambush us, but with where Michael and I stopped, they are still all in front of us, so we'll be able to track them more easily. I once again draw my sword and mentally ready myself for the battle that's about to occur when an idea strikes me.

"Michael, they can't fly or anything, right? They're still human?" I check.

"Good thinking. Just don't go too high. Remember that we took the caves rather than simply flying down here partly because of the risk of serious harm and possible loss of consciousness if hit by large pieces of debris when the edges of the crater break away. That risk still exists, even this far down," he replies.

We couldn't have used such a tactic in the caves, but out here, with sixty stories between where we are on the crater floor and the frequently monitored lip of the crater, we have the space and the freedom to use our flight abilities to our advantage. Unfurling my wings, I relish the relief it provides and push off my feet into the air. The vamps resist as much as they can by sucking in breaths of our energy in large gulps, but we use our wings to our advantage, dive bombing them and dispatching them one by one. Unfortunately, while Michael and I are dive bombing the vamps, we are being dive bombed ourselves by the green parrots that roost in the wall of the crater at night. I guess they don't like us disturbing their sleep. Either that or they don't like other winged creatures encroaching on their territory. Either way, the pretty green birds, although small, can be quite vicious when they want to be, and I find myself battling not only the vamps, but also the birds.

By the time the last vampire drops, my energy is almost completely depleted again, and I haven't a hope of sealing the Gate in my current state. The good news is that when I nearly crumble onto the floor of the crater, the green parrots seem to forget their grievances against me and return to their roosts in the crater wall. Note to self: in the future, don't fly near parrots.

"I need to rest again," I tell Michael.

He looks up toward the sky and then at the watch on his wrist.

"We have a few hours. Rest as much as you need," he says with understanding, and in response, I slide my pack off my back and under my head, quickly falling asleep in the middle of the crater floor.

Chapter 35

BRIE

Falling asleep wearing goggles, a gas mask, and a helmet is not recommended. Zero out of ten. Will never do again. I wake with a pounding headache, likely from the pressure of the helmet against my skull, and I feel like the straps of the goggles and the mask will be imprinted into the sides of my face for the rest of my life, however long that may be. As I try to think past the pounding in my skull, I realize my left hand is being caressed and I open my eyes to see Michael gently rubbing his thumb back and forth along the backside of my hand, his eyes glued to the movement and a pensive expression covering his face.

"Penny for your thoughts," I croak, my throat dry behind my mask.

Michael's face quickly blanks of any expression, all traces of the pensive look he had just seconds ago completely masked, and I immediately regret saying anything. Why is this so hard? I wish he would talk to me, share what he's thinking. He's always supportive and understanding. That should be enough, but my greedy little soul wants more. I want to know every part of him, every thought that crosses his mind regardless of whether it's good or bad. But I don't know how to tell him that without sounding like a crazy person.

As expected, Michael doesn't share his thoughts with me, instead removing a water bottle from his pack and handing it over to me with a caring smile.

"You should drink," he says. "How are you feeling? How are your energy stores?"

As I pull my mask down and gulp some of the water, I look inside myself to find that my energy stores are still alarmingly low. They don't seem to have replenished much while I was sleeping, which is concerning.

"They're not looking so good," I answer honestly. "What are the chances we can come back tomorrow and try again?" I ask hopefully.

"If we leave, Lucifer will just throw more at us the next time we come. I'm sorry Brie, but we have to do this tonight, or we'll miss our opportunity."

I sigh. It's not what I want to hear, but I get it. And he's not wrong. There is no doubt in my mind that Lucifer would bring more and more resources here to defeat us if given the opportunity. Nodding my head, I start to stand up. Before I put my pack back on, I turn to Michael, taking another chance that I'll probably also regret.

"A kiss for luck?" I say, my mask still pulled down and hanging around my neck.

Michael stares at me for a beat. Then two. His expression is unreadable, and I berate myself for daring to take such a chance when I knew I'd regret it. He's only kissed me on my cheek or my temple since that one real kiss when I almost died in The Cursed Forest of Massachusetts. I should have taken that as a hint. I'm totally in love with him, but he's still pining over his beloved Sabriel. Of course he doesn't want to kiss me. I'm not his Sabriel, I just have her soul. What was I thinking? Stupid, stupid girl.

"Forget I said anything," I backtrack. "My brain is tired and...."

And before I can finish with whatever embarrassed excuse I was going to make next, Michael yanks his mask down and swoops in, pressing his lips to mine with the kind of passion I've only experienced in my imagination. He kisses me like he's dying of dehydration and I'm the last drop of water on Earth. There's so much need and wanting in his kiss that I can't fathom how he possibly kept those feelings so locked down since we've been on this journey together. I part my lips and his tongue dances with mine as I pour all of my own need into the kiss as well. When we finally part, we're both panting for air and no joke, I'm slightly dazed by how amazingly intense and absolutely perfect that kiss was. He leans in again, slower this time and gives me a small peck on the lips followed by a radiant smile. Then, he gently pulls my mask back into place and whispers, "To be continued" right against my ear. Butterflies tumble around in my stomach, and I can't help the grin that appears on my face as I watch him fix his own mask back into place as well.

We both slide our packs back on and Michael takes my hand, almost as if he doesn't want our connection to end. I feel his thumb gliding against my skin again, but I realize that this time, he's not caressing the back of my hand, he's rubbing my hand near the knuckle of my ring finger. Where a wedding ring would be. Holy shiznits. I almost trip over my own feet when the realization hits me, and I quickly remind myself that I should be focusing on sealing this last Gate, as the wedding playlist that I've been adding songs to for the last ten years plays in the background in my brain.

As we walk closer to the lava lake, the air continues to warm and the smell of sulfur becomes overpowering, even through the mask. I remove my pack and kneel down near the edge of the lava lake, pulling a knife from my belt and carving the closure sigil into my palm. I picture my white angel light flowing from the center of my chest into my palm and press my palm to the ground, ready to finish this. But instead of watching the lava lake seal over, I'm pulled into a vision.

Three men, looking to be around mid-forties, drag a crying girl toward the lava lake. The girl is young, only around twelve or thirteen, with long dark hair and exotic features. She's the type of pretty that you know will only increase as she gets older until she turns into a stunning woman. The girl is shaking from head to toe, her bare feet dragging against the rocks, drops of blood leaving the evidence of the men's brutality in their wake. Her hair is wild, her eyes frantic, and she's wearing what appear to be pajamas, indicating that the men dragged her out of her own bed.

"Please," she begs. "Please, you don't have to do this! Please don't do this! I haven't done anything wrong!"

"You aren't the first sacrifice we've brought here, and you won't be the last, but you will be a sacrifice no matter how many tears flow from your eyes or how much you beg," one of the men replies coldly.

Another of the men raises his voice as he calls out into the night, "Accept this sacrifice and grant us mercy from your fury." And with that, the men lift the now wailing girl and throw her into the lava lake, before turning and walking away without an ounce of regret on their faces.

The scene disappears before my eyes and I come back to the present. That poor girl. How human beings can be so evil, I'll never understand. Knowing that my vision was far in the past and there's nothing I can do about it in the present, I refocus on trying to seal the Gate. The sigil in my palm healed while I was in the vision, so I re-carve it and once again feed my white angel light down through my arm, pushing it through the wound into the ground along with my blood.

I wait a few beats, but nothing happens. I expected the lava lake to seal over, but it's still burbling in front of me, completely unaffected. I remember the grotto in Turkey and how I had to stick my arm into the boiling water to close it. Is that what I need to do here? But sticking my arm into a lava lake...I don't know that I would be able to heal from that. What if I end up losing my arm? Would it regrow? But then I realize: it doesn't really matter. When the choice is between losing billions of souls versus losing one arm, there's really no choice, is there?

Steeling my resolve, I slide my hand from the rocky ground of the crater floor into the glowing lava lake. The pain overwhelms me immediately and I cry out. I can feel my arm disintegrating in the lava as I try to push out as much angel light as I can, but again nothing happens. Moaning in pain, I pull my mangled arm out of the lava and gasp out, "Michael, it's not working. It's not closing. Why isn't it closing?"

I can sense Michael near me, feel him stroking my back. I think he's talking to me, but my brain has shut out everything but the pain, so I can't make out his words. Through the fog clouding my mind, I remember the girl in my vision that was sacrificed by those evil men, and I hear Lucifer's whisper to me back when I closed the Gate in Ireland. He said he'd see me again soon. I thought he meant through the portals or that he would come to the Earthly plane to confront us, but now I think that I naively misinterpreted his meaning. What if he meant in Hell? That he'd see me in Hell. He must have manipulated this Gate somehow, so that the only way to close this Gate is for me to sacrifice myself into the lava lake, just like those terrible men sacrificed that innocent young girl. A pure soul in exchange for mercy from Hell's fury.

But what if I'm wrong? What if the pain has robbed me of my reason, and this is all delusion? What if I sacrifice myself and it still doesn't close the Gate? Then again, what if it would close the Gate, and I don't do it? That's selfish. One soul, willingly given, in exchange for the protection of billions of souls from the darkness that would corrupt them and drive them into an eternity of misery. I have to do this. It's not the just thing, but it's the right thing.

I try to block out as much of the pain as possible and slowly turn my head to see Michael. I look into his piercing blue eyes, that bring me comfort and the feeling of home, and I force my mouth to form the words I've been terrified of saying out loud.

"Michael, I love you."

Then, before I can think on it too much, I dive into the lava lake.

Surrounded by lava, my mortal body disintegrates. Without the pain receptors my mortal body held, my soul, in its purest form, doesn't suffer as it floats through the lava toward the Hell Gate. The Gate itself reminds me of a photo I once saw of a black hole in space. There's a brilliant glow of reds, yellows, and oranges spiraling outward in a spherical shape, and in the center of that glowing brilliance is just nothingness. A perfect circle of a black void. The glow surrounding it doesn't penetrate it and anything that gets too close is absorbed into it.

My soul floats toward the emptiness of the void and I send one last ping of love toward Michael. I hope he knows how much he meant to me. How perfect I think he is. How lost I was without him and how happy he made me during our time together. He truly is my soulmate, the other half of my heart, and it kills me to know that he's hurting right now because of me, but this is what we do, isn't it? We constantly sacrifice parts of ourselves for the greater good, and no matter how many good deeds we do, there's always one more sacrifice that must be made. They say no good deed goes unpunished, and whoever they were, they were right. Trying to do the right thing only ever ends in pain and heartache, but I still can't bring myself to turn my back on the side of good, because what kind of person would that make me? If I were to ignore the sacrifice expected of me, I would no longer be worthy of Michael's soul. I'd lose him either way, but at least this way, my light is still intact. As my soul crosses the threshold of the light ring surrounding the Gate, a blast of light envelopes me, echoing upward, and I know that the Gate has been sealed. Then, I'm enveloped by darkness.

I tumble out of the darkness and onto a cold stone floor, my soul taking on its angelic form as I land inelegantly on my side. I push myself up into a sitting position and glance around at the room I'm in. The hard stone floor I landed on is a dark slate gray, perfectly smooth with a matte finish. Three of the four walls in the room are made of an even darker stone, while the last wall is an accent wall painted a dark mahogany red. There are no windows, but there are some medieval-looking metal torches mounted on each wall, dimly illuminating the space. Beyond that, the room holds only one piece of furniture. A large, gothic-style throne sits upon an elevated dais in front of the mahogany accent wall, daunting in both its size and design, with metal spikes fanning out from its back. And on the throne's padded seat sits a smiling Lucifer.

When Lucifer sees that he has ultimately gained my attention, he slowly stands and descends the steps of the dais. Taking a few more strides toward me once he reaches the bottom, his smile grows wider the closer he approaches, until he pauses just a few paces away from me, towering over my still seated form. Lucifer kneels on one knee, caging me in with his body, and reaches out a hand to play with the ends of my now dark brown hair. Then, at long last, he speaks.

"Hello, Sabriel. Welcome to Hell."

Lucifer stares at me for a moment, releasing my hair and moving his hand to my shoulder, giving it a gentle squeeze, just like Michael used to do.

"Oh," he continues, "I almost forgot. Happy anniversary."

And with those two words, he finally breaks me.

Epilogue

MICHAEL

"**M**ichael, I love you," Brie garbles out through her pain, and then, before I can reply or react, she dives into the lava lake as though she's diving into a pool.

"No!" I yell, and lunge to stop her, but I'm too late and her body disappears beneath the lava before I can grasp hold of her.

"No!" I bellow again, and I fall to my knees in desperate agony for the woman who's owned both my heart and soul since the moment I met her. I crawl toward the edge of the lava lake, ready to throw myself into its depths as well, but before I reach the edge, a blast of lights permeates the viscous lava, and the entire lake hardens into solid rock. I wail, punching the newly formed rock with my bare fists, knowing that the Gate has been sealed and I can no longer follow my soulmate, at least not this way.

I must have unintentionally sent an energetic flare to my brothers in my distress, because Raphael lands by my side moments later, panicked.

"Michael, what's wrong?" he asks urgently, but I can't answer, too lost in my grief and despair.

"Michael, what's wrong?" he repeats. "I can't help you if you won't tell me what's wrong," he says, panic seeping into his words.

But I can't tell him. My mouth refuses to form such heinous words. Instead, I continue to break down uncontrollably, crying and wailing and punching the rock that's blocked me from the only part of my world that truly matters. Raphael watches me for a few seconds as I completely lose it, and then seemingly realizes that there's only one thing that could cause this type of reaction from me, and he looks around frantically.

"Where's Brie? Michael, where's Brie?" Raphael cries desperately.

My whole body starts shaking in response. No longer having the strength to pound on the rock any longer, I turn my head and meet Raphael's eyes. The whispered "gone" doesn't seem to come from me, although I hear my voice in the single word. Raphael's eyes widen and he shakes his head in disbelief.

"No," he says in denial. "No, that's not possible. She can't be...she can't be gone. It's...that's not..."

Raphael trails off, looking lost and broken, and I turn my head away from him to once again stare at the rock that's responsible for bringing my worst fear to fruition. I know Raphael was close to Brie too, but I can't deal with his emotions on top of my own. Of course, our healer is empathetic enough to understand and he scoots closer to me, pulling me into a hug as though he can physically hold the broken pieces of my soul together.

I feel Gabriel land near us a few minutes later. No doubt he already knows what happened from his visions. He walks straight onto the cursed rock before me without pause and kneels directly in front of me. His iridescent, baby blue eyes stare deeply into my own, and he says with a hard edge to his words, "This is not the time to break down, Michael. Brie needs you, so you need to channel this pain into action. You went down into Hell once before to rescue the souls that were kept there unfairly, you can do it again. You *will* do it again. We will bring our army down into Hell and we will rescue your soulmate before her soul is tarnished. Now, get up. We have an army to rally."

He's right. I've ventured into Hell before, and I can do it again. Only this time, Lucifer will feel my wrath rather than my mercy.

Since the day Sabriel's immortal soul was created, I have known that she was my soulmate. I have loved her and cherished her with every particle of my being for as long as her soul has existed, and now, I will bring her home. Even if I have to raze Hell to do it.

Author's Note

Thank you so much for reading <u>Trailing Darkness</u>. Writing this novel was truly a labor of love and I hope you enjoyed reading it as much as I enjoyed writing it. If you did love the story, please take a minute to leave a quick review on Amazon or Goodreads. It helps authors out so much!

I know some people hate cliffhangers, so if you are one of those people, I apologize that you are left in suspense. I debated a lot about ending the novel without a cliffhanger, but this was the only ending that really felt right to me. Luckily, the next book in the *Savior of the Light* series, <u>Encompassed By Darkness</u> has already been released so you don't need to wait to find out what happens next.

I did also want to comment on the sealing of the Gate in Chinoike Jigoku. I know this chapter wasn't as exciting as the others, but I wanted it to echo the hollowness that Brie feels after Callie's death, so that you could feel the same emotions she was feeling at that time. Overall, I hope you loved the story and the characters. More adventures await.

To stay up-to-date on future releases, join my newsletter at https://algordon-author.com/ or follow me on social media @algordon.author

About the Author

A. L. Gordon is an American author and self-described book addict. On the rare occasions when she is not reading or writing, you can usually find her making some of her own adventures with her dog.

If you want to stay up to date with A. L. Gordon's new releases, sign up for her newsletter at https://algordon-author.com/ or connect with her on social media.

Instagram: @algordon.author

Facebook: https://www.facebook.com/author.algordon/

Facebook Readers Group:
https://www.facebook.com/groups/algordon.author

www.ingramcontent.com/pod-product-compliance
Lightning Source LLC
Chambersburg PA
CBHW070622300726
48975CB00006B/1892